PRAISE FOR PROUD PINK SKY

"Tender and heart-breaking, *Proud Pink Sky* is centered on a Berlin that could have been—a paradisal Gay Republic that is not all it seems—and it's absolutely captivating, a perfect blend of reality and fiction, disquiet and hope, caution and celebration. Beautifully conceived and deeply affecting, *Proud Pink Sky* is a book you'll want to return to again and again."

—Calder Szewczak, author(s) of *The Offset*

"The conflicts and conversations—both micro and macro—will be achingly familiar to anyone who has been engaged with queer or trans movements in recent years, helping us to remember the vital need for coalition and solidarity right now. Please read this book!"

—Meg-John Barker, author of *Queer: A Graphic History*

"Drawing on an in-depth knowledge of queer history, *Proud Pink Sky* richly imagines an alternative world that is neither utopia nor dystopia. Barrett's vertical Berlin is a setting built on dreams, yet pocked with flaws, nuances, and squabbles that make it feel credible and strangely universal. Intriguing and occasionally shattering, *Proud Pink Sky* defies binaries in more ways than one, making it a compelling and welcome addition to the speculative Queer canon."

—Christian Baines, author of *The Beast Without*

"Redfern's fabulous 'what if?' envisions the queerest of timelines—a postwar Berlin that refashions itself as the world's only gay city-state. This electrifying tour through a would-be utopia riven by its own contradictory laws, traditions, and prejudices is at once deeply celebratory and critical. Like *1984*, its distant ancestor, the novel questions and probes but dares to hope for a happier, freer future."

—Brett Josef Grubisic, author of *The Age of Cities*
and *My Two-Faced Luck*

"To enter the pages of *Proud Pink Sky* is to be engulfed by a tidal power of masterful storytelling, morphing histories, and utopian imaginings. Boundaries of families and colonies, maps and guidebooks, words and sounds, dissolve into delicious, heady outcomes in this vital inhabitation of queer homelands. The crisp narrative pace combines with sensuous contours of language to remind one that to belong to an electrifying urban milieu is to also belong to its many troubled, unspoken intimacies and exiles. Redfern Jon Barrett has composed a virtuosic novel of fearless incantations."

—Gayathri Prabhu, author of *If I Had to Tell It Again*

"In *Proud Pink Sky*, Redfern Jon Barrett demonstrates that utopias and dystopias are not the opposites of each other—they coexist in the exact same space. As French philosopher Gilles Deleuze once said, 'Beware of the Other's dream, because if you are caught in the Other's dream, you are screwed.' With Barrett's eye for both history and prophecy, the Gay Republic of Berlin feels as lived in as a real nation. Though they've built an imaginative and thought-through alternative universe, they don't stop there; the yearnings and struggles of their characters are also true and engrossing. Barrett's novel is a compelling page-turning read and an important warning."

—Paul Gallant, author of *Still More Stubborn Stars*

REDFERN JON BARRETT

PROUD
PINK SKY

Amble Press

Print ISBN: 978-1-61294-253-7

Amble Press First Edition: March 2023

Printed in the United States of America on acid-free paper.

Cover design by Ann McMan, TreeHouse Studio

Amble Press
PO Box 3671
Ann Arbor MI 48106-3671

www.amblepresspublishing.com

This novel is a work of fiction. All characters and events
described by the author are fictitious. No resemblance
to real persons, dead or alive, is intended.

In loving memory of Richard Murray Vaughan:
Berlin is poorer without you.

MAP OF BERLIN

Excerpt from
The Honest Guide to Berlin

Official name: The Gay Republic of Berlin
Population: 24,549,100
Formed: 07 August 1948 (by UN resolution)

Common myths about the Gay Republic:

"Only men live there."
Rest assured, the Gay Republic isn't only for men—in fact, the bustling city-state is even divided into two federal zones: the gay male Senate House is located in Maytree in the west of the city, with the lesbian Assembly found in Delos to the east (see Government, p.16).

"Everyone is homosexual."
While it's true the Gay Republic was first formed as a haven for homosexuals, these days it's home to many different orientations. There have been straight residents from the very beginning (centred around the outer districts of Hetcarsey and Gajo), while bisexuality was legalised in 1969. For the most part heterosexual visitors will feel safe and even welcomed in the Republic, although public displays of affection are best avoided in more conservative areas and certain drinking establishments (see *Advice for Heterosexual Visitors*, p. 80).

"I need to speak Polari."
This is simply nix (not) true. Though if you keep your nells (ears) open you'll hear the gay tongue cackled (spoken) everywhere from street corners to government ministries, most of the population are immigrants to the smoke (city) and arrived with bijou (little) knowledge of it beforehand. That said, Polari is very easy to pick up, and you may even return home speaking a few lavs (words).

"The Gay Republic isn't safe."

Those exploring everything the Republic has to offer will find it a fun and friendly experience, particularly during the annual Pride Month festivities. It's true the city-state has developed a reputation as dangerous, particularly with regard to terrorist attacks, but in reality, these are low-level, sporadic incidents that the average resident is unlikely to ever encounter—let alone a tourist. That said, please stay alert in public, particularly around transportation hubs, and make sure to steer well clear of the slums to the south of the city (see *Ongoing Violence*, pp. 18, 20, 34, 55, 58, 60, 67, 81-83, 102).

HOMIES LOVING HOMIES

The Great British Kingdom

1998

1.

The wooden chair was hard and designed to dig between the shoulder blades. It was a seat for instilling shame: without armrests its occupant was forced to either hold their hands meekly in their lap, or else fold their arms in outright defiance. Placed at the very centre of the overstuffed, overly warm office, it directly faced the headmaster's desk: an antique leviathan of oak and walnut, crisscrossed with ancient scratches.

A sickly afternoon light fell through the window, glazing the stolid furniture and hiding the old man's face.

"Come on William, there's no need to drag this out."

William's hands were in his lap. His school shirt clung with sweat, sticking to sore bruises. He could have told the story in seconds: earlier that day he'd poured his adolescent heart onto a scrap of paper. He'd folded it, over and over, and dropped it to the bottom of his bag. No one was supposed to see it; no one was supposed to read it. But the usual boys had snatched his satchel, bellowed and jeered and tipped it upside-down, spilling an array of pencils, notebooks, a ruler, and, of course, the offending note. It lay on the scuffed wood floor like a prize, and a dozen hands had grasped for it. The note was read aloud.

His form teacher had arrived as William cowered on the ground, trying to shield his head from each kick.

"Well?"

"I don't know," William answered. He knew the headmaster wanted the truth, and he knew it was important he didn't get it. The truth would lead to no good. No good at all. The faded portraits of

1

Her Majesty Queen Elizabeth II and First Minister Powell watched him from their gilded frames, hung so high upon the wall that they almost touched the ceiling.

"I already know what happened, William. I want to hear it with your own words."

Confession, that was it. The other students had punched him to the floor and kicked him in the back, shins, gut. Now they needed his confession.

"Nothing happened."

"Then why did they attack you?" the headmaster questioned, with all the cold patience of authority. "They didn't just attack you for no reason now, did they?"

"I'm telling you, I don't know why."

"You wrote something. I want you to tell me what it was."

William felt sick. Everything smelled of shoe and furniture polish, and there was no other escape, no route free from this strange and dismal room.

"I wrote a note." He had to choke the words out.

"Now we're getting somewhere. What did the note say?"

He couldn't say it. There'd been no punishment for the other students, nothing more than just a few verbal barks from the form teacher. He knew it was important not to confess—not out there, not in here.

Several painful minutes passed before the bell clanged, followed by the distant stamping and hollering of the day's end. The sun's glow sank into shadow, highlighting the pocks and lines of the headmaster's face, his gaze as still and constant as the twin paintings. Finally, the old man stood, posture perfect, and flicked on a brass standing lamp.

"Before I came here, I was in the military. For a long time, we were stationed in the Cologne Republic. Things were different, back then," he added, lost for only the briefest moment.

"There was this one soldier in our unit. He looked a little like yourself: the slender, pale, nervous sort. More importantly, he kept to himself, always staying at the barracks, never joining our jaunts into town. He made us curious. Secrecy makes people curious.

"One evening we told him we were going out. We asked if he

wished to come with us—knowing he would refuse—then, instead of walking the three miles to our usual nightspot, we waited in some bushes and watched the gate. Eventually he stepped out of the barracks to begin his secret journey. We followed him.

"He arrived at a perfectly ordinary townhouse. We saw him knock on the front door and go inside. But we were soldiers, and that couldn't be the end of it. We burst in, expecting some hidden poker den, or else a backroom burlesque show, something we could understand. But he was in bed. With a man."

William couldn't look his headmaster in the eye. Instead, he squeezed one hand with the other, wishing this would end.

"For a few seconds nothing happened. Then one of us started shouting. Then we all were. He scrambled for his clothes, he tried to hide what he'd been doing, but we were sick with rage, William. We were unable to control ourselves."

The old man paused.

"All our training, all the discipline we endured, in that moment none of it mattered. Some rules aren't just enforced from above. Some are so basic, so fundamental to our survival, that they're enforced by human nature itself."

He stood; William mirrored him, legs near buckling with the effort.

"Regardless, I'm suspending you for a month. If I see you anywhere near the subject of your confused perversion, you'll be expelled. Do you understand?"

William nodded, his face burning with shame. He tried not to cry.

The school was the same as a hundred others scattered over the south coast of England: a grand, grey-faced, utterly symmetrical edifice topped with a greening copper clock tower. Few other structures could convey this same devotion to discipline, the same austere disdain for nonsense of any kind. Its narrow, brick-lined hallways were empty by the time William left the headmaster's office. It was already getting dark.

Gareth was waiting for him at the bottom of the school steps, beyond the high iron railings. On seeing William approach, he wrapped his hands around the bars like a criminal, his face a mask of mock misery.

"I'm glad this is funny to you," William greeted him. He didn't stop; he couldn't stop. So he kept walking down the street, Gareth hurrying along beside him. It took effort; Gareth was shorter and broader than the lean and lanky William.

"It was a joke, right, I was—" Gareth stopped mid-sentence. "William, are you crying?"

"No," William insisted. Yet when they were out of the school's visual range Gareth pulled his reluctant friend into a hug, squeezing him close. The street was empty, but net curtains and high hedges hid prying eyes, and neither dared hold the embrace for more than a few seconds. After pulling themselves apart they walked side by side through the suburb, one arm brushing against the other as their hands hung close, never quite touching.

"Did he tell you the soldier story as well?" Gareth asked. "Did you believe it?"

"It doesn't matter if it's true," William replied. "It makes no difference. We still can't see each other."

"Y'know," Gareth said, after a few moments had passed, "you'd be less of a target if you acted more like a lad. They can see how you walk, how you're holding yourself. They'd never've even found that note if you hadn't stood out in the first place."

William said nothing; he felt as though he were back in the stuffy head teacher's office.

"So, why'd you write it, anyway?" Gareth asked.

"What do you mean?"

"I *mean*..." Gareth paused his inquiry as they passed a woman struggling with two small children, "you've never written me a love letter before."

"It was a poem," William corrected.

The streetlights flickered on, bathing the road orange.

"A *poem*," Gareth teased, his arms spread wide in sham grandiosity as they crossed the quiet two-lane road. "I do feel special."

4

Grasping at Gareth's shoulder, William stopped him in the middle of the intersection. For the past few hours, he had clasped his emotions inside. Every pitch of shame, rage, and despair had dwelled and swelled within his skinny ribcage, and he could no longer hold it all within himself.

"Don't you dare, don't *fucking dare* make fun of me for that. I wrote it because I care about you. I care about you, do you *nell* me? Because I—"

"Keep it down." Gareth's tone was urgent and calm as he pulled William to the side of the street. "What happened today's bad enough, don't let them hear you using words like that."

"*Nell*," William cried. "*Nix, trade, homies—*"

Gareth placed a strong hand—a hand rough from sports and woodwork—over William's mouth, keeping the taboo flood inside. He spoke softly, his face almost touching his lover's.

"Right, if you keep talking like that, they'll send you away. You'll go to a special school at the other end of the country and we'll never see each other again." Gareth's eyes shone; his skin aflame in the glow of gas lamps. He slowly took his hand from William's lips, with the same uncertainty used on the familiar but potentially dangerous, a beloved pet gone rabid.

They walked the rest of the route in silence, listening to the evening birdsong from nearby trees and the clatter of pans from kitchens they passed. When they reached the corner they parted, Gareth glancing all directions before nudging William's cheek with a kiss.

Every house on the street had been built at once. Each came with a handsomely gabled roof, bay windows in both the downstairs living room and upstairs master bedroom, red-brick walls, and terra-cotta tiling. With an assuringly middle-class aesthetic, they were houses for people who valued comfort, yet saw pride as mankind's original sin. The Dovetrees' ascension to this street a decade before had been more than a move of house; it had been a change of status, a shift in the order of their world.

No one greeted William when he returned, and he was glad for it. He gently raised his jacket to the coat stand, placing his shoes beneath, all the while listening for signs that his parents had returned home earlier than usual, or that his brother had skipped the Boy's Brigade. Hoping he was alone, he crept up the stairs—running the tips of his fingers along the textured floral wallpaper—and slipped into his room. All that remained of the sun was a distant ink blue, retreating along the horizon as he pulled the curtains closed.

Waiting a few more moments for the creak of a floorboard or the kettle's gargle, he heard nothing. Satisfied, he turned on his bedside radio and brushed through the distant crackles.

A voice whispered to him, echoing across a thousand miles from a land that could scarcely be real. William removed his shirt as he listened, inspecting each plum-purple bruise across his chest and stomach, each berry-red graze.

... a space for those like us. More than anything, we provide safety. Not because it's kind, not even because it's bona, but because we have to. This is survival. It's not altruism. It isn't choice. Every year we take in thousands of homosexuals, providing space for the millions who would otherwise have none, a sanctuary for those in danger.

I don't need to cackle that we live on a hostile planet. We must barney for mere survival in a heterosexual world. Just look at the dozens of countries who refuse to recognise our very existence. We face proscription, jihad, and crusades. We are the victims of Christians, Jews, Hindus, Muslims, and Buddhists alike, detested by both presidents and dictators.

Yet to those homophobes I say: you can never win. Even when we were arrested for loving one another, you didn't win. Even when the priests and clergy made us fear our own desires, you didn't win. Even when Wilde was killed, his mortal body sacrificed for the crime of loving men, you didn't win.

You didn't win because you never stopped it. You never stopped us. Despite the laws and sermons, despite the mobs and police and prisons and death camps, you could never stop us from loving one another. The whole force of your churches and your states could never stop fruits from coming together. That is how weak you are. That is how strong we are.

And if tomorrow you destroyed everything we have built, if you rounded us up and killed us by the thousands, if you burned our bevvies and

6

took our children and preached our sin across the world, you still would not win. Because whatever you do, whatever extremes you go to, men will still love men. Women will still love women.

The front door slammed. Without thinking, William flicked off the radio and leapt into bed. Pulling the duvet up over his face, he squeezed his eyes closed, hoping his parents would leave him alone. Exhausted by the day's events, it wasn't long before he started to drift off, his leg twitching, his breath deepening, and his head flooding with images from a strange and distant land a thousand miles away.

2.

The breakfast table was the first warning. Ordinarily it was laid in happy chaos: toast rack askew, condiments clumped to one side, the teapot out of reach, and blobs of marmalade clinging to the cloth. Now everything was laid with militaristic precision: toast rack at the centre, teapot adjacent to his mother, the marmalade safely contained in a jar by his father. Rather than lying in a scattered pile, the toast was neatly arranged in a rack.

Only once had William seen such rigour; it was the day his grandmother had died.

"Good morning, dear," his mother chirped. Neither she nor his father took their eyes off him. His older brother stared sullenly into a half-empty mug of tea.

"You answer your mother when she speaks to you," his father ordered. Unlike his wife, he'd never felt the need to bury unhappy feeling with bourgeois pleasantries, a trait he'd held onto in his ascent from mechanic to management.

"Good morning, Mum. Dad."

"He's here, can I eat now?" his brother asked. Without waiting for an answer, he snatched a slice of toast and began buttering it with dedicated intensity, shutting out the room with his scraping. His mother offered William a slice and he took it, sensing the trap but seeing no means of escape.

"You won't be going to school today," she said, laying out the plainly obvious.

His brother sighed. "Do I have to be here for this?"

"We're having a family meal," she responded. "You need to be here as much as anybody. We all have to support William during his . . ." she paused, as the entire table waited to hear how she'd phrase it. "Troubles."

"For Christ's sake, he's not menstruating," his father barked, earning a sharp glare from his usually genial wife. William cringed at the situation he'd caused, looking to his brother for support, who in turn kept his eyes firmly on his plate.

"If you need to talk about anything, anything at all . . ." his mother continued. "William, look at me."

William did as he was told.

"You're not going through this alone. We're your family and we're here to help you. Everything will be all right, you'll see. On your wedding day we'll all look back on this and laugh."

"It's a bleeding joke all right, writing love poems to other boys." His father raised the butter knife, using it to gesture at William. "But you won't, not anymore. We'll be looking after your notebooks, your pencils and your pens. You spend too much time in here." He jabbed at the side of William's head with his finger. "And don't you go blaming us for any of this, either. We didn't raise you like that. You've picked up some funny ideas, somewhere."

William nodded, staring at his unbuttered toast, hating his father with an intensity only possible in adolescents.

"Don't think you'll spend the next month bunking off, either. Just 'cause you're not at school doesn't mean you'll be bone-bastard idle." His father stuffed toast into his mouth, leaving his mother to explain. She poured scalding water into William's mug.

"You'll be helping your father down at the workshop." (She never called it a garage.)

"Starting today," his father confirmed, grabbing another slice of toast.

Dread bubbled through William's stomach. The garage was located in the centre of town, past the long, low shopping centre and the imposing train station with its jack-and-crown flags. William had always avoided his father's workplace when he could, its mechanics full of jeering contempt for their boss's poetry-loving, nancy-boy son.

None risked outright hostility, no, but they'd hide things, they'd snicker behind his back. Once they'd taken a book of his, only for him to find it in the side alley, torn to fluttering pieces.

Yet where William saw despair his father found joy, his breakfast surliness fading as he drove past charity shops, old stone churches, and rows of family houses. He'd always wanted his son at the garage; this was his chance to mould a man.

They pulled up outside the cinder-block structure, the sun beating down on its hollow concrete bricks. Through the gaping entrance a pine-green sports car was hoisted aloft, three black-handed workers busy beneath. William followed his father toward the small corner office, but was directed back to the shop floor.

"You're here to redden your blood," his father cheerfully stated, guiding William by the shoulder toward the maddening complexity of car parts. "These ones'll show you what to do."

He gestured to the three men: two muscular blokes whose nametags read Jake and Matt, and a larger man called Freddy. All were coldly polite, which worried William even more than their usual bawdy hostility. They took turns, guided him with short, noncommittal grunts, first performing a task at breakneck speed, then undoing it and gesturing for William to do it himself.

Yet the first few chores were too complex, and the demonstrations too swift for him to follow. He suspected this was deliberate, but the tasks they gave him grew simpler, and simpler, until the one named Freddy handed him a smooth cylinder.

"Just get the oil filter on there. If you can't do that, you can't do anything. Go on, it shouldn't take a second."

William's hands shook; the filter slipped. He tried again, and then again. The filter clattered to the oil-smeared floor as he trembled with frustration. Of course, this would come naturally to Gareth, who could identify any make of car by its headlamps alone, and hoarded auto magazines as if they were rationed. But William knew nothing of engines; nothing would go where he wanted it to, and no matter how hard he tried he would never, could never, be in touch with his own hands like the three mechanics were.

Shutting out their irritated, half-amused groans, he took a deep breath and closed his eyes. Just for a moment, just to be somewhere, anywhere else, and, feeling calmer, he began to imagine what Gareth would say if he were there with him.

You're clever enough when it comes to books. Just stay calm, go slow. You can do this.

His lover's tone was quiet, soft, and so vivid it could have been real. Nodding to himself, William tried again. The filter slipped once more, but this time his hands trembled a little less, his heart beat slower. As the mechanics guffawed, he kept hold of that voice; gently correcting, never mocking. The grubby room was dark, his fingers numb and clumsy, but he worked diligently, never rising to the bait dangled before him. The only distraction he couldn't block out was his father, who continually passed by, watching with caution and then approval at William's stained hands and masculine quiet.

Eventually the day ended, tools downed with a hefty clank and clamour. He rode silent by his father's side, and when home he completed his schoolwork beneath his mother's vigilant glare. At night he collapsed into bed, too tired to listen to his secret broadcasts. Instead, he fell into an oily, black sleep.

The next day he summoned Gareth's encouragement again, and the day after that. More tasks, more mistakes, more imaginary comments from his real friend. Somehow, a week passed. Then another. Slowly, the distant land which crackled through the radio slipped away, and though he never said anything outright, William could feel his father's growing pride, expanding to fill the quiet between them. His mother was more verbal in her praise, rewarding his worn body with extra desserts while his brother sulked and grumbled.

Heavy work and heavy food. Each night another stack of schoolwork before the dense, undreaming sleep which stuck to him throughout the day, leaving his thoughts thick as treacle. Writing was a thin and distant dream, and after a while even the comfort of Gareth's voice slipped further and further away.

There just wasn't the energy to hate it; he couldn't even hate his increasingly proud father. There was a marble in the depths of his stomach, hard and immobile, a calcified ball comprised of guilt and an almost physical need for approval. Besides, he didn't want to upset his mother; he didn't want to see the strain of holding the family together etched onto her face. He didn't want to hear her cry late at night. He tried to be the man his parents wanted.

They were just finishing up one sodden evening, as the endless rain clattered against the garage's tin roof, the beat of a thousand tiny drums. Matt and Jake hurried off into the downpour, work jackets held over their heads, yet Freddy hung back. He worked side by side with William, directing him through the day's final tasks while his father waited in the corner office.

"There's something I want to say," Freddy said, suddenly and softly, his voice almost drowned out by the rooftop patter. William braced himself for some further castigation, but instead the mechanic took his hand in his oily palm. He squeezed it.

"It'll always be hard," the man said. "Don't think otherwise. But you're not by yourself. Even when you're hiding, you're not alone. Do you nell me, homie? Do you savvy?"

It was as though a stiff, grim mask had fallen from the mechanic's face, revealing a careful smile and kind eyes. With an awkward cough, he let go, then picked up a pencil and began scrawling something onto a scrap of paper.

"Look," he continued. "If it ever gets too much for you, if you ever need somewhere to go, you just come 'ere." He offered the paper to William. With a glance toward the office windows, William snatched the note and shoved it into his pocket.

As the office door opened and his father approached, Freddy's tone changed once more.

"You done a good job, boy, but you've a long way to go. Just keep listening to your father, he knows best."

"You heard the man," his father grinned. "Come on, let's get you on home."

12

William glanced back as they left; the mechanic's stony sneer had returned, as though nothing had happened. The warmth was gone, leaving no trace of the tender man who spoke the language from the radio.

3.

Our Republic was born to a world torn in two.

East and West.

Communist and Capitalist.

Left and Right.

A split personality had descended on humanity, a silent barney over economic organisation which threatened lives and livelihoods, borders and palaces, even our very survival. No one could deny our brave city-state emerged in precarious times.

Yet where did we fit in? Countless thousands of brave gay brothers and proud lesbian sisters had lost their lives in the fight for Berlin—for our independence, for our freedom—yet we found ourselves balanced on the edge of an iron curtain. We were five million homies rebuilding the ruins of a bombed-out smoke. We were, and are, a small land.

Yes, small! But while we were tiny, we loomed grand in the eyes of the world. There was no safety in our size or neutrality; we were not defended by obscurity. By our very natures we transgressed in a way more repulsive than the parasitic Capitalist, and more subversive than the dangerous Bolshevik.

Their cold war may be over; our little nation may have grown; but still we transgress. Still we repulse. For the hettie world we threaten the very foundation of our species—not merely the organisation of society, but of the family, of gender, of love itself. The great divide into which we were born was nix between East and West, Capitalist and Communist, Left and Right. In the end they all go home to their wives.

No. The true barney in our world is between the pure and the perverse. Straight and gay.

14

Hettie and fruit.

The speech drifted into advertisements, the radio's voice replaced by soft, jangling tones which gently floated across the room, over the bodies of the two boys.

"Don't fall asleep," William whispered into Gareth's ear, his breath tinged with wine. "We'll be caught if you don't get going soon."

It had been a month since they'd seen one another. A whole month, and when Gareth had appeared at the front door that evening William's heart had frozen. He'd forgotten how much he'd missed him, how much he craved his friend and lover. Awkward and uncertain, he'd briefly touched Gareth's forearm with his fingertips. A static rush had shocked his body.

"You shouldn't be here," he'd warned from the doorway, as the thrill of their brief contact subsided into a deep ache.

"Your parents went out for the night. I saw them go. Your brother is with the Boy's Brigade—I saw him go too, uniform and all. For once, don't worry yourself. There's no danger, there's no risk." His voice quavered. "William, I've missed you. I had to come see you. I had to."

Then he reached into his bag, pulling free a bottle of cheap white wine.

"Plus, we need to celebrate. It's over. You're back at school tomorrow."

And even though William was hardly thrilled at the prospect of going back, they'd celebrated nonetheless. In the giddy thrill of one another they'd swigged straight from the bottle, kissed in the hallway, clambered into his bed. Together they'd trembled like frightened explorers, scouting valleys and peaks with hand and tongue. When it was over they lay together in the dull lamplight, drifting in the luxury of space. Gareth's pupils flickered beneath his eyelids.

"I said stay awake. My parents will be home soon." William pressed his lips to Gareth's.

"I wish we could do this more often," Gareth mumbled, his throat clogged with sleep.

"Me too."

It was a risk, sharing the bed, but William had wanted more than a brief fumble. He wanted Gareth to know he still cared about him. That he was still there. Besides, his mother and father always arrived home from drinks with the Richards at eleven-thirty, which meant they still had time.

On seeing Gareth's eyes slip closed again, William kissed his neck and ran his hand down his lover's body, over the fleshy mound of his belly, hairy and pale even in the dim light. He kissed down by Gareth's armpit, then his arm, then his hand.

He bit his finger.

"Bloody hell, William!" Gareth jolted awake, pulling away. William choked on his own laughter.

"I told you not to sleep."

"Right, well I wouldn't dare sleep near you, you psychopath."

William dove forward to kiss his lips. Gareth kept his mouth clamped closed, making an obvious effort to contain a grin. William drummed his fingers over the sparse hair of Gareth's chest, moving them toward his armpits.

"Don't," Gareth giggled, his skin prickling. William took the offensive, thrusting his head forward and his tongue into Gareth's mouth.

"Yough uttergh bartharghd," Gareth groaned.

"George!" The voice of William's mother burst through the room like a gunshot. The two boys fell apart.

She was standing in the doorway, eyes fixed on the bed.

"George I need you here *right now*."

His father entered, still in his overcoat. On seeing his naked son he halted in shock, a blank white grief. Then his face twisted terribly, burning bright red, his lips a snarl.

"A whole month," he spat, striding toward the two boys. "A whole fucking month and now *this*."

He swung his hairy fist into Gareth's face. The dull thud toppled Gareth's limp body from the bed, striking the nightstand and sending the radio clattering to the floor. William leapt over to his lover, but was stopped by a burst of pain through his ear. The pain pulled him away, his father's grip dragging him from the room.

"That's it," he growled. "That's it."

William was hot with shame. His father threw his clothes into

16

the living room and told him to dress. When his mother appeared, he knew that Gareth was gone from the house.

He didn't ask after him, nor did he apologise. There was no point in speaking. Nothing could undo what had just happened, and if he spoke he would mouth the words of those radio broadcasts, he would ramble about love until his father beat him quiet. What they really wanted was confession. That's what they'd always wanted.

Guilt.

"Say something," his mother begged.

But he couldn't. The shame was fading fast, leaving a rage which burned his throat, his lungs, a fury so intense he gasped for breath. Fierce teachers and merciless students. Notes, taunts, fists. Gareth lying limp on the floor, the only person who ever really knew him, knocked cold. No, he couldn't speak.

As his father lurched forward, toward him, William grasped a nearby vase and hurled it straight at the burly man's head. Flowers fell to the floor.

William—

Hairy hands holding greying hair

Dripping crimson—

William, get back here!

A bag, his things,

His coat, the door—

William William!

The fresh air.

The suburb glowed silent and sinister, the yellow eyes of a dozen windows gazing down upon him. It was a cold night, and he walked quickly, heat spilling from his body as he wound his way down narrow, labyrinthine streets. Somewhere a seagull cried. He had to keep moving.

Gareth's house loomed like a semi-detached castle. William pushed open the gate, hauled himself up the front steps, and pounded at the door.

You had better leave.

He pushed past Gareth's parents to find his lover, whose face was already bruised and blackened, whose hand was warm in his.

"We're leaving, Gareth. We're leaving now."

You're absolutely not leaving with our son.

Gareth's eyes fixed on him, hurt and confused.

"It can be better." William had to choke the words out, force them from his burning lungs. "It can be better, I promise. I promise you, Gareth."

Then he and Gareth were running, Gareth in his dressing gown, his furious parents reaching for the phone. The two boys spilled from the house, down the street, past the houses, and into the park. While hidden among the trees, William gave Gareth his pullover.

"They'll be looking for us at the train station," Gareth warned, glancing through the dark as though they could be ambushed at any moment.

"I know somewhere we can go," William replied, fumbling for the scrap of paper, the mechanic's gift.

They avoided the main roads, ducking behind a Royal Mail postbox as the bright blue bursts of a police car rolled by. Slipping through the shadows of the street lamps, they hurried on toward the edge of town—hand in hand—until they finally reached the pub. Its windows were clamped with thick shutters, just a chink of light slipping out. William slammed his finger onto the buzzer by the reinforced steel door.

"How do you know about this place?" Gareth whispered. Before he could respond a tinny voice hissed through the intercom.

"Yes?"

"Please," William gasped. "Please, we need your help."

The intercom crackled.

The door swung open.

That was how William and Gareth spent their first night together. A double bed, warmth and privacy. Lying side by side, they entwined fingers while listening to the dark, to the soft noise of each other's breath. Slowly, William turned his head to examine his lover's face, the dim divide between chalk skin and purple bruise. Gareth shifted to face him in turn. Bit by bit they began to smile, and then laugh. It was a giddy, nervous, delighted laughter, one neither could control.

Excerpt from
The Honest Guide to Berlin

Overview: The Sights and Sounds of Berlin.

Berlin—the towering city-state which comprises the Gay Republic—is a focal point for visitors the world over. Its central districts were constructed as part of the Grand Say Oney ("Big Seven"), then the world's largest construction project, with reconstruction completed in 1952—replete with wide boulevards and a sensible grid system. However, over the next decades the metropolis saw a rapid and disordered expansion fuelled by an unprecedented wave of migration, characterised by an urban blight which is particularly prominent in the city's south.

Marvellous Maytree.
For new visitors, Berlin offers an imposing level of splendour and charm. The first point of entry will be the Berlin Grand Caravansera ("Berlin Central Station"), a multilevel transit hub located at the heart of the pleasant Maytree neighbourhood. Also known as "Daddyland," Maytree has greatly changed since it was known as "Mitte," and the grandeur of its 19th-century buildings is now rivalled by the city's high-rise skyline. Older gay men will enjoy Maytree's lavish restaurants and genteel atmosphere, with the district hosting the Senate House, the Gay National Museum (which dominates Museum Island), and Berlin's famous Memorial Square.

The Memorial Square commemorates the many thousands of homosexuals killed in the 1933 Schöneberg Revolt against the National Socialists, the brief victory of the gay brigades in liberating the city, and the subsequent flattening of Berlin by Nazi artillery fire. A series of tunnels run beneath the square itself, resulting in a claustrophobic atmosphere which may prove too intense for small children.

The Memorial Gift Shop offers a range of souvenirs, from "I Love Berlin" T-shirts to keyrings, all in a range of rainbow colours.

Exploring Gay Berlin.
The other gay districts lie to the north and west of Maytree. Hairier visitors will enjoy downtown Paw, a bear-dominated neighbourhood which is also home to the world's highest concentration of leather manufactories (smooth-chested travellers are advised to avoid this area entirely). The younger set will feel at home in Twinkstadt, with its impressive collection of nightclubs and the city's largest red-light district, which draws visitors from every part of Berlin. For those focused on fitness, Adonis is centred around the Olympic Stadium, boasting an impressive array of gymnasiums, sports halls, and health clubs—where guests can find everything from herbal supplements to illegal steroids. Beyond Adonis lies the National Park, a mass of forests and small lakes providing welcome respite from the noise and concrete.

Despite the dominance of Berlin's gay male community, lesbian visitors will also find themselves well catered to. Boasting the largest lesbian population on Earth, the state's economic core is undoubtedly Delos, whose arcades and plazas are filled with besuited businesswomen, politicians, and lobbyists. The Delos Assembly is conveniently located opposite Goddess Caravansera ("Goddess Station"): a significant work of second-wave feminist art, notable for the hundreds of sculptures depicting female deities which dominate the building's exterior. Summer visitors packing sunscreen and swimwear will enjoy the beaches of Flora Lake, which happens to be a focal point for the city's Femmes. The lake's eight-kilometre-long waterfront also hosts a variety of saleswomen, selling drinks, snacks, and marijuana cigarettes (please note the legal age for cannabis consumption is sixteen [see *Laws and Regulations*,

p. 78]). Those toward the "butch" end of the spectrum would do well to explore Diesel, a friendly, down-to-earth district which also serves as the city's industrial hub.

Trolling Out of Bounds.

It is advised that tourists avoid the poverty-stricken sectors in the south of Berlin: the quasi-official district known as "Q" is particularly prone to disorder and civil unrest. Wise visitors will also be vigilant while in hetero-dominated areas such as Hetcarsey and Gajo, where the high concentration of churches and mosques has done little to alleviate a spiralling crime rate.

NIX BOXES

The Gay Republic

1998

4.

When she was a little girl, Cissie had read picture books all about handsome princes and beautiful princesses, books which were, without exception, the only literature allowed that wasn't stamped with a golden cross. Once she'd learned these fairy stories by heart, Cissie's parents had gifted her animated movies, and so she'd watched and rewatched *Snow White* and *Sleeping Beauty* and *Cinderella* until the videotapes were chewed into buzzing, fuzzing static.

There must be some way of becoming one of these princesses, so she reasoned. She'd perch herself in front of the television set for hours, her brow furrowed in single-minded concentration, and after months of studious analysis she'd arrived at three conclusions.

The first was, to her young mind, the most appealing. According to the movies, each princess would summon small animals to do her bidding. For years Cissie dreamed of this animal menticide, of commanding mice and bluebirds and becoming dictator to all woodland creatures. It seemed a rather more substantial prize than marriage to some willowy prince.

Cissie's second conclusion was that she would need to be placed in mortal, supernatural danger. This prospect seemed quite exciting, particularly as her world—which was comprised, almost exclusively, of the cozy farm-style house in which she was raised—seemed rather tame and limited by comparison. If there was danger, well, at least something was happening to you. Besides, were she to die she would simply reappear in the Heaven her parents so often talked about, and which surely was much bigger than their small Ohio home.

Her third conclusion had been the least agreeable. There was no avoiding the fact that these stories always ended with a marriage, which in turn was sealed with a chaste kiss. Cissie could do without these princes, yet it seemed there was no way of acquiring queenhood and the corresponding royal superpowers without one. So, she approached the subject with an adult pragmatism, neither drawn to nor disgusted by these boyish regents. They were simply a means to an end.

These infant fantasies changed with adolescence. Ashamed of her blood-dotted underwear, she'd thrown all her clothes straight into the laundry hamper, and later that day her mother had sat upon her bed, patted the ancient quilt, and told Cissie to join her. With her thin face pulled tighter than Cissie had ever seen, she'd dished out opaque advice: *You're a woman now* and *This is our burden* and *It's part of His plan for you and your husband.* The shared prayer her mother led afterward lasted longer than the talk itself, and though Cissie still had no clue as to why she'd bled, she'd been left with the impression it was somehow because of men. It was surely a warning, her body cautioning her away from boys. Especially handsome princes.

Yet Cissie was an inventive child. Men were dangerous, that much was true, but perhaps women were safe. This led to the natural conclusion that she could avoid the terror of a prince by marrying a princess instead. So she'd invited her one friend, another homeschooled girl named Susan Michaels, up into the attic and into her old playhouse, which to grown-up eyes was an ancient refrigerator box with hand-cut holes for windows. With Susan safely inside, Cissie had sealed their relationship with a kiss.

Her friend's next words had opened the door to another world. *You're a dyke,* Susan had said, her little face stern with condemnation. She'd told Cissie that women who kissed women were dirty and sent to a special land far away. Susan knew so because her aunt had gone there, and once you left you never came back.

Of course, Cissie had been surprised. The idea to marry another girl was all her own, and it had never occurred to her that someone else might have thought of it first. Questions had piled upon questions. Why could you never return from this land? Why had it never been mentioned in any of her stories? And most importantly: Where was this other world?

Cissie had never kissed another woman, but nearly twenty years later this mysterious city would become her home.

Oh, it hadn't been her idea; her youthful curiosity had been fickle, and besides, what family woman would choose to live in homosexual Berlin? Yet Susan Michaels had been right about one thing: Cissie had never returned to Ohio.

At first, she'd wandered the crisscross streets, staggering around while gawking up at the crowded overhead transit lines, a foolhardiness which twice resulted in stolen purses. She'd only later learned said streets were part of Hetcarsey, one of Berlin's two straight districts. Though it wasn't pretty—in fact most of the tenements had a raw, unfinished look about them—it was thrilling, and so different from the wide boulevards and gleaming art deco towers she'd seen in the postcards. With millions of residents, Hetcarsey was practically a city unto itself, and while Cissie had since learned to walk with thief-deterring speed, she still marvelled at the noise, at the dizzying array of lives above and around her.

After six years she'd even honed her life to a fine routine. Not because she was a particularly precise person, but because the boundaries of her day allowed her to carve a cranny for herself, a Cissie-shaped hole in a dizzying, sprawling, unknowable city. After taking the kids to school (they would have a proper education, not the rote Biblical learning she'd received), Cissie was left with nearly two whole luxurious hours to wander, to chart this territory, to wallow in chaotic multiculturalism.

The balconies and their rows of dripping laundry; the shouts and catcalls in a hundred languages; the neon and printed and hand-painted signs, coating every blank surface as they boasted burlesque shows and suicide hotlines and international phone cards. Whole cultures were swallowed through the nose, Cissie breathing in curries and kebabs, won ton soups and matzoh balls, scents which spilled from greasy windows and roadside kiosks. All places have their own smell, and when she thought back to the United States, it was cinnamon and gasoline. Away from the food stands, Hetcarsey smelled of detergent, and sharp perfumes.

Despite her explorations Cissie always stopped at the district border, demarcated with gleaming steel rows of railway tracks.

"They stick us here, so they don't have to look at us," her husband Howard often mumbled, and though Cissie didn't argue with him (the city's politics were as peculiar as the city itself), she knew he was missing something important, something which had long grown precious to her.

"Don't get too comfy," Howard warned every single year. "When the work dries up, we're out of here."

By now it was a hollow threat; Howard loved his job. And though no family woman would willingly choose to live in the homosexual nation, Cissie had fallen in love with the sights and sounds of her neighbourhood. A Hetcarsey patriot, if such a thing were possible. In fact, so little had changed in six years that when the brewing unrest reached her district it took her completely by surprise. She learned of the city's conflicts only as they interfered with her routine. The struggle revealed itself in installments.

5.

That morning, like every morning, she woke at dawn. For a few moments she lay beside her husband, straining her ears for the surrounding city clamour: the flutter of pigeons nesting in concrete crevasses, the early-morning throng of the twentieth level skybridge. Passing just six stories beneath their bedroom window, the bridge was crowded with daybreak commuters and revellers staggering home, but Cissie didn't mind—the resulting din meant the apartment was cheap, and it comforted her to rouse so early with life all around. She hated nothing more than waking to still noiselessness.

After a few minutes she flicked on her small bedside lamp, knowing it wouldn't disturb Howard, who could sleep through a meteor strike. The bedsheet was bundled around his furry legs, his right arm slung above his head as though in victory, displaying a black nest of armpit hair. She watched his chest sink and rise, admiring his construction-worker bulk in a way she never could when he was awake. Even during sex Howard insisted on the dimmest light possible, ashamed of his fatherly belly and hair-splayed shoulders. She'd tried to tell him how much she loved his body, once, but he'd felt patronised. He immediately covered himself up.

A drunk bellowed from below, his cries rising like a siren. Taking this as her cue to get out of bed, Cissie pulled on her rough flannel robe, crept to the bathroom, and stood over the tiny sink, washing herself with lukewarm water. The apartment was old, though not quite old enough to be charming, and built before showers had become social custom; every evening Howard would squat in the tiny tub, turning the water grey with scummy concrete dust. For Cissie it was a luxury indulged in just once or twice a week. As the drain babbled, she brushed her matted auburn hair, peering into the tiny mirror, her nose practically pressed against the glass.

She ate her breakfast in small snatches as she cooked, Howard and the children wandering in to the sounds of sizzling and percolating, the smell of eggs and coffee. The kitchen was nothing fancy: the countertops were an unfortunate shade of beige and smudged with old coffee stains, but they allowed for an unobstructed view of the living room just as warm sun peered through the little windows.

The boys turned on the television set, flicking past reruns of gay soap operas and news broadcasts, and stopping at the cartoons. Howard kept glancing toward the set, making sure they weren't witness to anything too fruity. (Howard himself only ever watched football, and only ever on mute.)

"You're up early," he greeted, brushing his lips against Cissie's cheek.

"Thanks for letting me know," she teased as she placed the coffee in his hands. But he was already looking past her. His eyes were narrowed at the television, where a flamboyant pink cat danced around a streetlight.

"Children," Cissie distracted, "if you don't go brush your teeth the tooth fairy will come and yank them all out." She turned off the set as they raced one another to the bathroom, eight-year-old Thomas easily besting his baby brother, who shrieked with indignation. Howard was about to say something but sipped his coffee instead.

He never complained about the gays outright. Instead, he made his thoughts known through tuts and hand gestures, often accompanied by a small smirk or eye roll, something to indicate how well he tolerated it all. And yes, when it came to living in "their" Berlin, Howard really was *tolerant*: with all the quiet distance that implied.

His frown lifted.

"Hey—" he began, wrapping one arm around Cissie's waist. "Guess who we're building next."

It was always *who*, not *what*, and she already knew, of course she knew: it was a complex of interlocked deco-gothic towers designed by Philip Johnson. (*One of the greats*, so Howard had said.) The towers would have a symmetrical network of hi-flung walkways and rail lines arcing between them. Howard had mentioned it thirty-seven times,

30

but he always shone with such enthusiasm as he did so, and so she shrugged and listened and cleared away the dishes.

"It's Philip Johnson," Howard beamed. "An actual Philip Johnson."

Unlike her, Howard travelled far beyond the boundaries of Hetcarsey, working on the never-ending construction of the city itself, on tenement blocks and elevated train stations as Berlin spread upward and outward.

His work gave him pride. Sure, he was a construction worker and not an architect, but he could give whole sermons on each project, and Cissie knew all the names: Amaza Lee Meredith, Bruce Goff, Paul Rudolph. Howard may have been perplexed by the lives of lesbians and gays, but he enthusiastically admired their architects and planners.

"They invented hi-urbanism," he lectured, the talk so familiar Cissie knew it word for word. "While back in the States we were building endless wastes of cookie-cutter homes, here they were using space the best they could. Sure, Japan and Singapore might have copied them since, but nothing rivals Berlin. Twenty million people all in a single city. You've gotta admit it, Cissie," he playfully taunted, "they've certainly got talent."

Truth was, they were all too distant for Cissie to form any real opinion either way. She had no reason to hate the gays, and in fact she too held a vague admiration for all they'd accomplished, for what they'd built. But they were so exotic, with all their castes and categories and rules. And she so rarely saw them in her neighbourhood.

What was there to hate? What was there to love?

"Philip Johnson will fire you himself if you don't get moving," she warned, whisking his coffee cup from his hands and swigging the dregs. "Then what will you have to brag about?"

With Howard gone, Cissie took the children's hands—Jonah on the left, Thomas on the right—and walked them to their schools. Gripping each tightly as they wound and wove their way through the morning crowds, she first delivered Jonah to the Chanting Chavvies Infant Academy, itself a small, squat building dwarfed by its peers. Then she walked a further four blocks and rode the packed elevator to take Thomas to the Gildy Journo Middle School.

With his mother all to himself for a few minutes, her older son ranted and rambled, speaking with a self-important authority which was almost comical coming from an eight-year-old. A miniature version of his father.

Then she took Howard's battered spare work boots for repair. With the hanging trains rumbling overhead, she meandered her way through Hetcarsey's lower streets, toward the district border. Prerecorded chants wept from the neighbourhood's crowded minarets, and nothing at all seemed amiss until she dropped off the peeling boots.

On a stretch of wall by the cobbler's someone had spraypainted nonsensical words:

Nix Boxes.

And she thought nothing of it until she saw the same words at the ground level of the Hermannstreet station, rendered in bright blues and purples:

Nix Boxes.

This time it conjured a memory of herself as a little girl, climbing into a box with holes for windows. Sharing her first kiss.

Nix Boxes.

The words were there on the shutters to a post office; they were scrawled over the side of a ramshackle mosque.

Nix Boxes. Nix Boxes.

Perhaps it was some local complaint, or the name of some gang of wispy-moustached teenage boys. Yet she kept walking, on into a nearby Catholic neighbourhood, and there it was. Over the sidewalk, under an ironwork bridge, on the wall of a rickety church.

She asked the cobbler about it as she collected the boots later that day, but he answered with a noncommittal shrug. "It's not our problem," his young assistant replied. "Not our problem," and nothing more.

That evening she thought of asking Howard, who must know something, what with his working all over the city. But he'd arrived home weary and dusty with concrete, so she'd presented his newly mended boots, run his bath, and said nothing.

6.

His fingers lingered on her stomach, lightly brushing the fuzz of hair she hadn't removed. From other men, Cissie knew, the gesture might have been critical, but Howard never criticised her body. Though his own physique both embarrassed and repulsed him, he adored hers with every small action, always fascinated as though seeing it for the first time. With his fingers, his eyes, his tongue, he examined her in ever-loving detail as the morning commuters gabbed outside the window.

He pressed his nose to her belly, running his hands down her thighs, and though Cissie reciprocated with her usual array of shivers and moans, her mind kept conjuring questions, ones she'd never thought to ask. *Is this what they do together, when it's two men?* She groped and then gripped Howard's shoulders, feeling the thin T-shirt he'd kept on. He brought his mouth to hers, his lips soft, moving to her neck, her collarbone. *Do lesbians make the same sounds? Do they kiss like we do?* He pressed his body to hers, muscle and sinew beneath a cotton-poly blend, sheens of sweat soaking together.

Does it feel the same for everyone?

"Mom. Mommy."

Husband and wife sprang apart at the elastic twang of Thomas' voice.

"What is it, sweetie?" Cissie asked, breathing deeply to bring her panting under control, pulling the bedsheets to herself. Howard sat bolt upright, clearing his throat.

"Jonah threw up."

Howard looked to Cissie; Cissie to Howard. They rose together, Howard taking her hand as they went to the boys' room to inspect the damage. He squeezed it lightly, almost imperceptibly.

"It's everywhere," Thomas proudly announced.

"Better than a cold shower," Howard joked at the sight of Jonah's orange-splattered bedsheets.

"Oh, you poor thing," Cissie cooed, kneeling to her younger son. He was sitting, legs dangling from the side of the bed, his skin cold and clammy as she pressed her palm to his forehead. "You must have swallowed a stomach bug."

"I don't want any bugs in my stomach," his older brother declared.

"You get a wet cloth for his head, I'll change the sheets," Cissie instructed her husband. Howard gently lifted their sickly son from his bed and onto Thomas'.

"Not *my* bed," Thomas whined. "I don't want him in *my* bed."

"It's time for you to have breakfast," Howard replied, scooping the older boy up and carrying him to the kitchen.

Cissie sang while tucking Jonah into his brother's bed. She made up the words every single time, and the tune was always the same, but it never failed to calm her youngest son. Thomas had grown up and out of her songs, but not Jonah, not yet.

Don't worry a bit
We all get sick
But I bet you feel better already . . .
She tickled his tummy, and he squealed in delight.
So close your eyes
And later you'll rise
For now just stay in your beddy.

Jonah's grin faded as he sank into sleep, his mother planting a kiss on his clammy forehead.

Back when she and Howard had met, Cissie had been a model daughter—and yes, *model* was the operative word, for she'd done her fair share of that. Lecherous, nicotine-stained men with their cameras and grunts and premature jowls. It wasn't much: there'd been a magazine ad for pocket calculators, school bags, work which fit a wholesome image.

At first, she'd been thrilled, certain that being a model (even a model for back-to-school equipment) would make her the most popular girl at church. This fantasy had sustained her until she'd found her pictures papered all over the bathroom stalls of the church youth centre, engorged, oversize penises scrawled across her wholesome smile. The teenaged Cissie had heard the savage giggles of the other girls and realised that she would always be a joke.

She'd donated her pay to her mother and father, who in turn had overlooked the inherent blasphemy of the camera lens. There was no doubt in Cissie's mind that her parents' poverty had grown alongside their religious fervour; when she was three her parents had attended a Billy Graham rally, and they'd returned so full of the Lord's Light that her mom had quit work the following Monday, that she might fully dedicate herself to home, family, and the moral rectitude of her only daughter.

The family had struggled by on her father's single income till she was around eight, when her father had resigned from his job in the local library (*"Too much smut, especially for the children"*) and then been fired from his grunt work at a nearby book warehouse (*"Those memoirs were filthy, they should have thanked me for pulping them"*). Even with no job he'd still donated ten percent of his former income to the church, a tax for maintaining the family's respectability.

When worried, her father quoted the great Graham himself: *"When wealth is lost, nothing is lost. When character is lost, all is lost."* Her parents hid red-lined utility bills from their daughter, and from each other. Meanwhile Cissie had tried to hide her parents from the other kids. She never mentioned her mom or dad.

As for Cissie herself, there'd been little remarkable about her. She hadn't smoked or taken drugs or had improper intercourse. (Though she had, in a reckless moment, allowed a boy named Billy Buckley to touch her left breast.) Cissie's policy had been to keep her head down, not to draw the attention of either her zealous parents or the cruel kids at church, and to simply race through her childhood years toward the precious line of adulthood. Then she would be free to make her own decisions.

Yet Cissie was to rebel, and, as with millions of other teenage girls, she did so by dating—as it had been with her parents, and their parents before them.

She was seventeen when she met Howard, working on the roof to the annex where she'd once gone to Sunday school. He'd been up a ladder, a tight torso and lusty grin, and she hadn't been disgusted. She'd even teased him, and he'd come down to her level then taken her student-model hand into his big, grubby, hairy one. He had led her to his place—what was she thinking? —and touched her all over. She had let him and didn't know why. She never knew why. But she gasped with pleasure as those hairy hands touched her skin.

Howard never spoke much about the past, he'd just told her he had moved into town the month before, doing odd jobs for good and Godly folks. But there was no fervour in his voice, no condemnation in his gaze, and, for once, Cissie could relax. She could enjoy herself with him.

Of course, her parents had taken an instant dislike to the well-spoken, strong-minded young man five years older than their daughter, whose collar was sometimes blue, sometimes white, and often coated in grey, unwashed rings. When they barred him from the family home, Cissie simply went to his rickety one-room apartment above a tailor shop. She'd scrub his clothes in the small bathtub as Howard talked and talked, sometimes squeezing her tight, sometimes pressing his hardened crotch against her while kissing the back of her neck.

Meanwhile her parents' mortgage notices had piled behind the bureau and stacked behind the television set, unacknowledged until repossession loomed. Then they gave away spare furniture and old crockery, piling their earthly belongings into worn cardboard boxes. Their plan was to relocate to a religious community in Oklahoma, and Cissie would join them. It was an order.

"But you're eighteen now. You're a free woman. Move in with me."

As always with Howard it wasn't a suggestion, it was direction. That was how she thought of his instructions: *direction, heading somewhere.* Different from the orders of her parents, which had held her in place so long. Howard watched her, waiting for a response. He'd been naked but for an unbuttoned, freshly cleaned shirt, and she had leaned forward, pulled the shirt back, and kissed his small hairy nipple. She didn't know why.

36

But she did leave them.

Her father had jabbed toward the ceiling with his all-knowing finger as her mother clutched a handkerchief to her own mouth, as though Cissie's sins were airborne. Cissie didn't even own a suitcase. She'd packed some spare underwear into a plastic bag and worn everything she could. She'd stumbled over boxes and then waddled down the front lawn in the July heat, her parents' fury bellowing away behind her. She'd walked straight into that small one-room apartment, into Howard's waiting arms. They'd married two weeks later.

"Make way!" Cissie called, holding the sick-soiled sheets at arm's length. "Biohazard coming through."

Thomas giggled as she threw the laundry into the bathtub with one arm dramatically outstretched. Even Howard slipped a sly smile as he scraped butter onto blackened toast.

Glancing at the cat-shaped clock and realising how late they were, she took the slice from Howard's plate and placed it into his mouth.

"You get going, I'll take care of things here."

Howard's reply was muffled through charred bread, but Cissie knew what he was asking.

"It's fine, really. I'll just ask Ms. Fortier to look after Jonah while I take Thomas to school."

Howard's next mumbles were equally indistinct, but the grunts were shorter, more obstinate.

"She says we can ask for her help any time," Cissie insisted. "Besides, she's just a harmless old lady."

Howard had swallowed enough to choke out, "No one ith harmleth."

"Except you, hon," Cissie teased, taking the coffee cup from his hand and hurrying him toward his coat and shoes. "And don't worry, I'll make sure she doesn't corrupt Jonah too badly. Nothing a few years of therapy won't fix."

"What's wrong with Mizz Forrer?" Thomas asked, mangling Ms. Fortier's name. Cissie winced; he heard too much, he was at that age

37

where repeating adult secrets was a form of currency. So, she insisted his father was joking—a private joke, not one he would understand—and herded her husband out the front door. Peering into the boys' bedroom she heard the light, even breathing of her sleeping younger son, then took Thomas' small hand in hers.

Each floor to the building was a different colour. The lobby with its rows of grim elevators was a starched shade of white, while her floor was a light shade of raspberry. As Ms. Fortier only lived three storeys above, they took the stairs, Thomas counting the steps as they ascended: "One, two, three . . ."

The next floor was a deep ocean green. Prayers swept from the hallway in a language she couldn't understand, though she heard the word *amen* furiously repeated. She squeezed Thomas' hand tight, hurrying him a little. She had nothing against the religious, not really, but she could hear her parents in that piety. She could hear years of sharp judgments and bad decisions.

". . . nineteen, twenny, twenny-one . . ." Thomas chanted, not even noticing.

The next floor was a cheerful saffron. They passed a woman edging her way down the stairs, a baby slung across her chest, five barbarous children clawing at her legs. Cissie shared a sympathetic glance with the stranger, secretly glad she'd stopped at two.

". . . forry, forry-one, forry-two." They'd reached the twenty-ninth floor, painted a deep royal purple.

"Here we are," Cissie announced as they stopped by Ms. Fortier's door. "Do you want to knock?"

Thomas had started rapping his fist before she'd even finished the sentence. After some rattling the door creaked open a head's width, with only Ms. Fortier's peacock blue and green eyeshadow and pencil-drawn eyebrows visible behind the heavy chain. On seeing who it was she unchained the door and opened it wide, her gown flowing from her arms like limp wings, swirls of those same blues and greens spread over an ocean of black. The subdued warble of an old record player drifted from her apartment.

"Cissie-girl, what a surprise," she greeted Cissie in her thick French accent (at least Cissie presumed it was French, she'd honestly never

38

asked). Ms. Fortier held her arms out in greeting before peering down at Thomas. "And you brought your husband Howard. Hello, Howard." She took his hand and shook it.

"That's my daddy," Thomas giggled. "That's not me."

"Thank goodness for that," Ms. Fortier replied.

Cissie was used to these barbs about her husband. Ms. Fortier and Howard held a mutual grudge, though it wasn't exactly clear why: their dislike had been immediate, more powerful than logic or social niceties.

She's a whore, Howard had proclaimed once, after they'd both had a few drinks. At first, she'd thought he was kidding, but he was wearing his *I'm-deadly-serious* frown, the same one Thomas had begun to mimic. *Or at least she was, a long time ago.* Cissie hadn't known what to say to that, so she'd said nothing.

Ms. Fortier lit a cigarette, sending a lilac plume of smoke above their heads.

"I hate to ask this—" Cissie began, but Ms. Fortier waved her hand, slicing through the small cloud. Thomas watched with wide-eyed wonder.

"Cissie-sweet, I would be happy to spend some time with little Howard here."

"It's *Thomas,*" he interjected, deeply amused by this routine.

"Oh, this one needs to get to school," Cissie informed her neighbour, who sent another delicate plume up toward the ceiling. "It's Jonah needs watching. He's a little sick."

"Why of course! And I know just the thing." She hurried inside and came out with a small pack of peppermint bonbons. "You can even have one, Howard."

This time Thomas took one without correcting her. Cissie handed her keys to her neighbour and took her son's hand. He was already late.

"Thank you thank you thank you," she called back, racing toward the elevator.

Then came the next installment of the strange conflict. They rode the elevator to the Gildy Journo Middle School, only to find it closed. There had been no warning, but a small sign in the doorway informed parents of the school's "temporary" relocation to the Hephaestus Physical Academy. Memorising the listed directions, she guided her son across the seventh-level skyway, holding his palm tight through the bustle of Hermannstreet station's tenth level, down the elevator to the ground, and on toward the austere-looking academy. It was an old building: a five-storey tenement with nineteenth-century decals, so ornate it looked for all the world like an overdecorated cake.

A security guard met them at the door, gruffly asking for Cissie's ID, which she nervously handed over. She'd never been asked to show her ID before.

Cecilia Parker. Born 10/10/74. Red hair, brown eyes. Heterosexual.

The man waved them through. Inside, the class was crowded but well-behaved. The teacher offered Thomas a cookie, though she had no explanation for the sudden change, nor did she know how long it was for.

"I'm sorry," she informed Cissie, clearly anxious to get back to the class. "You know as much as I do." She turned, then turned back, adding a hushed, "Trouble with *them*," as though that told Cissie anything. Cissie nodded along like it all made sense.

But her confusion followed her home. Jonah still slept soundly, the colour already returned to his cheeks, while the living room ceiling was draped in lazy formations of smoke, an old paperback open and face-down to Ms. Fortier's side. Together they flicked through the forbidden news channels, hunting for some scrap of information on school closures.

Instead, they watched a report on sexual assaults in Hetcarsey; the resignation of a Gay Patriot senator (who'd cheated on his husband with a woman in a public bathroom); and the results of the Maytree district's annual *Festival de Tapas*, broadcast from an unending array of tables laid down the central reservation of a grand boulevard. Well-dressed, well-groomed gay men nervously stood by their creations.

Ms. Fortier lit another cigarette. She offered it to Cissie, who glanced toward Jonah's bedroom door before taking it between her fingers.

"You must have heard *something* about what's going on," Cissie implored, taking a drag.

"I never know what's going on, my dear thing. I merely react to the world. It saves time not to try and grasp it all."

Cissie sucked on the cigarette, sulking.

"Look," Ms. Fortier continued, "if you're so desperate to learn what's going on, why not find out for yourself? Have you ever even been to the rest of the city?"

"Of course," Cissie lied, feeling somewhat defensive against her worldly neighbour.

"You can't close your eyes then complain about being blind." Ms. Fortier glanced at the clock before slowly lifting herself from the couch and stubbing her cigarette onto a saucer. "Anyway, I must be off. If I don't leave before your husband arrives, I'll turn into a pumpkin."

On reaching the door, she turned back to Cissie.

"And don't look so worried, poor thing. They're gays, not wild dogs."

7.

Every Saturday Howard took Cissie and the children grocery shopping. To Howard this was an act of great kindness: hauling bricks five days a week come freezing sleet or blazing sun, and then kindly taking the family to the supermarket on his day off. And though Cissie appreciated the gesture—or more precisely, the *thought* behind the gesture—she secretly hated this weekly ritual.

On weekdays she was free to roam where she wished, to stop and even to marvel, but not on Saturdays. On Saturdays Howard monitored his family incessantly, controlling everything they bought while giving off disapproving murmurs. She didn't like the way he guided her by the arm and manoeuvred her through the weekend throngs, and she could see the glimmer of fear in his eyes, the way he puffed out his chest like a terrified little boy in an alien world.

"Jonah, take your mother's hand. This way. Quickly. Thomas, don't stare. I said *don't look*. Keep up, Jonah, we're leaving you behind. Walk faster. *Jee-sus Christ.*"

Of course, if they needed the odd toothbrush or bread loaf, Cissie would nip to the store in their own building, a small twenty-four-hour shop run by a friendly Hindu family, located where the skyway intersected with the twentieth storey. Stocked with pre-wrapped packages in all possible tongues, the noisy exchange mostly served the last-minute needs of foot-bound commuters, and the prices reflected the fact.

So, the bulk of the Parker family groceries instead came from BonaMarkt, a basement-level economy supermarket right by Britz Park, the block-wide square of lawn which served as Hetcarsey's only public garden.

In accordance with family tradition, Cissie dressed the squirming children in their starchiest shirts, taking care neither to stain nor fray her practically pristine shopping dress. The Parkers rode the elevator with all the appearance of wedding attendees, though if Howard noticed the glares and glances as they walked toward the BonaMarkt, he certainly didn't show it.

Black and grey crows skulked about Britz Park, their heads angled to the grass, pecking for insect prey. The park itself held a few waiting demonstrators, but they were too far away; Cissie couldn't read their signs. She glanced back at the scattering of protestors before following her family down the ramp, into the stale concrete aura of the underground supermarket.

Usually, Howard guided the cart down each halogen-lit aisle, the children clinging to the sides and "helping steer" as Cissie found the rice or potatoes or mustard. But not this time. This time the BonaMarkt was more crowded than usual, and she noticed as they approached the tall shelves, the products were scarce. Shoppers pursued the few jars of preserves or loose apples with brisk efficiency, the scene polite but frantic.

"Thomas, Jonah, don't let go of the cart," Howard directed, his knuckles strained white against the handles, his eyes wide with barely concealed anxiety as fellow shoppers whisked by. When Cissie touched him on the shoulder, he flinched.

"It's too crowded here," she explained. "You take the kids to the 'copter." She pointed to the coin-operated helicopter ride in the far corner of the supermarket. "I'll finish up and meet you there."

She could taste sweat as she kissed him on the cheek.

The checkout queue stretched all the way around the store, and though she strained her ears for news, she caught only rumour and gossip from the hetero customers. The closest she got was some young man speculating that supplies had been interrupted. Well, she could have worked that out for herself.

When she finished an hour later, Howard and Thomas were waiting by the helicopter ride. Little Jonah was asleep in the seat. Exhausted, the four made their way back up to the street.

Feeling a rush from the fresh air and finally free of the basement store, the two boys frantically giggled and poked at one another, weaving and winding their way around Howard's legs as he ordered them to *behave*.

But Cissie was distracted. The few demonstrators at Britz Park had swelled into the hundreds, spilling over nearby roads as megaphones whined to the sky. Before, the mood had been relaxed; now it was thick with tension, the mob jostling against the police cordons on each side of the square. Behind were rows of police cars, *Lilly Law* emblazoned over the sides.

"Howard."

Cissie and the children stopped, marvelling at this strange new sight—for better or for worse, the police were a rare sight in Hetcarsey. Howard took the lead, directing his wife and sons back down the concrete ramp and away from the troublesome scene. They passed the entrance to the BonaMarkt and carried on toward an underpass which led to the far side of the block. Walking quickly, but not running, they were surrounded by the tunnel's fluorescent advertisements. The walls boasted deodorants and cookies, sports shoes and oatmeal, everything which had been missing from the supermarket. Two husbands grinned as they served their children soup, their teeth white as sugar.

They were midway through the tunnel when the light at the far side dimmed. A line of police officers marched into view, riot shields gleaming with the reflected aquamarine glow of a shampoo ad.

Cissie turned; from the supermarket side there echoed the chaotic chanting of the mob. Both exits were blocked. Making brief eye contact with Cissie, Howard told them to *wait there*, then hurried toward the police line.

The formless chanting grew louder, coming toward them. Jonah had already started crying, a reedy, frightened wail, and Thomas put an arm around his baby brother's shoulders. Cissie placed the meagre shopping on the ground and knelt to her youngest. She started to sing, the usual formless tune and nonsense words.

If you stop your tears
I'll hide your fears
To be stolen by stray cats and foxes
So calm your cryin'
It'll all be fine

Nix boxes nix boxes nix boxes.

She was surprised at the meaningless words which fell from her mouth, but there was no time for distraction—Howard remonstrated with the bemasked officers, hands flailing with frustration. Her heart stopped as two of them broke formation, one grasping Howard's arms, the other cuffing him. Then the rest of the line advanced, toward her and the children.

Jonah clutched her left hand, Thomas her right, as Cissie ran back the way they'd come in, toward the supermarket, toward the mob. The crowd was already in the tunnel; a balloon of paint spiralled toward the colourful advertisements, splattering over the white-toothed soup billboard.

Cissie held the children tight, trying to push her way through the seething throng. Jonah's cry intensified, a terrified wail as she pulled them to and fro, hunting for a way past as bodies battered her arms and shoulders, surging all around. Some of them were armed with clubs and baseball bats, others with signs and banners, the concrete air thick with whistles and screams. The advertisements shone between shadow-like bodies, shining green, shining teal, as bandana-mouthed protesters grappled with the police. She couldn't even hear Jonah's wail above the screaming roar, but she held his hand as glass crunched beneath her heels; a young woman on the ground was dragged back up by another. Bricks bounced from gleaming shields, shining coral and saffron.

Which way was she facing? Which way was out?

A stone hit a man in the forehead, blood gushing from his eye as a grey-yellow cloud swelled between them all, a rising marshmallow, acid fog flooding her mouth.

She covered the children's faces with her arms. Her own face was wet. Was she bleeding or crying?

A hand tugged at her dress, dragging her backwards. Cissie grasped her children's arms hard as she could, fingers cramping as she stumbled back, unable to see who was pulling her. She struggled, but the stranger's grip on her clothes was too strong, too firm, and she couldn't even see where they were going, where they—

Daylight. Bright sun between blurry high-rises. Cissie's knees buckled, but the hands caught her; her ears were ringing but the children were there. Jonah to her left, Thomas right. Her eyes stung, her vision smudged, her lungs were on fire. But there was no crowd now, just clean air and the soft breeze of the park.

"Are you all right?" A woman's voice. A blurry blob with a Spanish accent. Cissie's eyes burned. She could hear the children sobbing; she ran her hands over them, terrified they'd be wet with blood. But they were dry, they were both dry. Where was Howard?

"Open your eyes. Open them properly," the woman barked. "Do you speak English?"

Cissie nodded, opening her eyes as wide as she could, everything fuzzy and out of focus. Something yellow appeared in front of her, something spurting into her eyes. More stinging.

"Lemon juice," the woman explained. "It'll help with the tear gas." Was she whispering or shouting? "Now the children. Open your eyes, children, please let me help you."

"Jonah, Thomas, listen to her," Cissie begged, stroking the blur of their faces. "Listen to the nice lady."

"Here, sit down," the woman instructed, helping Cissie to a bench. She felt Jonah and Thomas grasping her, their cries growing more shrill, then softening. "Breathe deeply. Can you tell me your name?"

"Cissie. Cissie Parker."

"You're doing very well, Cissie. My name is Ramona. Ramona Palomar." As Cissie's eyes began to clear, she could make out long dark hair, a smudge of a face.

"You're all fine, you've just had a bit of a shock. I have to troll away now, they'll be searching the area. Leave as soon as you have the strength. And breathe."

Then she pressed her lips to Cissie's—who kissed another woman for the second time in her life—and with that, the strange woman was gone.

Excerpt from
The Honest Guide to Berlin

Citizenship Law.

The Gay Republic's history toward migrants is a surprisingly complex one. The Constitution has guaranteed "sanctuary to all homosexuals" from the very beginning, with most of the original residents made up of those liberated from concentration camps. They were soon joined by arrivals from around the world, with particularly high rates of migration from Western Europe, North America, India, Brazil, the Philippines, and Japan. However, the 1950s saw a moral panic over migrants lying about their sexual orientation, and campaigns led by conservative gay newspapers led to the controversial Migrant and Asylum Act of 1953. The Act makes same-sex marriage a requirement for full citizenship, a law which remains to this day.

Marriages must be arranged prior to entry and take place alongside visa validations, with foreign "civil partnerships" converted into full same-sex marriages during this process. Breaking the marital contract within the first five years (reduced from ten years in 1976) can result in deportation should either individual fail to provide adequate proof of their orientation. Divorce, adultery, or voiding the same-sex marriage contract via gender subversion (see Trans and Genderqueer Individuals, pp. 81-83) may also result in visa cancellations and expulsion.

Those not currently in a same-sex marriage may apply for a temporary residence permit, which will need renewing every five years. Applicants can apply for citizenship and residency at the nearest embassy or consulate, the latter of which are often located in one of the Gay Republic's dependencies (see *Shared*

Administrative Zones, Overseas, p. 18).

Shared Administrative Zones, Overseas Territories, and Enclaves.

Though the Gay Republic itself only comprises Berlin and its surrounding territory (a total land area of just over 1300 km²), the city-state is in a unique position, possessing a number of overseas dependencies. Around two-thirds of these are co-administered by the Republic and a third authority, whereas the rest remain under the full administrative control of the gay state.

The history of these dependencies stretches back to the DISS (Disrupted Immune System Syndrome) epidemic of the early 1980s. Widely regarded as the most profound event in the Republic's short history, the epidemic led to a catastrophic loss of life and total economic standstill. Though numerous probable deaths resulting from DISS occurred throughout the late 1960s and the 1970s, it was Berlin's Ministry of Health which first recognised the disease and identified the retrovirus VAI (termed Viral Immunodeficiency Disorder, or VID) in 1982. At the same time several heterosexual nations refused to acknowledge DISS cases within their own borders, with many informally referring to the illness as the "Berlin plague."

Meanwhile, the Gay Republic saw what were amongst the most wide-ranging social support networks and grass-roots citizens' initiatives Europe had ever seen. Though much of the government was thrown into chaos during this period—seeing regular impeachments, recalls, and snap elections (see *Political History*, pp. 130-132)—the vast majority of state funds were directed toward medical institutions, with the Republic leading the world in DISS research. Alongside the introduction of universal health care, the 1980s also saw the establishment of thousands of foundations, hospices, shelters, and counselling services—

known nationally as the "Great Embrace" ("Große Umarmung," "Gran Abrazo," "Fantabulosa Aruma").

By contrast, many of the planet's gay-majority cities and communities were frustrated by their own governments' inaction during the crisis. These mostly urban areas fell into increasing disorder, seeing riots and localised revolts alongside demands to join the Gay Republic, which they saw as better defending their own interests (it should be noted that the Republic already had strong ties to many of these enclaves). Many panicked national leaderships, eager to be seen protecting heterosexual voters and fearing the astronomical costs of dealing with their worst-affected areas, would ultimately relent. These full or partial secessions, brought by a series of legislative acts, referendums, and civil conflicts, have become known as the "Great Break" ("Große Abgang," "Grande Abbandono," "Fantabulosa Exita").

The Gay Republic's current shared administrative zones, overseas territories, and enclaves include the Castro, Porta Venezia, Shinjuku, Barrio Norte, San Telmo, Le Marais, Zona Rosa, Eixample, and Brighton.

ANYTHING GILDY

Brighton (Shared Administrative Zone)

1998

8.

The flow of cars had stalled, traffic baking beneath a sinking sun. Large vans and small lorries made up the bulk of the vehicles, with the odd car squatting between like a lost child at a grown-up party. Noisy seagulls screeched and swooped overhead, circling over a line of shimmering metal stretching all the way from Brighton to the small border town of Lewes. Eight miles of sweating, swearing drivers guarding cargoes of fruits and vegetables, bread rolls, cheeses, refrigerated meats and fish, books, mops and dustpans, shirts, socks, bedframes, insulated piping, paracetamol, and a thousand other odds and ends, all heading toward the razor-tipped fence.

Beyond lay the vast radio masts, ramshackle towers, and noisy streets of Brighton.

At first William had been on anxious alert, wincing each and every time the car stopped, tense with the worry that their parents—or the police—were close behind. But nothing had moved, no one was chasing them. He glanced toward the pub manager, who patiently waited in the driver's seat of the stuffy Ford Fiesta, his attention entirely devoted to a battered paperback. Gareth had fallen asleep two hours ago, mouth agape and head rocked back against the window.

It had been four hours since they'd last nudged forward.

Gareth snored. Each breath in was abrupt as an objection; each breath out a gentle sigh. His slack lack of expression revealed how stern his face looked when awake. Stern and certain. William wanted to hold him but didn't dare; strangers could see into the car as clearly as he could see out.

How many of those in the surrounding vehicles were *family*? He'd learned that word from the pub manager: "You're with family now, don't you forget that." On seeing the two exchange glances, he'd elaborated.

"One of us, a fruit. We look after each other. All fruits are family."

But William couldn't tell if the man in the adjacent van was family; nor the man striding between cars, pink with sunburn; nor the woman erecting a tent on the grass verge by the road. None of them made eye contact. Each waited in isolation, smoking cigarettes and blaring music from open windows. For a moment it felt as though they'd been there forever, alone and waiting, no origin, no goal, just hundreds of lonely people and their cells of iron and aluminium.

There's little more exhausting than doing nothing. His mind fuzzed into noiseless static, and he awoke just as they were passing through Brighton's gate. He nudged Gareth awake, and for a moment Gareth looked bewildered, before his face set into its usual rigidity, his guard against the world.

Neither William nor Gareth had ever been to Brighton before. Nor had anyone they'd ever met. Its existence had always lingered at the periphery, hinted at, but never spoken of. William's father had sometimes made a crude, drunken sneer about *them there*, or tutted at a newspaper article, at the naked depravity of *that sort*. Most of the time these references came with a gesture, always to the west, a magnetic revulsion.

The town itself was both alien and familiar. Brighton's seafront shared the same genteel architecture of any English seaside town, its waterfront flanked by the same white hotels and their Regency flourishes, the same tart-sharp smells of seaweed and vinegar salting the air. Yet behind the seafront were warrens of narrow alleyways, ramshackle apartment blocks housing hundreds, residents spilling in and out of doorways at all hours. Men openly kissed each other in the streets; women kissed women. Meanwhile, a surprising number of tourists braved their way into the city, delighted and scandalised as they took photos and lapped ice cream.

The car moved slowly as the evening dimmed into dusk, careful not to scrape against the signposts and lampposts which lined the narrow, one-way streets. They stopped outside a nondescript brick building, and the pub manager gave two sharp bursts of the horn, blasting William from his daydreams. This was no soft farewell; their rescuer said goodbye as a formality, the procedure routine. William wondered how often he did this run, and how many passed through Brighton's gate.

Inside they were greeted by a kindly, yet harried, middle-aged woman, who ran through the rules as she walked them through threadbare hallways and into what would be their quarters for the next month.

"That's how long it'll be, give or take. Don't you worry, my duckies. They'll sort you out, they always do."

She unlocked the door to a small room with a double bed and was gone by the time they'd turned around.

Most of the shelter's residents were young. Most had been there less than a month. That evening they shared stories as they ate, elbow to elbow in the little dining room, relaying personal histories in sad mumbles and wild gestures. Some of the stories were already well-worn, but they were handled with care. They were the most precious possession most of them had.

There was another couple in the room next to their own, two young men who'd walked all the way from south Wales. They'd walked until their feet had bled and their shoes fallen apart. One of them held the shredded footwear aloft as a sort of trophy.

The single man staying in the room opposite had escaped the family farm in his father's Land Rover. A gunshot had shattered the rear window, showering the back seat in glass. But he'd got away, that was the important part. He'd sold the four-wheel drive as soon as he'd reached Brighton and bought his own gun from some shadowy vendor. Just in case.

A young woman on the floor below was covered in cuts and bruises. She showed them off like tattoos, proud of what she had survived. She lifted her shirt and showed off her stomach, a collage of blue and purple welts.

William and Gareth had been through little by comparison, but the others around the table still listened with sombre intensity, wincing and consoling just the same. The two took turns, filling in details the other missed: being suspended from school, William's father, the vase, their escape into the cold night. Someone poured acrid shots of some cheap, clear liquid, and by the time they'd finished they both felt lighter, their story made real by the telling, their burdens shared among the group. Then someone poured another round—the third, fourth?— while someone else told a dirty joke, and the conversation slipped toward lighter topics.

William tipped his head back and drank, feeling the burn from his throat down deep into his belly. He was actually looking forward to the future and couldn't remember having ever felt that way before. Everything was warm, everyone inviting.

You're with family now, don't you forget that.
All fruits are family.

9.

Gareth woke up alone and hungover, his head sore and belly empty. Bright light poured through the open curtains, as did the harsh cries of gulls as they hunted the alleyways for open bins. Hopping up from the bed, he pulled on a shirt and stumbled to the shared bathroom. The hot and cold taps were the old-fashioned, short-spouted pillar type, and he struggled with the stiff metal till a cool, clear stream spilled out; sticking his head right in the basin, he slurped till he'd had enough.

Then he went to pick up breakfast. William was still downstairs in the common room—which reeked like an abandoned distillery— where he'd passed out in an armchair the night before. William was never much of a drinker, and now his face was smothered with makeup, which the girl on the floor below'd applied as a drunken joke. At first Gareth'd thought it was funny, but now the ruby lips and rouged cheeks made his sleeping lover look like a circus attraction, somewhere between clown and bearded lady.

Still, Gareth kissed his forehead before braving Brighton's busy morning streets. Dodging dawn drunks and delivery bikes, he followed the smell of fresh bread, wondering how long they'd be in the shelter, how long it would be till he could restart his life.

The thing was, Gareth'd never needed rescuing. He knew how to handle himself. When it came down to it, it was all about blending in, not standing out as a victim. How to bend when the breeze blew, so William said one time (that being the sort of thing William said). After all, if you don't stand out, you're left alone. No one picks a victim from the background.

In fact, it was Gareth who'd rescued William, the very first day they'd met. It was a Thursday afternoon, he'd always remembered that, and there'd been a fight in the chemistry labs. Two thick-as-shit

57

classmates were caught hurling blobs of mercury at each other, and the whole class was held behind for lunch. By the time Gareth'd grabbed his tray and got to the canteen it'd been almost empty. But only almost, because a mob of seniors crowded around a boy seated at one of the tables. They were sneering and jeering and spewing insults, like lads do when in packs, but the weirdest part was that their target was just staring into space. That silence was driving the swarm into a frenzy, until one of them reached out and smacked his victim in the head.

The boy flinched. His lip wobbled, eyes wide and shining with shock. It annoyed Gareth: allowing yourself to be bullied, looking terrified, asking for trouble. But then those eyes'd looked to him, *seen* him, and Gareth was no longer part of the background. Without even thinking, he'd stepped forward and slapped the attacker, branding a bright pink handprint onto his face. He didn't even know why.

Of course, the group could've piled on him, but they'd been looking for a hunt, not a fight. Gareth was broad (chunky, even), and solidly built. The seniors'd been caught by surprise, and they fled, shoving him aside and yelling *faggot* as they went.

But the other boy stayed, hiding his face with his sleeve.

"Don't cry," Gareth'd said, because what else could he say? "What's your name?"

"William," the boy sniffled.

"Don't cry, William."

They'd grown attached, after that. Despite being one of the lads, Gareth'd always been something of a loner. Not that he'd thought of himself in that way. He'd honestly not given it much thought at all, not until William. William'd tell Gareth about the stories he'd read, and Gareth would watch the wild movements of his hands and the faraway look in his eyes. It made him feel warm. Warm like basking in the sun or huddling by a fire.

At first, he thought he didn't have much to offer in return, but he'd shown William his car magazines. The two looked at the pictures together, fingers touching the glossy pages. Fingers touching. He knew William wasn't really into cars, just as William knew he wasn't into literature, but they'd shared it all anyway. The passion was the point.

They'd endured puberty around the same time. They'd been

curious. Gareth couldn't remember who'd started it, but they'd both trembled, they'd both nervously undressed and then carefully touched each other. They'd kissed, awkwardly, clumsily fumbling about, learning each other's bodies and never really being sure if they were more friends or lovers. It was new, it was exciting, and it was completely forbidden.

They'd helped each other survive. Right up until that poem. When William wrote it, he'd broken a kind of agreement. He'd left Gareth's protection and put them both in danger. He hadn't told William, what with his being suspended, but the next month at school'd been unbearable. All the work he'd put into managing things, his knowing what people wanted and how to avoid trouble, all of it'd been wrecked with that one note. The taunts and shoves and swift kicks were constant, and though he'd done his best not to blame his careless friend (his naïve friend, his stupid friend), a little bit of anger got stuck in his gut.

It didn't help that while Gareth was living a nightmare at school, William was working at his dad's garage. Which happened to be Gareth's dream job.

Even so, it might still've been all right, things might've gone back to normal, but then William hurled a vase at his dad, and that'd been the end. The end of their old life, the end of fitting in. Everything Gareth'd learned, everything he'd tried to show William, all of it gone in an instant. This was William's way, not his. Words written on paper for all the world to see.

Then came the weirdest part, the moment it'd all tilted completely upside-down. *William went and rescued him.* William, who'd taken his hand and run out into the night. William, who'd given him his pullover and held him when he'd shivered.

Gareth's head had cleared by the time he returned to the shelter clutching a small wax paper bag of warm rolls. Finding the common room empty, he trod his way up the stairs to find William peering into a small mirror, his face still coated with makeup.

"Better wash that off before breakfast. You look like a—"

He stopped mid-sentence. He'd only meant to tease William, but William'd flinched and then left for the bathroom, nodding to himself.

"Good morning to you too," Gareth mumbled. Chewing on a fluffy hunk of warm bread, he fiddled with the bedside radio. Somehow the room looked more and more shabby, overlooking old bricks and murky windows, the walls layered with mould, the carpet scratchy, the sheets a worn grey. But it didn't really matter—it was all temporary, it was something they had to get through.

There was so much to learn about the gay world, and over the next weeks they each took their own approach: William went to the Pavilion Library, burying himself in books like it was a full-time job and then regurgitating what he'd learned to Gareth. History, literature, politics, sociology, anything he could find, he devoured.

In contrast, Gareth explored the place. He wandered over to the bevvies—gay-speak for bars—learning what he could from watching people, listening to their conversations, hearing what they had to say. And yeah, the bars were exciting. They were loud, sure, but not violent like the ones back home. Instead of fighting, the men inside went to one another for temporary affection. Gareth'd said no when asked, but just being asked made him feel good.

His favourite was The Hard Heart, a ramshackle pub on Queen's Park Road filled with the teasing and hearty laughter of groups of gay men. He wondered how long it'd be before they too belonged.

At night he and William found each other again, relishing the double bed and space and sex and giddy freedom.

"Did you know they have different parties in Brighton from the rest of the British Kingdom?" William asked as they walked down the noisy seafront, past fairground rides and carnival acts. When Gareth didn't answer, he kept talking. "The Liberals and Conservatives are there, of course, but there are all these others, the same ones as in the gay city. There's the Gay Patriot League, the Demetan Union—"

"That's great," Gareth muttered, pulling William out of the way of a group of whooping straight women. They were clearly on a hen party, all wearing matching bunny outfits. "But you can't learn about people just by reading. Experience comes from *doing*. You know, getting out there, seeing it all with your own eyes."

"I *am* experiencing it," William protested.

"Mmm-hmm," Gareth replied, seeing no point in arguing. "So, what do you reckon? Will they think we're good enough for the gay city?"

Without answering, William took hold of Gareth's hand. They kept holding hands as they passed the pier with its arcades and chip shops, the slate-grey sea roaring to their right. They were lucky to have each other, they both knew that. Even so, it was strange to see other pairs of men also walking hand in hand, and Gareth had to look down at the ground or up at the cloud-patched sky just to keep from staring. They only let go of each other once they reached the consulate, a large white Victorian hotel which guarded the crowded shore, all grand columns and regal austerity.

Once they'd checked in, they waited side by side on a leatherette sofa before being called into a small office. It was all going well, until the bored official read out the requirements for citizenship.

"We really need to marry each other?" William asked, his voice bouncing off the oak-panelled walls. Gareth winced.

"You don't *need* to do anything," the official told them. He was prim, terse, and seemed deeply irritated by William's reaction. He sorted through the papers on his desk as he replied. "No one's *forcing* you to move to Berlin. By all means stay here, or feel free to go back home to your loving families. I'm sure they'd welcome you with open arms."

"Is there no other way?" William asked. Gareth didn't say anything.

"You could get a work visa," the man sneered, "which I'm sure would be easy for you two, with no formal qualifications and no work experience."

"But—" William began.

"But what?" Gareth interjected. The man behind the desk was no longer looking at his papers and instead stared at William.

"Well, I read we could go as an 'uncategorised couple.' On a temporary visa." William rushed out the words as though he were running out of breath. The official frowned.

"Or, we could just get married," Gareth mumbled. The official nodded at him in approval, though that didn't matter. William was his life. He was the only one he'd ever opened up to, the only one who'd seen him, really seen him, and still Gareth had no idea how William really felt in return. Fact was, he'd never even had a chance to see the poem—it'd been snatched away and read by everyone except him, and he wished he knew what was on it, what that scrap of paper said about him, 'cause he needed things to be clear, he needed a label to wrap around what they had together. After all, he'd given up everything for William, he'd left his home, his family. He'd let himself be rescued.

He was in love with William, he'd just never really said so out loud. And what was wrong with marrying the person you loved? Wasn't that the whole point?

10.

William did love Gareth. Of course, he did. And it wasn't some cheap love at first sight. It had been slowly, carefully built over time, the two of them bound together not only by affection, but the comradeship which naturally arises from shared injustice. There was nothing and no one but Gareth, a statement which was all too literal now they were in Brighton, and William thought it was obvious, this love which spilled from his skin like sweat.

"Can't we just get married?" Gareth asked, his voice small and hard as he perched at the edge of their shared bed.

"Maybe—maybe someday," William consoled, aware of the flimsiness of his response, seeing it in Gareth's pained grimace. Yet whenever William had thought of marriage it was always with dread: bound to a wife he'd never want. He couldn't think of a wedding without recalling his parents' marital photographs, photographs which had ostentatiously decorated the hallway of the family home, framed reminders of his future, a wordless threat he'd passed by each morning on the way to the bathroom. They'd been a constant reminder of his own perverted inadequacy, a demand for him to surrender himself in front of a crowd of witnesses, to confess. Always to confess.

He did his best to herd his stray thoughts and explain himself. His palms were damp.

"It doesn't feel right. My parents were married. Your parents were married. I don't want that to be us."

"It would never be us," Gareth countered, gazing intently at his knuckles, hands cradled in his lap. "Our marriage wouldn't be theirs. This isn't about them."

It would be easier just to agree. It would be simpler. But this was already about them, because he saw in Gareth that same heavy

63

expectation, that same pressure to live someone else's life, on someone else's terms. He loved Gareth, but would Gareth love William if he weren't everything he expected?

There was that first morning in Brighton, when he'd awakened clad in lipstick, rouge, foundation, eyeliner—things which had been long forbidden him—and when he'd caught himself in the mirror it was as though he'd had a vision from another world. A world where he could explore the thousand possibilities of a free life, where whatever he felt on the inside could be worn on his very skin, where he could be whomever he so pleased.

You look like a—

Gareth hadn't finished the sentence and hadn't needed to: it was the expression that really stung, that look of mockery and disgust. It had only been a brief moment, but for the first time William had been afraid of Gareth. For the first time he'd realised that Gareth, too, needed him to adhere to certain restraints.

"Please know that I love you," William was flustered. "But . . ." He swallowed. "But I don't think I can get married. At least, not right now."

They were silent, then, William standing by the window of their temporary shelter, Gareth with his head in his hands, each trapped in position until William asked, "Could you accept that? Could you be with me anyway?"

To which Gareth mumbled, "I think so."

So they filled out the temporary residency forms, declaring themselves: other. And that was that. There was little to do but wait.

11.

It is said that our nation formed fifty years ago, when the UN finally recognised the homosexual resistance as the official government of Berlin. Others say it began in the Revolts of '33 and '34, when the gay brigades— volunteers from all over the world—took back control of our smoke and forced the Nazis off to Munich. It could be said that we were formed even before the War, when we made Berlin the homie capital of the world: the city of a thousand gay bars and a million gay residents.

But, you see, dear listeners, they would be wrong. Correct on paper, perhaps. But wrong in spirit.

Because our origin goes back even further than that—and as we stumble back beyond the 20th century, let us halt for a moment in 1888. Here we varda the dolly Oscar Wilde and Jane Addams, both in their prime, engaged in deep discussion with the old auntie Karl Heinrich Ulrichs. We varda them as they codify the disparate aims of a hitherto distracted and leaderless movement, surrounded by stacks of newsprint and letters and old magazines as they gather decades of diatribes, distilling them into one single text. An explosive text. A text which chanted for a homeland free from persecution.

They called it The Homosexual Haven.

Yet we're still nix at the beginning, even as we sprint back past the multitude of secret bevvies and meeting houses of the early 19th century, spread across London. Paris. Berlin. San Francisco. We're close, but nix there yet.

No, in order to find the founding of our great Republic we need to go all the way back to 1726, to London's "molly houses." These were the gay bars before there were gay bars, where fruits would meet and romance, where they drank and fell in love. And we need to focus on one particular molly house, one run by Margaret—also known as "Mother"—Clap.

At first Mother Clap's molly house may not have seemed anything special: it was another bawdy, run-down carsey of uneven plaster and broken bricks catering to the smoke's closeted clientele. Such places lived short lives before being infiltrated by spies and Lilly Law. Then the arrests would begin, and docile fruits would hang from nearby gallows.

But nix this time. On that fateful journo in February 1726, Lilly Law barged right on in. Only this time the guests did not flee, and neither did they cower. First, they threw coins, jeering at the corrupt constabulary. Then they threw bottles and chairs. They trolled through the streets, shouting and chanting, letting all of London savvy who they were. They were the Molly Revolt.

And they were crushed, tortured and hanged as an example to all. Their screams flooded the smoke's dockyards. They savvied it nix, but the spirit of our Republic was with them, even then, all that time ago. It was founded in their bravery, and though Mother Clap was burned along with her molly house, its ashes drifted across oceans.

We can't savvy the names of those killed that February, but we should savvy them as our first founders. The ones filled with the courage we would need to stand up, to declare ourselves an independent...

William turned down the radio as Gareth entered the room, cradling a round, un-iced cake and two miniature bottles of fizzy wine. At first William was confused, having completely forgotten his own birthday, then overwhelmed by Gareth's small kindness. Together they toasted his eighteenth year, drinking straight from the bottle.

But there was more than one reason to celebrate: their plane tickets had finally arrived, and so with their second glass they toasted their final night in the shelter.

"Hold on," Gareth ordered, rummaging through his backpack and pulling out a flimsy disposable camera. "We might want to remember this someday."

Cheek to cheek they grinned, dazzled by the flash. They downed the wine and went out in a jubilant mood, carrying their bottles with them, clasping free hands together as they breathed in the salty sea air.

"Goodbye, Brighton," William said.

"Hello, Berlin," Gareth added. The bottles chimed as they clanged them together. And no matter how much Gareth protested, there was still one thing William needed to do.

They wandered in search of a telephone booth. The weekend was already well underway, drunken celebrants streaming from party to party, chattering and whooping as they staggered down the narrow streets. A group of young men passed them by, one lusting after Gareth with a none-too-subtle backwards glance before disappearing into the giddy throng.

The old red telephone kiosk squatted in the corner of a quiet alleyway, bathed in the light of a sickly bare bulb. Motioning for Gareth to wait outside, William entered the piss-reeking cubicle, slid the correct change into the slot, and dialled. The receiver was shaking in his hand.

A voice answered, distant and small.

"Hello, Dovetree residence."

"Mum."

There was silence on the other end of the line, then a juddered intake of breath.

"George. George, it's William. Darling, please come home. Whatever's happened we can still work it out, we can work it out as a family. Please, William, we've been worried sick. Your father—"

"—had to have three stitches," his father's voice interrupted as he snatched the phone. "Thanks to his son and his sick little friend."

"Just come home," his mother's voice distantly pleaded. "Please, just come home."

"Well?" His father demanded. "What do you have to say for yourself?"

"We're leaving for Berlin tomorrow," William answered. "I'm calling to say goodbye."

Awful as it was, he could never have left without calling them. He glanced toward Gareth, who patiently waited on the other side of the glass.

"No you're bloody well not," his father ordered. "And you're upsetting your mother. No son of mine would move to the faggot city."

Faggot. It was the word the others at school had bellowed and jeered, as he'd shielded his head from each kick; it was the word the mechanics at the garage would say in hushed voices when his back was turned, but he'd never heard it from the man who'd raised him. On hearing the slur he knew he'd never see his father again.

Gareth tapped on the glass. He looked worried.

"We turned a blind eye to more than you're aware of," the voice barked from the other end of the line. "You're coming home, you hear me? This ends now."

William's knuckles clenched white against the telephone. He heard Gareth open the booth's door.

"I said, do you hear me, William? Do you—"

Wrapping one arm around William, Gareth took the receiver and gently hung up the phone.

The two exited the booth into the soft autumn breeze. Already the conversation, his father's outrage, his life of fretting and hiding—it was all drifting into the past. The air was filled with coloured lights and Friday-night noise.

"I think it's time for another drink," Gareth offered, playfully drumming his fingers against William's waist. "What do you say?"

Without answering, William grabbed Gareth and pulled him close. It was a full five minutes before he let go.

Excerpt from
The Honest Guide to Berlin

The History of Lesbian Berlin.

Berlin has a rich lesbian history, one which easily rivals its gay male counterpart. In fact, the city had the greatest concentration of lesbian meeting places on earth prior to the rise of the Third Reich, with Weimar Berlin boasting several dozen lesbian bars, the vast majority of which were located around the Schöneberg district (now part of Paw, the city's bear neighbourhood). These establishments catered to all manner of cultures, hobbies, and even fetishes—from sports to pipe smoking. Much like the lesbian regions of Berlin today, women flocked from all over the world to partake in this vibrant culture.

The lesbian world of pre-War Berlin was far from homogeneous. The early 20th century saw the formation of several working women's clubs, mainly for women factory workers and domestic servants, which were typically rowdy, bawdy establishments with a fiercely political culture. These stereotypically masculine working women came to be known as "diesels," and were often denied access to the middle and upper-class venues (particularly migrant diesels from ethnic minority backgrounds). The scene was home to various far left syndicates and provided the bulk of the lesbian brigades during the gay resistance against the Third Reich, playing a crucial role in driving Nazi authorities from the city. Today, diesel culture thrives in the aptly named Diesel district, to the far east of Berlin.

Women from well-to-do backgrounds were no less organised. Though fewer in number, their greater economic resources were used to establish grand private clubs, in which their lesbian clientele were encouraged to gather and network: many figures, such as American migrant Julia Morgan, sought to rival the lesbian scenes of fin de siècle Paris—and succeeded. While at first "duke" was used as a disparaging term both by diesels and a hostile heterosexual upper class, the term was reclaimed following Swedish writer Selma Lagerlöf's novel Rika Duka (Kingdom of Dukes). Alongside the "daddies" (their gay male equivalent), the duke establishment was instrumental in the founding of the gay republic, so much so that the lesbian Assembly is located in the duke district of Delos, close to the heart of the city.

Younger, trendier gay women dominate Flora, which is located around Flora Lake (formerly the Müggelsee). With its inhabitants known as "lipsticks" for their perceived focus on appearance, this scene is newer than those in Diesel and Delos but demonstrates a determination and vibrancy all its own. Several of the world's leading fashion labels are located in Flora, alongside artistic communities, modelling agencies, magazine publications, and even a small movie industry. Of course, the lake itself proves the area's greatest tourist attraction, with a beach promenade several miles long which features outdoor performances throughout the summer months.

LIPSTICKS, DUKES, AND DIESELS

The Gay Republic

1991

12.

Seven years ago—seven years before the riot—Howard had been waiting in the departure lounge at Cleveland International Airport. Howard was drinking a cocktail.

He was drinking a cocktail because there was nothing wrong with a man drinking a cocktail. Sure, he liked beer, but he was going to go work in the gay city, so he'd get used to how the gays did things. And the gays liked cocktails. He wasn't sure what food they liked, or many other things, but it was his first time outside of America, and he was going to go and experience it with an open mind. When in Rome. He even took a certain pride as he sipped the reddish-pink drink, because really, none of his friends would have done that. Even the lady bartender had given him a weird look.

This small rebellion, coupled with the potent fusion of booze, made him giddy. He ordered another as he chewed at the straw.

Howard had only met a gay once before, although looking back, it was probably just something they'd all assumed. Like dumb schoolkids do. Jack Henry'd been the kid's name, and Lord, he'd had a rough time. Looking back, Howard felt sorry for him, though back then he'd only felt the same contempt as the rest of his class. Everyone picked on Jack, or so he could remember. The girls would giggle at him, the boys beat him, and he didn't know which was worse. Then one day Jack disappeared, and even though he'd been a daily outlet for all their teenage anger and frustrations, no one even seemed to notice. Life went on; a new target was found.

"There you are. I've been looking all over for you, buddy."

Rob clasped his hand to Howard's shoulder. Howard up and pulled him into a brief hug, rigorously slapping his back as he did so.

As he pulled away, he glanced at Rob's hairline: in retreat, creeping back up his forehead in a way which worried Howard for his own. Otherwise, Rob was tall and broad and gooder than good: he hadn't picked on poor Jack Henry. A gentle giant, so Cissie called him.

You take good care of him now, she'd told Rob with a wink.

It hurt, the idea of spending a whole three months away from her and baby Thomas, but he sure was happy for his friend's company. Besides, the money was good, and Christ knew there was precious little work in Ohio, not for guys like him.

Or Rob.

Thing is, back when they were kids Howard had been kind to Rob, and maybe that made up for how he'd treated Jack Henry. Rob was from a bad family, and when shit'd hit the fan Howard had taken him in, even let him sleep in his bed while he took the floor. He'd listened to all Rob's problems, nodded along and doled advice, even given the odd hug. Rob had needed someone, and it'd felt good to be needed. It had been a pattern, as they'd grown and sprouted hair all over, as their voices cracked like broken dinner plates. Howard had been his rock, sure and steady.

"Lemme buy you a drink," Howard offered, gesturing to the airport bar.

"What're you drinking?" Rob asked, glancing down at the sugary pink-red mess that was starting to make Howard feel sick.

"A Cosmopolitan. I'm getting ready."

Rob nodded, as though his friend were making perfect sense.

"Then I'd better get one, too."

Berlin was like nothing he'd ever seen. The Ohio suburbs, with their sprawling lawns, rows of single-storey homes, and low-rise big box stores now seemed like an endless horizontal plane. A world in two dimensions. As he and Rob stepped out of the airport they gazed up at towers on towers on towers like hapless tourists, shrunk small with vertigo as walkways and elevated rail lines soared overhead.

The city looked like something from his childhood comic books, and the child within him marvelled at this strange new world.

Throw 'em all together and this is what the gays could build.

And not just the gays. As they wound their way through lanes of traffic and angry-honking taxicabs he realised that he, too, would be adding to this impossible city. That his two hands would leave their mark. There was pride in that.

It was Rob who found the company bus; Howard couldn't have found his ass cheeks with both hands. He was surprised by how many of the people around spoke English, though often in some unknown dialect, peppered with words he couldn't comprehend. There were other languages too, and from his limited Spanish he knew that was also mixed with the same odd vocabulary.

The bus buzzed with chatter as it pulled away from the station. They were off to Delos, in the lady half of the city. In fact, Howard was surprised by how many women there were; when he'd imagined gays he'd imagined men. Truth was, he hadn't given lady gays much thought. But of course there were lady gays. Why wouldn't there be?

Finally the bus hissed to a halt, depositing them at the builders' barracks which would be their home for the summer. It wasn't much (their quarters were sparse) but it was clean and comfortable. The dormitories were long and narrow, a single line of single beds, and he and Rob found two free ones at the far end of the room. Howard set down his bag and sat upon the sheets. They were cool and crisp, and reminded him of home.

Dinner took place at a long and noisy table. Most of the other construction workers were American, mostly from the Midwest. All of them were straight. He talked with Rob as they wolfed down grits, cornbread, fried chicken, biscuits, gravy, and mashed potatoes— deliberate Americana, clearly designed to preempt homesickness. In fact, it was all arranged, to Howard's mind, like some sort of summer camp: they were given Xeroxed pamphlets with directions to the nearest English-language cinema, the American grocery store, and the American Working Person's Club. Sure, it was a nice enough gesture, but Howard wanted to explore the local culture. He was in a foreign land, after all.

Then someone cracked a crate of beers, and by the end of the evening some of the men were slurring so bad the words piled up like cars slamming one into the other, crumpling into one big mess. But not Howard. He went to a small room just off the dormitory where there was a payphone, and dialled the number to his distant family. This is what they'd arranged, that he'd call when he got there, and then once a week.

"It's really something here," he told her. "Really something."

"I'm proud of you, hon," Cissie replied. "Just take care of yourself. I'm too busy to find a new husband."

Her voice was small and distant, but so sunny and soft it warmed his whole body, from his ears to his feet. She put Thomas on the line.

"Dad," he squealed. "*Dad dad dad dad dad.*"

And the sound of his little boy's voice lifted him higher than any of Berlin's towers.

They had the next day free, so over breakfast Rob suggested they take it easy: explore slowly, he said, take it all in gently. The worst thing is to be overwhelmed.

So, Howard and Rob wandered through the lesbian state beneath the blazing summer sun. Already the buildings seemed to have shrunk just a little, were less colossal, less imposing than they'd seemed the day before. Down an alleyway a crow pecked at a recycling dumpster, though for the most part Howard tilted his head upward as he walked, this time not as a tourist, but as a construction worker. Someone who appreciated good architecture. Someone in the business.

Rob, though, he took in everything at street level, watching the people around him and pointing them out to Howard. The pair passed women clutching expensive purses to their chests and wrapped in fashions they'd never seen—outfits nothing like the ones they were used to, all dramatic shapes and big pockets (neither Howard nor Rob had ever seen pockets on a dress). A lot of other women wore suits, with hair swept up like Victorian schoolteachers, swinging hefty briefcases: *Dukes*, Rob whispered. Then there were women walking hand in hand, or arm in arm, and though women friends back home did that, here it meant something different. Howard tried not to stare, all the while aware of how close he walked to Rob, of the tricky space between them. It was tough, figuring out this new world, and how he should act in it.

"Just think," Rob pointed out, "we're going to be giving these people a place to live."

"Ain't that something," Howard mumbled in reply, hiding his own enthusiasm. Of course, he was excited, but he couldn't show that to his friend. He wasn't sure why, exactly, but it felt shameful, like being naked.

They reached the grand, gilded entrance to a hotel, six revolving doors set side by side. Around the doors heaved throngs of women, some alone, some in pairs or groups, some chattering and some silent, but all with the same tense anticipation, like sprinters before the starting gunshot. Noisy buses pulled up, spilling more congregants to the sidewalk. Before Howard could stop him, Rob was asking one of the women what was going on. She had a strange accent, but she was friendly, explaining to the two shabby-looking workmen that the global conference for second-wave feminist-something was in town.

Rob looked passive, neutral as a Swiss. When they reached the next block, free of the buses and swarms, Howard asked his friend what he thought of it all.

"We shouldn't judge right now," his friend replied. "We're still taking it in. Don't think. Just watch. There's all the time in the world for opinions."

They only turned back when darkness spread across the sky, the streets glowing with light. By the time they reached the compound the others were halfway through dinner. The warm room buzzed with eager chatter as Rob and Howard collected their portions. One of the men threw out a joke about the queers, and Howard noticed a shadow spread over Rob's face like an eclipse. There, then gone.

That night it took him longer than usual to get to sleep, lying on the hard narrow bed as Rob snored close by. For a while he pictured Cissie, her lips painted red, full and soft when he kissed them, full and soft on his dick. He was pleased to feel it stiffen at the thought of her.

• • •

The work was tough, and the days were long, hefting and hauling beneath the scorch of the sun, or else drizzling rain. The pay was good. There was no complaining about that. But there were still some things Howard found strange. For one thing, he wasn't used to working with women. Sure, there'd been female secretaries, but he wasn't used to digging and hauling and lifting alongside them. He was working with some South African girl, though *girl* didn't exactly fit. She came up and introduced herself right away—"Anneke"—hand outstretched, shake as hard as any man's.

And that wasn't the only thing. These women were their *supervisors*. Not only was Howard surrounded by women doing things he'd never seen a woman do, but the women were in charge. Some even played practical jokes on the men: one poor guy opened his lunch pail to find a plastic prick inside, growing like a tumour out of a skimpy pair of panties. And of course, the women roared like it was the funniest god-damned thing on Earth.

It's a different culture, or so Rob kept saying. But it was hard, being so sweaty around them. He started to feel ashamed of his body, of his own dripping skin and stinking pits, in a way he'd never felt around the guys. And the South African woman—Anneke—was under him all the time, grabbing some tool, needing this or that. She was sweaty too, he could smell her, like hot pea soup. Something about that just wasn't right.

They were working in Flora, a district wrapped around a huge lake and lined by a long nudist beach. Each lunchtime the guys made their way to the sand, hollering and roaring, as raucous as they would've been back in the States. Flora was also flooded with pretty young lesbians, and the men would exchange glances and jokes as they passed naked girls. It was a way of relieving frustrated tension, Howard could understand that, though the full lips and perfect hair of passing girls only reminded him of Cissie.

Of course, they were the only large group of guys at the beach in among the young couples and homosexual families. They attracted glares from the mothers, but they didn't care. One particularly warm day they charged into the water, dicks flapping, concrete dust swirling about the surface as they swam and splashed like happy children. As ever, Rob hung back. He and Howard watched from a distance, perched on opposite ends of a beach towel.

Two young men eyed them as they passed by.

"Do you suppose they think we're a couple?" Howard asked his friend. It wasn't the first time he'd wondered, but it was the first time he had asked.

Rob just shrugged. What did it matter?

Howard thought it over, squinting at the water which may as well have been the sea. *We are what people think, at least a little. So, if someone thinks you're gay, does it mean, in some small way, that you are?*

Anneke returned from lunch in a grim mood, her nostrils flaring as she hauled and grunted beside Howard. So far, the two had barely spoken, but now she chastised and corrected him, a few words at a time. He was too slow, and then too fast; he didn't assist enough, or else he got in the way. She didn't like the way he smelled.

"You smell too!" he finally snapped, and for the briefest moment he thought he saw her smile. She said little after that, returning to her usual quiet, but Howard felt that in some small way he'd been tested. He just didn't know if he'd passed or failed.

He called Cissie every week, without fail. Thing was, he always stored up all the petty angers and frustrations, ready to reel them off to his wife and bask in her sympathy, but, when it came down to it, he never could.

"I don't know why you always want to talk about *my* week," Cissie said, voice still tinny and distant and wonderful. "Each one just runs into the next: cooking, grocery shopping, playing maid to our hellish little boy."

"I don't care," he told her. "Tell me everything."

He couldn't waste those calls with his gripes and complaints about the gays; those minutes were too precious. All that mattered was her voice. That she was there, even if thousands of miles away. Every time he hung up the grimy receiver, he felt cold again, and the irritations which hadn't mattered five minutes before needled at him.

79

He tried to talk to Rob, who would surely understand. He tried several times.

"But think of what *we* must look like," his friend responded over a beer. "Problem is, we're so alike, us and them."

Howard snorted. He was growing a little tired of this priggish liberalism, this puritanical need for correctness. *Saint Rob*, the others called him: ever understanding, ever tolerant. Just once he wanted to share a stupid, thoughtless joke with his friend, something to help him cope with this strange foreign culture. Something to show he was understood, at least. He thought of the plastic penis in the lunch pail. If the lesbians could tease, why couldn't they? After all, he didn't mean anything by it. Live and let live.

Howard's tension was only released at the rowdy dinner table, lost among dirty humour and lewd comments about the work women: the bulls, the diesels. He didn't join in, not directly, but he enjoyed it. He laughed from the sidelines. Meanwhile Rob kept quiet.

"If we hadn't been told they were women, I'd have guessed they were a bunch of shaved bears," someone chimed, rewarded with a chorus of guffaws.

That night, when Howard went out with the boys, Rob stayed in the compound. The same the next night, the same for many nights after that. Gradually, gradually, they stopped talking. The other construction workers weren't so bad, and now when they went to the beach, Howard joked and splashed about with them, ready to relieve a hard day's work.

Then everything changed.

"You've a call," one of the men yelled, waking him before the 6 a.m. alarm. He made his way past the beds of grumping, sleeping workmen, his head fuzzy and heart pounding. What had happened? Something was wrong, something with his family.

Then Cissie's voice, ever-tinny, ever-distant as Howard blinked through the pale morning light.

"I'm sorry," she apologised. She did that too much. "I know it's early there; I got a separate clock to keep track—"

"Cissie," he blurted. "What's wrong?"

"I'm pregnant."

The world stopped. Pregnant, pregnant, the word grew larger. *Pregnant.* He was going to be a father again. Pregnant. Thomas was going to have a little brother or sister.

Howard thanked God, surprising himself. But he meant it. After all, hadn't God been good to him? And his family? He laughed like a delighted child, a silly, simple joy.

But Cissie sounded tired.

"Honey. What are we going to do?"

The question stuck to him. He turned the situation over and over, examining it from every angle. The plan had been to spend just three months in the gay republic, to use the money to buy his wife and child the things they needed, to save a little for a rainy day. Now there was another mouth to feed, another little body to clothe, another growing mind to buy books for so it could grow up to be something greater than its old man.

That night he told the guys. They whooped and cheered, taking him to a nearby bar and buying beer after beer until the world spun, joyous and dizzy. All night they called him Daddy Howard, though that meant something else here. Besides, he was already a daddy.

As always, he said little to the work women, the diesels who grunted alongside him all day. But the guys must have said something to them instead, because Anneke came and shook his hand, a stoic nod of the head as congratulations. Thing is, he didn't know what to make of it, but the gesture was nice. The gesture was fine.

He didn't tell Rob the big news, there was enough to think about. Besides, Rob didn't even eat with them anymore, he got his food outside with his new gay friends. He'd find out soon enough.

The next call to Cissie was at the usual time, on the usual schedule. And Howard gave the answer to their puzzle, the only one he had, the one which stared them both in the face. Thing is, despite the discomfort, despite all the jibing and joking, a few of the other guys had already admitted they were coming back to Berlin full-time. Maybe it was even *because* of the jokes, which helped them deal with this alien world, where so many things were upside-down.

The pay was better, and new gays were coming in every day. They'd always need construction workers.

Honestly, he was surprised by how quickly Cissie said yes. How she leapt on the idea like a cat pouncing on a mouse. But he was pleased, of course he was pleased. Better to face your fate with a smile than a frown. And what was keeping them in the States, anyway?

It all spun by after that, his life a blurry cycle of work, drinks with the boys, calls to Cissie. The calls punctuated his routine, and they planned and planned in a way they never had before, when life had simply happened to them. There was furniture to sell and permits to sort, a thousand tiny things to build their new life.

Then the strangest thing happened. He was on a regular shift toward the end of his contract when Anneke approached and held out her hands, offering something.

It was a tiny romper suit, one her wife had made. She turned away before he had a chance to say something, some awkward, stumbling thank you, and he was glad of the consideration. There was an understanding between them, him and Anneke.

The romper suit was blue, and he hoped for a boy.

Before he knew it, he was back at the airport, drinking a beer in the departure lounge. Returning to Ohio one final time, and when he came back to Berlin, it would be with his family. He raised his glass in silent toast.

"Howard."

He didn't need to turn around to know it was Rob. Rob who no longer had the receding hairline, his head having been shaved by some queer barber, who now boasted a beard and looked every inch *Saint Rob*.

"Robert."

Really, he didn't know where this hostility came from. But he couldn't fix things with Rob even if he wanted to. The guy had made his choices, and Howard had made different ones. Besides, they wouldn't even be living in the same country anymore. What was there to mend?

"Things have been strained between us, I know that." Rob's scalp flushed red. He was clearly uncomfortable saying it. "But I do still consider you a friend. Things have been strange here, but when we get home—"

"I'm not going home, not for long," Howard interrupted. "Me and Cissie, we're coming to Berlin full-time. I can provide for her here. I can show her parents—"

He cut himself short, remembering the distance between them. "I can give Cissie a good life here, that's all. The life she really deserves."

"Well congratulations, Howard," Rob replied. "For that, and the new kid. I hope it works out for you."

Howard could hear the break in his old friend's voice.

"Yeah, you too."

Howard didn't look back up, but he could hear the man he'd known so many years walking away. And truth was, he took a grim satisfaction in it. In knowing that he could be a helpful, loyal, even kind person, but if you betrayed him, well, then you saw how brutally unforgiving he could be. That despite how gentle he was most of the time, he was no pushover. There was comfort in knowing that, there really was.

Howard drained his beer. His stomach lurched. But he had a beautiful wife and a healthy boy, with another on the way. As for the gay city, well, it was still distant and strange, but at least he had it figured out. Whatever came their way, he could deal with it. Whatever happened, he could protect his family.

It was, after all, his most important job.

Excerpt from
The Honest Guide to Berlin

The Gay "Language."

Visitors to Berlin will notice that Polari dominates everything from signposts to casual conversation. This might be confusing at first, but it's easy to master once you've got the hang of it, and many visitors find themselves still using Polari phrases once they return home—much to the surprise of their friends and neighbours! Though it's one of the official "languages" of the city-state, Polari is in fact a form of slang, and Polari terms are used with a variety of different languages. For example:

English (unaltered):
Hey neighbour! Want to go to a bar?

Polari English:
Hey homie ajax! Want to troll to a bevvie?

Polari German:
Hallo Homie Ajax! Willst du in eine Bevvie trollen?

Daunted? Don't be. Few gay people can immediately converse in Polari on arrival in the gay republic, and no one expects it of a tourist. For the most part Polari-speaking residents are patient and happy to help teach you their "language"—perhaps in exchange for a drink or two.

A Brief History of Polari.

Polari has its roots in Parlyaree, a slang used among European carnival performers since the 1600s. Once in Britain it made the transition from fair to theatre, where it mutated into Early Polari with the addition of cockney rhyming slang. Acting was a profession common among "sodomites" at the time, with the new language providing safe cover for dangerous talk. By the time the molly houses arose almost a century later, Polari had become widespread in the underground gay scenes of England's larger cities. Over time, a variety of terms from Romani, backslang (backwards words), sailor slang, Italian, and Yiddish were added to the expanding Polari vocabulary.

Unsurprisingly Polari dominated many of the gay private clubs which had become widespread by the Victorian era. When Oscar Wilde, Jane Addams, and Heinrich Ulrichs penned *The Homosexual Haven* (the first treatise calling for a homosexual homeland) they made sure to create a Polari translation of the document. Variants on Polari became common in Paris, Milan, San Francisco, and of course, Berlin—where the gay "language" was commonly heard in the streets and cafes of the Weimar capital. When the gay brigades formed in resistance to the Nazi establishment, Polari was used to give orders to the regiments. It was even part of the constitution for the new gay republic.

Today Polari has become thoroughly mainstream among the planet's gay havens, with movies, books, magazines, and even newspapers being published in the slang. However, its ad hoc, free-form days are over: Polari is now officially controlled by the Polari Grand Carsey, a government institute which regulates vocabulary and terminology. Over the course of its long history, Polari has gone from an ever-changing, underground dialect to an official state tongue—but through it all it has remained the "language" of the gay people.

OF BEVVIES AND GARTERS

The Gay Republic

1998

13.

Cissie had never seen Ms. Fortier's apartment. Well, that wasn't quite true: she had peered in through her elderly neighbour's doorway, noted the dark wallpaper in the hall. It was striped green and white, and was, to Cissie's mind, entirely incongruous for a small apartment perched within the bowels of a high-rise—it reminded her of movie-set Victorian homes, or haunted house rides. Covering the wallpaper were old picture-portraits, in appropriate ovals and squares, scratchy, monochrome faces trapped within.

She had asked, once, if the pictures were of friends or relatives. *Of course not*, the older woman had tutted, *but I know their faces better than anyone.*

From her vantage point in the doorway Cissie had also glimpsed a polished oak hatstand, a small armoire, and a fancy bucket stuffed with a ridiculous assortment of umbrellas. The combination of wallpaper, pictures, and antiques made it look as though Ms. Fortier's hallway had been transported from a bygone century and transplanted into their concrete stack of a building. It gave her the impression of someone playing at being an old woman, in the same way a child plays at adulthood: with cliches and objects too big for them.

Why had she never entered her friend's apartment? For the simple reason that Ms. Fortier had never invited her inside, and Cissie—raised in a cozy farm-style home which had been resolutely and absolutely cut off from the world—had never dared invite herself. Of course, that didn't mean she hadn't wondered. In her fantasies this bizarre hallway extended back to a colossal manor house, so grand and opulent that it defied both their building's cement shell and indeed physics itself, spilling out into parlours and maid's quarters, drawing rooms and— Cissie's favourite part—a grand conservatory of glass and wrought

89

iron, soaring over a steaming jungle of plants.

This imaginary abode was somehow comforting, the thought of such opulence lying three floors above her own worn yet beloved apartment. Like a magical world hidden in the back of a wardrobe, or at the bottom of a rabbit hole. And she would have left Ms. Fortier's home to her own imaginings, had her own world not changed so much. Had Howard not changed.

Once rescued by the Spanish stranger, Cissie and the children had meandered back to the apartment. Slowly, carefully, Cissie led them on, her ears straining for shouts or chants. For danger. Jonah clutched her left hand, Thomas her right. Yet the surrounding streets had been more or less normal—people scurried to and from jobs, a street seller with a shaved scalp sold vegetarian meatballs—all as though the world weren't imploding just a few streets away.

After twenty minutes of walking, she'd even felt silly. She and the children were fine, it was Howard who'd been handcuffed and taken away by the police. So, she'd straightened her back and walked a little faster. Sensing this shift, the children had calmed, and Cissie had bought them ice cream. By the time they returned to the apartment the children were loud and giggly, their faces smeared bright colours. Cissie unlocked the door, hoping to see her husband.

Howard wasn't there.

The children watched television (unmonitored and uncensored, they'd flicked through the channels in nonsense abandon, grasping the forbidden worlds in two-second jumps) while Cissie pored through the phone book and called the local police station.

Then another.

Then a third.

They all used the strange gay words. None would tell her anything. So, she'd left the children with Ms. Fortier and was about to scour the city in person when Howard stumbled into the lobby.

For the longest moment she and her husband simply stood and stared at one another, drowning in relief, unable to move. Then Howard darted forward, wrapping her in his arms, hard chest and soft belly enveloping her. She'd drowned in his presence, and she'd been glad to.

It took her another few days before she'd realised that the Howard who'd returned wasn't *her* Howard.

For one thing, this new Howard smiled so much less, and when he did it was with his mouth, and not his eyes. Then she noticed that this new Howard took no delight in going to work, that when she asked about the latest building project, he'd given nothing more than a shrug. The only time he strung more than two or three words together was during family prayers, which now took place before every meal—even breakfast—and, with hands clasped and head bowed, Cissie would patiently wait for it to end. She tried not to think of her parents.

Once, when she snuck an eye open during the Lord's Prayer, she caught him staring at her and the children. His face was entirely blank.

At first, she'd continued her usual routines, but by the fourth day (or was it the fifth?) after the riot, Howard had taken Jonah and Thomas to school. He'd picked up groceries after work. He insisted she stay safely at home.

No, not insisted. Not even directed. It had been an order.

"It isn't safe. I feel better knowing where you are."

She'd hoped that when the bruises on her knee and the small cut on her cheek had faded that this new Howard would too. That he'd soften and calm. So, she'd obeyed his strange orders. She'd spent her time reading paperbacks and cooking dinners and cleaning behind the fridge, and as each day passed the apartment had shrunk smaller and smaller, until it felt as though she'd be crushed between the living room wall and the kitchen counters.

Out of desperation, she broke her old taboo. She knocked on her elderly neighbour's door and invited herself in. Just to be somewhere else. To escape into the magical mansion which lurked upstairs, and which she knew could not be real.

"Cissie sweet! There's no great secret. You could have come over whenever you wanted."

Ms. Fortier handed her a cup of tea laced with some syrupy sort of liquor, and Cissie, too polite to object, took it in small sips. Ms. Fortier drank from her own cup, looked disgusted, then added liberally from a cut-glass decanter on her side table.

Cissie was too busy drinking in the contents of Ms. Fortier's apartment to focus on her neighbour's daytime libations. At first, she'd been disappointed to find the apartment the same size and shape as her own; there was no secret, mystical palace waiting on the twenty-ninth floor of her tenement. But once the childlike fantasy had been dispelled, she discovered things more wondrous, not in the length and breadth of the place, but in the detail. Whereas Cissie's home was filled with all the crud and clutter of a hectic family, Ms. Fortier's was draped in memories and adventure. Every wall had some different hanging or mask or painting or poster or photograph from Africa and Asia, from the Americas and all parts of Europe. Antique coffee tables held figurines and ornamental ashtrays, books, and lamps in at least five different styles. The floor was carpeted with rugs in Latin and West Asian fashions. It was as though a museum had been ransacked: the delightful mess was both appalling and amazing, with nowhere for the eyes to rest. It was either the apartment of a woman who'd endured a life of adventure, or one with a particular penchant for antique markets and souvenir stalls.

"Are you shocked, dear thing?" Ms. Fortier inquired, sipping what was evidently a much more satisfying gulp of tea.

"It's a lovely apartment."

"I mean about your husband's change. His new behaviour."

Cissie was about to ask how she knew, but *of course* Ms. Fortier knew. Though Cissie hadn't seen her since the day of the riot, Ms. Fortier would have assumed something was the matter from Cissie's uncharacteristic intrusion; by the trembly, nervous way she clutched her teacup. Howard was the most obvious cause. Besides, she might even have seen him taking the children to school or returning home with bundles of the wrong groceries.

But strange as it seemed even to Cissie herself, it wasn't really Howard that bothered her. To Cissie's mind, Howard's changes were a symptom, not a cause, and were most likely—hopefully—temporary.

He'd also been a little strange when he'd returned from his first working visit to Berlin several years ago, but he'd soon gone back to normal.

No, what bothered Cissie was the world outside their small apartment, the events which circled their building like cats stalking prey.

"It's not Howard that shocks me. It's here, it's Berlin. I thought I had a grip on things, but now I don't know what to expect. And if I don't know what to expect, how can I protect myself? How can I protect the children?"

"Well," replied Ms. Fortier, taking another sip of her liquor-laced tea. "It sounds like you need to learn more about the city, so why not go right to the source?"

"The source?" Cissie took a large swig from the delicate cup, grateful for the mystery liquor's warmth as it coated her stomach.

"A lesbian bar, darling. Go to a lesbian bar and talk to people. One in their own territory, say, in Delos. No, no, Flora. It's prettier there."

The warmth was gone. Cissie's stomach was now a solid block of ice.

"I've never been to Flora. And I don't even look like a lesbian," she declared.

"You've lived here, what?" Ms. Fortier asked.

"Six years or so."

"Six years!" the older woman exclaimed, one hand to her heart. "And you still think they all look like bull dykes and the bearded lady? Sweetness, if you say you're a lesbian, you're a lesbian. Just get that haunted look off your face and you'll be fine, I promise you. Especially with me by your side."

"You'll be there, too?" In all the years Cissie had known Ms. Fortier, she'd never seen her elderly neighbour leave their building.

"What?" Ms. Fortier exclaimed. "You think I wouldn't go to a bar? You think I'm too old? Well, we'll see who's old."

14.

Cissie awoke that morning even before the dawn chorus of the twentieth-level skyway. She was already uneasy. She got up, brushed her hair in front of the little bathroom mirror, and ate her breakfast in small snatches as she cooked for Howard and the children. As the edges of the eggs flapped and bubbled about the frying pan, she thought over Ms. Fortier's suggestion. Part of her was curious, of course. She did live in the gay city, after all, and what had she seen of it? All these years and she'd barely left Hetcarsey. How had the time gone so quickly?

She chipped at the borders of the eggs to keep them from sticking. The other part of her was nervous. She'd never gone anywhere with Ms. Fortier, let alone to a place like that. Yet she already knew the story she would present to Howard.

"I was thinking of having a girls' night up at Ms. Fortier's place," she said, as she placed the plate of eggs before her husband. She wouldn't be discovered—there was no chance Howard would ever venture up to Ms. Fortier's apartment—but was her voice as fake as it sounded in her head? She wasn't used to lying.

"It's just been difficult being cooped up in the apartment, and I thought—"

"Of course," Howard replied, his mouth full of egg. "You need a break."

Cissie hadn't expected it to be so easy. Without realising it, she'd relied on Howard's objections to substitute for her own.

"I mean, I honestly don't mind cancelling, if leaving you with the children is too much trouble. Really."

"Honey," Howard responded, swallowing his food and placing his fork upon the table. He rarely addressed her with terms of endearment, and Cissie felt edgier than ever. "I don't know why you'd want to spend time with that—" he glanced toward the children, who were fighting over the cereal box, "—*knowledgeable* old lady. But I can take care of the kids, once I'm done with work."

"Oh really," Cissie said, turning away to prepare more coffee, hiding the anxiety which surely lined her face. "You don't have to do that. I can say no. I don't mind at all."

"Go," he replied, pushing his chair back and walking over to her. "You work yourself to the bone for this family." He wrapped one arm around her, then the other, nuzzling her neck from behind.

"Gross," Thomas exclaimed.

"But you work hard, too," Cissie replied, ignoring her son's outburst.

"I know I've been a tad distant lately," Howard confessed, releasing her from his embrace. "I've just been worried, after what happened. And you've been so good about it. I don't always think I deserve you."

Before she could say anything, he issued his direction.

"Go have fun tonight. Please."

That evening she met Ms. Fortier at her door. Her palms were sweaty, and she was relieved when her friend and neighbour didn't take her hand in greeting. Instead, Cissie patiently waited as the older woman applied blusher and lipstick. Then she waited as she mused over the right handbag, from a closet holding at least a dozen. By comparison, Cissie only had two: her good one, and her everyday one.

"You never had children, did you?" she asked, gazing at the array.

"Not true. I had a boy. I loved—" Ms. Fortier corrected herself, "—I *love* him very much. He died a long time ago now."

She finally selected a green and gold bag, holding it up and examining herself in the mirror.

Cissie burned with shame, a dull ache spreading through her whole body at the thought of losing either Jonah or Thomas. Ms. Fortier remained frozen before the mirror, her eyes resting for just a moment on Cissie, who only managed to say, "I had no idea. I'm so sorry."

On hearing the words, Ms. Fortier dismissed the green and gold bag, and returned to her collection.

"Be careful, sweet thing, in making presumptions about people." Her voice was thick and heavy in a way Cissie had never heard before. "After all, you're a young housewife from a part of America most of us in Europe have never even heard of. There are plenty of things a person could presume about you."

Before Cissie had time to take offence Ms. Fortier continued, her voice warmer. "Would anyone guess you're on your way to a lesbian establishment? Darling, tonight we will do away with presumptions. Tonight, we are sapphists.

"Oh, get that look off your face," she added, "I don't mean *littéralement*."

She picked up a red leather purse as though she'd wanted it all along, and ushered Cissie from the front door.

Bracing themselves against the evening's chill, the two women left the building at ground level and took the main avenue. When Cissie had first heard they'd be living on Amity Boulevard she'd imagined a grand street lined with trees and breezy European cafés, not ramshackle market tents housing sex workers and fortune-tellers. When she walked past with Howard he'd mutter beneath his breath, whereas Ms. Fortier seemed to know each of them intimately.

"Charlatan," she commented, pointing a long gold nail toward a tent marked *Oracle* as a light-rail train passed overhead.

"Expensive," she noted, the nail directed at a stall labelled *Tarot*.

"Not worth it," she remarked at a booth advertising *Erotic Massages*.

"How many 'erotic massages' have you had?" Cissie asked.

"I keep my ears open to local information, Cissie dear."

"Some might call that gossip," Cissie replied.

Ms. Fortier playfully jabbed her in the side.

"Everyone is interested in gossip, my sweet. It simply depends on what kind."

The two women boarded a near-empty bus bound for the lesbian district of Flora. The only bus Cissie had ever ridden had been the one which had taken her to the airport, and in truth she was more than a little glad of her friend's company as they took their seats side by side.

Together they watched the city roll by the windows. Cissie's fists clenched as they reached the border, marked by a stretch of sixteen train tracks which sliced through the southeastern part of the city, a no-man's-land between buildings. As the bus crossed a narrow bridge over the tracks, she gazed upon the shimmering silver trains snaking beneath.

The streets on the other side were a far cry from the clamour of Amity Boulevard. Already Cissie could tell they were quieter. More genteel. The apartment blocks shrank as their windows grew. The litter lining the sidewalks transformed into neatly trimmed grass and high hedges. Though the rows of buildings were still fairly tall (at least eight stories, as far as she could tell), the atmosphere gave the image of Paris, a city she'd only seen in movies. It was exciting. Like an exotic vacation.

"Close your mouth, dear. You look dead."

She noticed the advertisements change. A billboard sprawled over the side of one building was emblazoned with an ad for toothpaste: a smiling family headed by two women, all with glaring white teeth. Then, by an intersection, one for cola. This featured a young, pretty, short-haired girl, swigging from a can while watching another girl pass by.

"It's like another world."

"Keep your voice down, sweet. It *is* another world."

Finally, Ms. Fortier rose, and guided them from the bus. Though the street was rosy with twilight, most of the stores were still open, and the area hummed with sedate activity: young mothers strolled with their children, who bothered flocks of pigeons; new girlfriends giggled and kissed one another; old women sat on benches in pairs, watching the world in the way only the elderly ever do. Cissie had never seen so many women in one place before.

In keeping with their surroundings, she chose to take Ms. Fortier's hand in her own. Ms. Fortier glanced at her in surprise, then focused her attention on the street before them. Her face displayed an obvious, though slight, satisfaction.

"The bar is around here somewhere."

"Do you remember the name?" Cissie asked. The two broke hands to weave around a herd of children, shepherded by two young chaperones.

"It's been such a long time," Ms. Fortier called to her over the heads of the passing infants.

"So, you don't remember?" Cissie raised her voice to compete with the excited babble.

"I—hold on, let's try this." Ms. Fortier reached over and grasped Cissie's hand once more, pulling her through the miniature crowd toward a doorway, the words *Sacred Weave* hand-painted above. "This sounds familiar."

There was no display window—most of the street's establishments were located on the second storey, up a series of steps. They entered to find shelves and shelves of wool, in every colour Cissie could name (alongside several she couldn't). The place was empty but for a middle-aged woman behind the counter, a long trail of knitted wool snaking around the floor. If it was a scarf, it was for a giraffe.

"Excuse me," Ms. Fortier enquired. "I was wondering if you could direct us to a bar."

The woman slowly looked up from her strange craftwork, as though this change of focus took a significant amount of effort. With a laboured swing of her hand, she indicated down the street. Her Russian accent was thick as treacle.

"Take your pick. Many places." On seeing their hesitation, she added, "Just walk."

"Thank you for your time," Cissie chirped, but the woman had already returned to knitting.

"It's the names, dear," Ms. Fortier explained once they were outside. "Any one of them could be a—how do you say?"

"Euphemism," Cissie replied, directing Ms. Fortier toward a place labelled *Legs Apart*. Once more they climbed up the stairs, this time to discover a store devoted to stockings, tights, and winter socks. Ms. Fortier bought a pair of navy-blue nylons.

They entered a print shop, a liquor store, and a bakery, each with a name which could easily be that of a bar, at least to Cissie's eyes. With each one, she took the lead. She'd come this far. She was determined to find an actual drinking establishment for gay women.

Finally, they found *The Stuffed Rose*, which Cissie suspected was a flower shop. However, they climbed the stairs and ascended into a cloud of smoke. It was one of those establishments which took care to look effortless, which had spent a great deal of money in fashioning trashy ambiance. Pink fur lined almost every surface—the walls, the bar, even the seats. Cissie imagined it would be a nightmare to clean.

"What'll you have?" the young woman behind the bar inquired. "We have a special tonight, 'Bloody Mother's Ruin.'"

"We'll take two," Cissie ordered, before glancing over to Ms. Fortier. "If you like?"

"You take charge," Ms. Fortier replied, watching Cissie with a look of proud fascination, as though she'd taught a dog to speak English. Once served, Cissie picked up the drinks and started carrying them toward a nearby booth. Ms. Fortier stopped her.

"We have to separate, Cissie my girl. What will you discover if you spend the night in conversation with me?"

The thought of going solo frightened Cissie, but still thrilled by this foreign adventure, she nodded all the same. As Ms. Fortier took her drink and seated herself at the bar, she made her way toward the empty booth. Alone.

It was still early evening, and the place was quiet. From a vantage point which allowed a clear view of the door, Cissie sipped her drink slowly, watching women enter in couples and pairs. One small group nattered away in German, another in a language she'd never even heard before. She weighed each guest, wondering which were open to approach as the stools and benches were taken, one by one.

Glancing toward the bar revealed Ms. Fortier in deep conversation with the bartender. She caught Cissie's eye and raised her eyebrows, willing her to talk to someone. And she'd almost, *almost* drummed up the courage to do so when a woman approached her booth, speaking in an accent she couldn't place.

"May I sit here?"

She wore a sensible suit, with an equally unremarkable shoulder-length haircut. For some reason this surprised Cissie: she wasn't sure what she expected, but she hadn't banked on them looking so familiar. So normal. Were it not for her blonde hair the woman could have been her sister. Cissie had never had a sister.

"Please," she replied. "I'd love the company." She sipped at her beverage in a way she hoped appeared lesbian.

If she wants to go to bed, just say you're taken, she told herself. *After all, that much is true.*

The woman grinned. Once seated, she sighed and kicked off her shoes. It seemed a strange way to attempt romance.

"How are you?" Cissie could hear the strained formality to her own voice.

The woman grunted. "It's been a long journo. At work."

"Your accent," Cissie remarked. "Australian?"

"Close, but you're still a good four thousand kilometres out," the woman replied, closing her eyes and sinking into the cushioned seat. "I'm from New Zealand, originally."

"And what is it you've been working so hard on today?" Cissie asked. The question animated the woman, sparking a grumpy enthusiasm and pulling her to an upright position.

She was a "vaggerie carser"—that meant travel agent, a profession which animated Cissie in turn—she'd had so few chances to travel, and she'd never even thought of the gay city's residents going on vacation, seeing as Berlin was a sort-of refuge, its residents hiding away from the world. As she gulped her drink and ordered two more, the woman explained the difficulties in operating a gay travel agency.

"Very few countries are safe havens for our kind," she explained. "People want an authentic, local experience, but mostly we can only offer a compound they can stay in. Little fruit-friendly bubbles. And even those aren't really safe—some new 'family values' politico gets elected, or some warlord seizes power, and the carseys are burned right to the ground. In some cases, with the tourists still inside. We've had people beaten, stoned, imprisoned for decades. The insurance alone—" She began rubbing her temples. "And people still go, even with the travel warnings."

"But there's trouble here, too," Cissie prompted, trying to shift the conversation to the danger she'd glimpsed. The riot.

"Not the same. Even with the violence, it's not like many people are killed. They're not *tortured*, and I can give you a list of places where they would be. Besides, show me a country that doesn't have different sides that barney once in a while."

Cissie wanted to ask what exactly the "sides" were, but to do so would out herself as straight. So she allowed a pause between them, hoping the woman would elaborate. Instead, she went to fetch yet two more drinks.

"It's my shout," she insisted. Cissie looked around for Ms. Fortier but couldn't spot her in the now thoroughly crowded space. When the New Zealander returned, she asked Cissie about her profession. Knowing that the easiest lies are those with a veneer of truth, Cissie explained she was a housewife, looking after two young children.

"You don't see many single-worker families here," the woman exclaimed, raising her glass to Cissie's. "And you don't have to look so guarded. I know you're hetero."

"It's so obvious?" Cissie sipped at her drink to hide her surprise.

"Plain as journo. You're a good actress, but we savvy our own. You're hardly the first straight Berliner whose curiosity got the better of her."

"So why are you talking to me?" Cissie asked.

The woman threw her head back, her laugh full-bellied.

"Because you seemed like good conversation. And I didn't have to worry about rejecting a drunken advance at the end of the night."

"Just get a couple more drinks in me," Cissie teased, joining her companion's good-natured cackle.

Though the conversation was certainly engrossing, it didn't reveal much. The woman assumed knowledge Cissie didn't have, and mostly referred to "us" and "them"; though "them" in turn referred to straight people, co-workers, and groups Cissie could only guess at. Yet she had fun, and by the time the New Zealander stumbled to the door (having announced an early start the next morning), she was also acutely drunk.

"Do you know Ramona Palomar?" she suddenly shouted after her. It was an afterthought, recalling the lemon juice-wielding saviour who'd rescued her from the riot. But the woman was already gone. Cissie realised she'd never even learned her name.

She staggered her way through the unsteady, swaying bar, trying to keep her balance as the floor rolled beneath her. The place was still busy, and as she pushed and prodded her way through the bodies, she issued slurred apology after slurred apology. She eventually found Ms. Fortier seated near the bathroom.

"Cissie!" she exclaimed. "Sweet thing, you look unwell. I better take you home." She stood and took Cissie's arm, guiding her through a swirling world which came in snapshots, like browsing a photo album: the fluffy pink walls, the hazy street, the lurching bus, the sixteen tracks, the dizzying towers of Hetcarsey, the raspberry-painted hallway outside her apartment.

"Take your shoes off, so you don't wake your family," Ms. Fortier instructed, bending to help free Cissie's feet. "You'll feel this tomorrow, my dear."

She left Cissie with a small kiss to one cheek, then hustled toward the elevators. Cissie wandered toward her apartment, one hand clutching her shoes, the other sliding against the wall. She carefully took out her key and unlocked the door.

The living room lights were blazing. A group of men were standing in a circle, red-faced and shouting angry *Amens!* which faltered as she walked in. They turned to her one by one, annoyed and confused by the interruption.

There were Bibles on the carpet, by their feet.

"What—what's going on?" Cissie asked, dropping her keys to the floor, suddenly, sickeningly sober. "Howard. What is this?" She could already feel the throb of a headache.

Howard walked over to her. "I guess we ran a little late, is all. It doesn't matter." Turning back to the group, he added, "Just a moment, guys." He then took Cissie's shoes from her and guided her to the bedroom, closing the door behind them. They perched side by side on the edge of the bed.

"Howard?" Her voice was thin as skimmed milk. She couldn't look at him, she couldn't acknowledge the scene she'd walked straight into. The fervour, the Bibles. She was afraid that if she looked upon his face, she would see her father.

"It's just a couple guys I know from work. We want to help each other," he said, with the same sullen tone Thomas sometimes used. "To look after our families."

Worse, he sounded as though he'd been rehearsing the explanation. She didn't know what to say. So she stared at her feet, at the spaces between her toes.

"We *need* to come together," Howard continued. "After what happened, I realised how alone we are. How vulnerable. How isolated. What we need is community. Like-minded people who share our values. It's the smart thing to do."

Her head was spinning; still she said nothing; still she examined her feet.

"What do you want from me, Cissie?" His voice cracked, hurt and defensive. He'd taken her silence as condemnation, but still, she couldn't speak, still she couldn't look. "You and the boys could've been killed. There's a big, messed-up city out there, tens of millions of folks all at each other's throats, and we're in the minority. When they're done turning on each other, they'll come for us. We have to look after our own."

Cissie cradled her face with her hands. Howard stood.

"You could've been killed," he repeated, his voice now soft and remorseful. He left the bedroom without another word, returning to the blazing lights and Bibles.

Cissie collapsed backwards onto the bed, trying to tame her swarm of thoughts, riding waves of nausea. But through her haze she held on to one simple resolution: she was going to keep control of her family. She'd no idea how, but she promised herself that.

By the time she returned to the living room the assembled men were gone. Howard was sitting alone in the corner, watching the football game on mute.

15.

Perhaps Howard was just building walls. He did that sometimes, unconsciously, doing without knowing. For all his strength, he was frightened. Sometimes that fear would make him close himself off, but she'd seen it, before, in his eyes. A faint glimmer, a little boy who wants to be held and helped and doesn't know how to ask. It had happened when he'd lost his janitor job; it had happened when his father died. Eventually he would re-emerge, once his shelter grew stale with loneliness, once the fear had passed like clouds brisking across the sky. So it had been, and so it would be.

But the group. The group was new. It echoed with the righteous self-destruction of her parents, and worse, it meant the prayers weren't just a phase. In fact, they grew ever more frequent. They got longer, too, and she'd try to keep the children from fidgeting, blocking out the memories of her parents' home, of those prayers which had housed unsubtle criticisms:

Please help Cissie try harder in her geometry classes.
We ask that you bring Cissie wholesome friends.
Remind Cissie to honour her mother and father.

They would sneak glances at her as they prayed, wary looks that made her feel like a caged animal. A strong animal, in a particularly flimsy cage. And there had been prayers for every circumstance: not only before dinner, but prayers for the morning, prayers for a Sunday, prayers for going to bed. This was how they'd communicated with her, how they'd conveyed their desires.

In your grace, we want Cissie to know how much we care for her. How we want only the best for our daughter.

This was how they'd told her they loved her. Via faith. Omnipresent, overshadowing. And despite their objectives, their prayers had failed to push her toward the Lord. As they'd fervently mumbled their wishes to an unseen God, she'd dreamed of escape. Only of escape.

She'd succeeded, of course. To a marriage, to a new land. Or so she'd thought. Now the prayers had followed her, all the way around the world.

"I'm just trying to find some order for our lives," Howard defended, when she'd asked him not to do it again. His voice had been thick with puzzled hurt, and she'd felt guilty, while just as stuck as before.

"He's made a boys' club so he can feel like a man," Ms. Fortier advised the very next day, tapping her cigarette into a bowl shaped like an elephant's head. "His ego was bruised. Men lose their minds when that happens. Don't worry, sweet thing. It'll pass."

Cissie hoped so. Though Howard didn't bring anyone to the apartment again, he disappeared for the evening, every Tuesday and Thursday. Off to the circle of men, with their cardigans and their hollering and their cheap paperback Bibles.

16.

R. Palomar-Detante, Apartment 1115, San Fran Boulevard, Maytree, BERLIN

"Hello?"

"Hello, I'm sorry to be calling you out of the blue, and you don't know me, you wouldn't, but my name is Cissie Parker."

"What can I do for you, Ms. Parker?"

"Well, I was wondering if I could speak with Ms. Palomar?"

"There isn't one. This is Mr. Palomar."

"Oh, I'm sorry to bother you."

"Can I ask what this is abou—"

Cissie hung up the receiver and crossed the number from the phone book. She turned to the next name.

R. Palomar-Malouzat, Apartment 002, 976 Lederweg, Paw, BERLIN

"Bonjour."

"Hi, my name is Cissie Parker. I was wondering if I could speak with Ramona Palomar. We met in the street. Well, it was actually a tunnel, there was a riot—"

"Pardon, madame, je ne comprends pas. Polari-vous Francais?"

"Oh, I'm sorry. Jermer apple Cissie Parker. Commentee apple too?"

"Raimond Malouzat-Palomar."

"Oh, never mind. Bon-jorr."

At first the wrong numbers had only increased her determination, but now it ebbed, little by little, with each call. It didn't make sense, Cissie knew that, but she couldn't shake the vague feeling that the woman who'd saved them at the riot could help her once again.

If only she could find her.

R. Palomar-Hilton, Apartment 1483, 12 Shelleypark, Delos, BERLIN

"I swear to the gods, Susan, if you don't stop—hold on, I'm on the phone. Hello? Hello? Who is this?"

"I'm sorry to bother you, but my name is Cissie Parker. Thank God I'm finally through to a woman."

"What?"

"I'm looking for—"

"Jesus cunt-busting Christ, is this some sort of weird phone pickup thing? I thought it was bad enough with the bevvies, now people are calling my *house?* Are you looking for Susan? She's been playing around, hasn't she?"

"No, I just—"

"Susan, your slut is on the phone. I absolutely fucking swear, if you've been cheating on me . . ."

"Hello, this is Susan Hilton-Palomar. Who is this?"

"I'm Cissie Parker, I was looking for Ramona Palomar."

"Well, you've got the wrong number, and now my wife thinks I'm having an affair. So thanks for that."

The line went dead.

Cissie had exhausted the possibilities of the phone book. All she knew of this Ramona Palomar was her name—and it was even possible that Cissie had misheard it. The gays and lesbians often seemed to have double surnames, but the woman had only given one. It was doubtful she'd ever find her.

The walls of the apartment were closing in again, subtly, almost imperceptibly, inching toward her as the hours rolled on. Seated at her perch by the telephone, she watched the twentieth-level skyway from her living room window, noting the scalps of passersby: the women sporting flakes of dandruff; the balding men decorating themselves with flimsy comb-overs; teens with gelatinous globs of hair gel.

Then: impossible. A woman with a sweep of long, dark hair.

107

It couldn't be her—the city was home to millions of women with that same dark hair—but Cissie bolted from her chair, throwing on a jacket and grabbing her purse. She ran to the elevators. She pushed the button. Too slow . . . it was still ten floors away. She'd take the stairs.

Floor twenty-five.

I need to catch up. I need to catch up . . .

Floor twenty-four.

Hurry hurry hurry!

Floor twenty-three.

It can't reasonably be her. You're being completely irrational . . .

Floor twenty-two.

Come on come on come on!

Floor twenty-one.

Cissie's heart heaved as she reached the twentieth-level lobby, shoved open the doors to the skyway, and stumbled outside. Palms pressed against the glass barriers of the high platform, she could breathe again. Traffic hummed from below. The world seemed huge. With each gulp of breath it grew, expanding all around her, more space, more air, more places than she could ever explore, more than she could hope to understand. It was the first time she'd left the apartment in days. She felt tiny and wonderful.

But she couldn't see the woman with dark hair. She ran along the high pedestrian bridge, dodging midday strollers as she realised she was still wearing her house shoes and no makeup. Not that she cared. Not at all. She felt giddy as a child, the city open before her as windows rushed by. This wasn't like anything she'd done before; she ran without knowing where she was going. She ran.

Arriving at one of the skyway's intersections, a high-rise junction with an elevator and food stand at its centre, she tried to guess which way the woman had gone. Left, right, or onward? Left, right, or onward? Right, she might have gone right, Cissie decided, almost colliding with an elderly man and his dog.

"Vorsicht!"

"Sorry, so sorry."

"Bist du meshiginer?"

The old man's voice faded behind her. Cissie didn't slow. She couldn't remember the last time she ran anywhere. She reached another fork, this one three-way. She coughed on air, gasping. Left, or right? Left, or right? Left.

Now she walked, her limbs deadening, her spirits sinking. Realising she was no longer in Hetcarsey, she took an elevator and rode it down to street level, her ears popping as it sank downward.

On the ground, it was all different. In Hetcarsey the buildings were quick-built concrete slabs, but here they seemed to have been built piece by piece, as though they might never stop, never be finished. It had never really occurred to her how most buildings represented a single vision—that of an architect, most likely—which was then realised by people like her husband. But there was no such singularity here, no tidy, hierarchical cooperation. From the looks of it fifteen stories would be built according to one idea, for one function, and then the next ten would be another style entirely, an effect as jarring as seeing two different bodies stapled together; Frankenstein meets urban planning. Cissie felt as though she were in a different city entirely.

"Excuse me," she asked a passing stranger before she could stop herself. "Where are we?"

"Er, we're in Berlin," the young woman replied, her accent suggesting she was from some part of English-speaking Africa. She walked on before Cissie could harass her any more.

Had she been gay or straight? Cissie was having a hard time telling. Her legs were sore. Now that the rush was over, she could feel her normal thoughts and fears creep-creep-creeping back in. She would head home the moment she found public transport, she told herself, yet she saw none; in fact, there were few vehicles of any kind on the cracked roads. The cold wind whipped her legs, her feet icy in thin slippers.

It was a few more blocks before the sky darkened. Overhead spread a solid concrete canopy. Up above the buildings, vast pillars rose up to meet it.

A bridge! she realised. They were beneath a huge bridge, so wide it covered the whole neighbourhood, blocking out the sun, the rain, everything. She could hear the soft rumble of trains and traffic like distant thunder.

Her throat grew tighter and tighter at the gut-cramping realisation that not only did she not know where she was, she wasn't even sure where she'd come from.

An intersection. Left, or right? She chose quickly and at random, not giving herself time to panic. Each street looked alike in the twilight beneath the bridge. Ramshackle buildings stared down, like vultures waiting for prey.

No, that was eagles. Eagles had prey. Vultures ate things that were already dead.

Left.

Cissie stopped. The street had the same discordant tenements, the same rows of laundry hanging between them, the same concrete bridge above—but facing her was a rough brick wall, stretching from one side of the street to the other. Was Berlin split in two? Surely, she'd have heard about that. She walked from street to street, following the redbrick wall, until she heard voices. Several voices.

She came to a large, wrought-iron gate, in front of which crowded a mob of women. They'd surrounded someone with dark, flowing hair, and Cissie's heart leapt as she realised it was the woman she'd seen from her window. The one she'd been following.

"Hey, we're just talking to you," a member of the group spat. "We just want to ask some questions."

Their target stood perfectly still, refusing to respond, and it was sending the others into a frenzy. They poked and taunted, working themselves into a mad dance of anger and mirth.

"Tell us who you are," another demanded, grabbing her by the elbow. "Do you think you're a real woman?"

Having spent so many days smothering her frustrations all while cooped up inside a tiny apartment, Cissie flared with rage. She knew bullies when she saw them, and without a second thought she marched right up to the group. Surprised by her approach, they broke their circle, inadvertently releasing their prey, who slipped away through the gate.

"*What* is going on here?" Cissie scolded, the same sharp, granite voice she used when one of her boys was in deep shit. "Hey." She pointed to one of the group, a stocky woman with buzz-short hair.

"You. What were you doing?"

"Bona evening," she greeted in return, a slight smile playing on her lips.

"Don't you *'bona evening'* me!" Cissie ordered. "I asked you a question, and I want you to answer it."

"We're just here," the woman replied. "Just meetin' people."

"Well why don't you *'just meet people'* nicely?" Cissie demanded. "Why couldn't you leave that poor woman alone?"

"She's not a woman!" one cried.

"We're not doing anythin' to you," the one with the buzzcut answered.

"I don't want you doing anything to *anyone*," Cissie scolded.

"Yeah?" Another challenged. "That's a shame, 'cause it's what we're here for. Real women protecting real women."

"You're protecting women by harassing them?" Cissie raged. "I've half a mind to call the police."

She'd played the wrong card. The group hooted with laughter.

"Lilly Law won't come down 'ere," the buzzcut one gloated. "They don't care about the freaks. An' what about you? Are you an actual bio woman, or are you one of them?"

"She's a bleeding-heart sex traitor, is what she is," another spat.

"We'll just see, shall we?" Buzzcut gloated, grabbing Cissie's purse and yanking it from her arm. She pulled out Cissie's ID, holding it up in the dim light and squinting at the laminate.

"She's real. Deluded, but real."

She dropped the card into the purse and the purse to the ground. Sidling up to Cissie, she spoke in a low voice, as though taking her into her confidence. "Seriously, sister, I'd leave if I was you. You don't need to get involved and goin' through that gate right there would only confirm you as a gender extremist."

The others snickered.

"Then I think that's exactly what I'll do," Cissie replied, scooping up her purse and barging past. She marched right through the open gate to the world beyond the wall.

"Your choice, hon," Buzzcut cackled after her. "You can't say we didn't warn you."

111

17.

Cissie expected some kind of transformation once she'd passed the gate—but at first, she noticed nothing it all. It was only once she'd walked a minute or two that she began to see the cracks in the paving, the roads rocked with potholes, the complete absence of motorised traffic. With the sky obscured by the bridge's underside it was neither night nor day, and light came from all sources: streetlamps on mobile generators, tiki torches belching flame, huge dripping candles, buzzing hot pink neon. Cissie's shadow shifted and split as she walked.

The woman with dark hair must have come this way, though the further Cissie went the more she questioned if she were Ramona Palomar at all; even through blurry tears she had seen that Ramona was short and stout, while the person she'd spent the afternoon following was tall and slender. Graceful, even. But she was here now, and this place was as good as any when it came to finding answers. She kept going, her face bare, hair matted, and sodden, worn slippers slapping against the rough ground.

All was quiet until she rounded a corner onto a busy main street. The neighbourhood suddenly burst to life: bicycles fought with hand-drawn carts for space over the pocked tarmac, while trestles lined the sidewalks selling everything Cissie could think of: food, construction tools, cosmetics, all hawked in the dim light among a cacophony of human voices.

She kept walking, weaving and winding around men and women—as well as those who seemed to be neither. Or both. People wore everything from homemade dresses to tatty three-piece suits. There were groups of men—she thought they were men—with made-up faces. Though her instinct was to gaze at anyone and everyone she passed, she clung to the one useful piece of advice her pious mother had given her:

When you stare, you shame yourself. It shows your ignorance to the world.

So, she let her gaze drift over the people, settling on her surroundings instead. The buildings were worn, with patchy plaster and exposed brickwork, yet decorated with colourful, abstract murals and spirals of ironwork. There was a giant red stiletto hanging above the entrance to a store dedicated entirely to large-size women's shoes, and a looping neon sign advertising hormone treatments. Cissie no longer felt the claustrophobic squeeze of her apartment, yet neither did she feel the exhilaration she'd experienced running along the skyways. She found herself curiously, passively open to the world about herself.

The crowd thickened, cramming the narrow streets, but the buzz of chatter was calm and cheerful, and Cissie found herself following the stream of bodies all flowing in the same direction: down the bumpy road, through a courtyard and into the wide-open front of what looked like a bar, only without the "bar" part. There were mismatched benches, chairs, and tables, and while it was all admittedly shabby, something about it comforted Cissie. It was, to her mind, like an open clubhouse. A cabaret theatre without the lighting.

A short man with red hair struggled through with a tray of drinks, placing tiny glasses into palms. Cissie accepted one and fumbled for her purse, something to pay him with, but he was already gone. She had no need to worry; Ms. Fortier had shown her that she could blend into unfamiliar surroundings, and she tipped the drink down her throat.

At the far end of the room was a small raised platform—a makeshift stage—upon which someone was already speaking; he was Black, bearded, and smartly dressed in a waistcoat and matching jacket. Hisses and hushes shushed the crowd until his voice could be heard above the clamour. He spoke in a lilting Irish accent.

". . . you all for coming. I savvy that you're worried, a lot of us are worried, but if we take bona, sensible measures we can make ourselves that bijou bit safer. We can stand our ground. Because we're also Berlin . . ."

A few cheers erupted near the front as applause scattered across the room. Those near the back chatted among themselves. More and more people were jostling their way forward, and, not wishing to be crushed among the bodies, Cissie edged her way to the side of the room.

"... and this smoke is ours too. We savvy better than anyone how hollow it rings when they cackle about *love* and *freedom*. We savvy their obsession with dividing everyone into homie and palonie. We savvy how they'll hurt others in the name of family, security, tradition. And who was there fighting alongside them to liberate Berlin in the first place? Who ... ?"

A hand smothered Cissie's mouth, muffling her cry of surprise. A voice seethed into her ear, the accent Italian, Sicilian maybe.

"You're coming with me. Right fucking now."

Sharp nails dug into Cissie's arm as she was led outside; twisting her neck just enough, she could see the furious scowl of the woman she'd been following.

It definitely wasn't Ramona Palomar.

The alleyway was dim, illuminated only by the decapitated head of a traffic light. Stuck permanently on green, it gave both skin and the surrounding brickwork an eerie, alien glow.

"I'm sorry, I don't understand," said Cissie, once the woman had released her grip. "Am I not allowed in here?"

"Well, that depends on *why* you're here. You are cis, right?" the stranger asked. "I've nix ogled you before. And I'd bet multi dinari that you're straight."

Cissie was confused. "What do you mean, *Ciss?* How do you know my name?"

"I mean *cis*, as in the opposite of trans," the woman said, slowly, as if speaking to a child. Cissie had heard the term before, somewhere, though she'd no idea what it meant.

"Trans?"

"Wow, chica. You really are straight."

"Will you *please* just tell me what it means?" She'd meant to sound authoritative but wound up whining like Jonah on bath night. Even so, it worked: the stranger visibly relaxed in the face of her ignorance. If

Cissie didn't know better, she'd have suspected the hint of a patronising smile.

"Fine. But only because you helped me get away from those pazza palonies outside." She paused. "The angry-looking bitches?"

"I remember."

"Well, I am trans. And trans means not fitting into certain gender norms. Maybe born into the wrong lacoddy. Maybe being neither homie nor palonie. There are lots of ways to be trans, but there's only one way to be cis."

"Oh," Cissie murmured. It all made less sense than ever. And now that she was out in the fresh air the back of her head throbbed with a dull ache. In the dusk beneath the bridge, it was impossible to know what time it was; she imagined Howard's panic at her disappearance, him clumsily comforting the children, him fretting and praying all alone.

"I think I need to get on home. I have—"

"Oh no," the woman replied, "no no no. Nix possible. We lock the gates at night. You've seen why."

"So, I'm stuck here?" Cissie leaned against the wall as the fuzzing headache swelled. "What am I supposed to do now?"

The Italian stranger inhaled as though she were about to speak, then stopped herself. Instead, she peered at Cissie as though she were an exotic animal. Her dark, judgemental gaze was edged with thick liner, her olive skin tinted a whitish jade by the light.

"You're nix from the Radfems, are you?"

"Radfems?"

"Maybe it was all an act," she accused, a sharp nail pointing at Cissie, "over by the gate. Maybe your little confrontation with those bitches was staged, a way to set me up."

"Please," Cissie croaked. "I have nowhere to go and apparently I can't even leave. I don't understand any of this. I just wanted to help."

"And before?" The woman raised her eyebrows. "When you were following me? Was that to help also?"

"You saw that."

"I saw that."

Cissie took a deep, quavering breath; she'd nothing left but the truth. "I thought you were someone else, someone who helped me when I was in trouble. And, well, things haven't been going so well since then, and I thought . . ."

She trailed off. After all, what had she expected? To be rescued again? Cissie had always considered herself a capable, practical person, one who could sort out her own problems. She was embarrassed to admit she felt overwhelmed by her own home. That she feared her own husband and his newfound faith.

"I don't know, honestly. I thought maybe she could help me again. I really didn't mean to cause any problems by coming here. I don't even know where *here* is, and I certainly don't know my way home."

The woman regarded Cissie for a few more moments before speaking. "You live in Hetcarsey?"

Cissie nodded.

"We can point you in the bona direction tomorrow. For now, you'll stay here. There are beds upstairs, in the gaffercarsey."

"Gaffercarsey?"

By way of an answer, she led Cissie back to the building with the makeshift stage, though the platform was now occupied by a small woman singing with a thin voice, and only a few patrons lingered. Too exhausted to argue, Cissie followed the stranger upstairs into a large, darkened room sheltering eight beds—three of which were marked with bags, clothes, and books, and one which already contained the bundled shape of someone sleeping. She was pointed to one by the window. Cissie had never slept in a dormitory before, but, surprised by how exhausted she felt, she kicked off her shoes and sat down upon the springy mattress.

"Thank you. Really." She wasn't raised to be ungrateful.

"Just don't give me reason to regret it, hettie palonie. It's happened before." She seemed to remember something. "Oh, and my name is Fiorella. Bona handle, no? Anyway, ask for me when you wake up." She lowered her voice.

"And don't go telling everyone around here that you're cis. Not everyone is as friendly and welcoming as I am. Especially not with what's been going on."

"What has been going on?"

"Bona nochy, chica." With that Fiorella departed, leaving Cissie with only her thoughts and the faint music sifting up from downstairs.

Excerpt from
The Honest Guide to Berlin

"Q"

So say that I love him
And yes, palonies too
Say we should be as three
And cackle vows anew

Say we troll down main street
In three in three amor
Be bibi in your bevvies
Be brazen and deplored

Then dash me from the dickey!
So lell away my wills!
And still I'll charper clevies
With bagagas in my lills

Now say I'm nix a lady
Can't stand the fit of 'man'
For all the fun's found in between
That strange old borderland

Say I cackle in a deep throat
Look dolly in my drogle?
With riha spread across my chest
And muck around my ogles!

Then dash me from the dickey!
So lell away my wills!
And still I'll charper clevies
With bagagas in my lills

—Q, Anonymous*

Though the ramshackle appearance of Q may bring to mind the nearby district of Hetcarsey, the dangers should not be underestimated. Home to Berlin's "uncategorised" residents, the neighbourhood is a haven for bisexuals, pansexuals, and those subversively identifying as "queer," as well as those in unconventional and otherwise illicit relationships (see *Same-Sex Marriage*, p. 101). A haven for civil unrest and organised crime, the district's infamy was affirmed by the notorious 1954 film *Am I Not a Stranger?*, in which a gangster (played by Rock Hudson) moves to Q with both a husband and a wife—a practice which remains illegal to this day.

Visitors are strongly advised against travelling to Q, but those with sufficient reason should notify both their embassy and the Republic's Grand Carsey for Registration at least three weeks ahead of time. Successful applicants will be provided with an escort for the duration.

* The above poem is included here for factual purposes only and does not represent the opinions of either the author or The Honest Press. Unauthorised replication or recitation of this poem within the borders of the Gay Republic is forbidden.

THE FRUIT SMOKE

The Gay Republic

1998

18.

One final hurdle and the running could stop. Their lives could begin. William watched the city from the plane, and though he'd seen countless pictures of it during their time in Brighton, nothing compared to actually viewing the grasping towers and crisscross of intersecting bridges from above, a fortress more intricate and delicate than anything he'd ever seen. He was surprised by the amount of greenery surrounding the fragile city-state, as though at some magical line the towers were turned into trees, without the usual band of suburbs.

The two boys arrived exhausted. Flights between Brighton's small airstrip and Berlin were frequently delayed by the air traffic controllers of the Great British Kingdom: a constant, continual campaign of minor harassment which had resulted in being held up half a day.

Now they were on the ground, and this final stage felt the longest.

"Homies and palonies, please nanti dashing from handbags. Handbags on their tod will be battyfanged. Help lilly, keep your ogles and aunt nells open."

The static of the tannoy crackled through Immigration. This section of the airport was comprised of a vast slick-white hall, whose pristine blank spaciousness enforced something like a religious experience, an impression bolstered by hushed quiet and rows of banners billowing above. Some were rainbow flags, the rest displayed stylised silhouettes of same-sex couples holding hands.

Below them waited the real couples, though not all were same-sex, and near none held hands. Instead they checked through bags, scribbled on last-minute forms, bickered and whispered with crumpled foreheads as circles of sweat stained their clothes. Mumbled fragments in two dozen languages scattered through the hall. English from New York, English from Australia, Polynesian French, German, Spanish.

123

Gradually the worn couples in front moved on and on, until the gates were finally visible. In front of the gates were rows of tables, divvying up the line.

Five more minutes. William glanced once more at the damp document clutched between his fingers, fingering the seal, then the embossed lettering.

Temporary Residence Permit
WILLIAM DOVETREE
and
GARETH JOHN POOL

Beneath lay the details of their lives—where they'd been born and when, their parents' names, the hostel which had housed them in Brighton, the address of the consulate. By their "relationship status" was a simple "U," which William took to mean either Unknown or Uncategorised. By "sexual orientation" there was simply "Q."

They held hands as they approached the desk, William's palm damp with nervous exhaustion, and though the middle-aged clerk seemed friendly on approach—flashing each of them an ingratiating (if slightly artificial) smile—he frowned when handed their papers. William felt the grip on his hand tighten.

The clerk set the document down and stared at the two. It was obviously an appraisal of some sort, of body or clothes, or both. William's discomfort drove his gaze downward, toward the floor's uniformly tiled rows. Gareth stared straight back.

"Income?"

His question was so blunt and sudden that it took a moment for William to register it.

"Oh. Erm, none," he admitted.

The clerk nodded.

"Savings?"

"None," Gareth answered, sharing in the shame.

The clerk sighed, languidly tapped at the computer's keyboard, and printed an address: Carsey 15, 112a Pogey Street. Without a word he handed it to Gareth, along with a sealed envelope with *500 dinari* printed on the front, then dismissed them with a wave of his hand. Neither knew if they'd passed or failed this mysterious exam.

"This is it," Gareth declared, holding the printout aloft as they walked through the gates. "This is our new home."

Once free of the airport they stumbled to the nearest licensed cab. The driver's ID was visible through the plexiglass, his stern, laminated face staring out above a rainbow seal, while the taxi itself stank with sweat, slick leather squeaking with every movement. Located at the outer edge of the city, there was little out the windows as the taxi sped away: little but grey airport buildings, sky, and trees. They handed the address to the driver, who informed them they'd have to travel to the far end of Berlin.

After a few minutes, buildings rose from nowhere, blocks bigger than the pictures, the streets deep as canyons, humbling the tiny cab, inducing in William an impressed vertigo. It was like nothing he'd ever seen.

"This should be Twinkstadt," he whispered in wonder, hoping to pass along some of the knowledge he'd absorbed from the hostel's small library. Pressing his neck to the window, he strained to see glass and concrete walkways slicing across the sky, the rush of a train carriage sliding overhead. There were colourful apartments from the fifties, poured concrete from the sixties, and brown glass towers from the seventies, all coated in unlit neon bulbs, spilling upward side by side toward the painfully clear sun. The streets were dominated by boyish, fey-looking youths wearing bright prints in every colour they could name. William felt a stab of envy. The car passed bevvie after bevvie, nightclub after nightclub, and dozens of discount supermarkets.

Crawling on through traffic toward the centre of the city the pavements grew neater, the buildings more ornate. The towers boasted neo-Gothic and art deco embellishments; several doorways were gold in colour, others silver or bronze, with uniformed doormen guarding each one. There were smart poodles on designer leashes. Here the men looked a little older, but they carried the confidence generally associated with the young. Their facial hair was trim and neat.

"Maytree," William whispered to Gareth. "Each district is like its own metropolis."

Gareth didn't respond.

Sometime later, the people outside the cab transformed once more: trousers shrunk into shorts, pressed cotton turned into leather, slim hips widened. The trim facial hair of the men grew out into bushy beards, while women disappeared almost entirely. Slung over some ten stories of a plain-looking hotel was a brown banner sporting a pawprint, above two-storey red letters spelling G-R-O-W-L. On one street corner, among flocks of sparrows, a group of young chubby-gutted men in white vests and thick body hair posed in spotless Levis, pouting through their beards as they awaited customers.

"Zoo cubs," William pointed, once more trying to engage Gareth. "We're in the bear district."

"And what district are we living in, again?" Gareth asked, as though finally noticing his presence.

A sharp cackle burst from the cab driver. William noticed his beard and bald head, the mass of hair splayed about the base of his neck. He was a bear.

"You're in Q, my little lullaby cheats," he began, savouring his answer. Neither William nor Gareth knew what a "lullaby cheat" was, but it sounded patronising. "You know, where they park the in-betweens? Savvy, those that are not really here nor there, not hettie nor lady, not one thing nor the other? The indecisive. What a sharda! You boys should've spent more time in the bevvies, back in the old country. Learned something."

The driver giggled to himself. William scowled, uncomprehending but fully recognising the schoolyard tone. Gareth continued staring out the window.

"Nearly there, my chavvies," the driver continued. "Almost home. No thews or gams outside the cabouche, please."

The broad roads and grid patterns devolved into a tangle of narrow streets, each curving and jutting from one another at odd angles, a dark, medieval layout of high-rise buildings. Each was a mess of cheap construction, to the extent that William couldn't discern which were

126

complete and which unfinished. Arrays of colourful, hodgepodge banners and lighting systems sparked from walls and rooftops, competing for space.

It was a place of make-do. Those waiting at bus stops or hawking wares from market stalls lacked the plush uniformity of the other districts: some looked normal, some looked like hippies, and some were strange as carnival acts. Women coated in tattoos, bearded men in tank tops.

"Don't judge," the driver mocked, bringing the cab to a halt. "These are your people, now."

Despite the mirth he'd demonstrated throughout the entire ride, he seemed sombre as they exited the cab, and said nothing by way of goodbye.

William and Gareth found themselves on a near-deserted street, huge tenements towering over the narrow road. William clutched at the scrap of paper reading *Carsey 15, 112a Pogey Street*. They were outside a forty-storey building (he counted the windows), a hodgepodge architectural design which appeared to have been built in several stages.

For twenty minutes they lugged their cases around the lobby of 112 Pogey Street, then around the front, unable to find the entrance to 112a and fretting over the possibility of having been assigned a fake address. It was only when Gareth noticed a small alleyway to the side of the building that they found it: a glass-walled elevator. *112a.*

They dragged the luggage into the waiting lift, only to find two buttons: *ground* and *rooftop*. Well, they were already at the ground, so Gareth leaned over and swatted *rooftop*. Though the button didn't light up, the elevator began its shaky ascent, the rutted street falling away beneath them.

William braced himself for the worst—after all, the building was haphazard, and who could tell what shape their apartment would be in? Why were they headed to the roof? Despite Gareth's coldness throughout the journey, he wrapped an arm around William's shoulders as the elevator slowed, only letting go once it came to a halt, some thirty or forty floors high.

They were standing to one side of a long, narrow rooftop of grey flagstones, one side lined by a row of crumbling brick cottages. These terraced houses were small and rough, yet cheerfully painted, and faintly absurd given their location. It wasn't what either had expected.

A brisk wind whirled around them, slipping in through the gaps and crevasses of surrounding towers. Except for a few lines of flapping laundry, and the wastebins squatting outside each front door, there was no sign of the other residents.

"Which one is ours?" Gareth asked, raising his voice in order to be heard above the wind.

"Fifteen," William answered. "That orange one on the end."

They passed houses one through fourteen, glancing toward the windows, most of which were obscured by roller blinds, Venetian blinds, pleated curtains, or, in one case, yellowed nets which were a little too close to those draped across the suburbs of their hometown. They reached the house at the end. Their house. William held his breath as Gareth pushed the key into the lock.

The house was divided into two single-room levels, each with a huge grime-smeared window at the far end, exposing motes that danced in the dimming light. It looked as though the place had been left in a hurry, with clothes still in the drawers and dust-covered dishes left to dry by the sink. William was relieved to find it a far cry from the stuffy, austere formality of the Dovetree household, the kind of place which would be advertised as "cosy" and "unique" if you ignored the brown stains on the floorboards and fingerprints over the walls. Together the two quietly poked and prodded around their new home, sorting abandoned bric-a-brac into piles and opening windows to disperse the musty smell.

Downstairs was made up of a yellow-tiled bathroom and storage cupboard, while upstairs housed a little kitchen-cum-lounge and fold-out sofa bed. Beyond the large upstairs window was a small balcony, which they climbed out onto.

In front: towers and towers stretching into the distance, a mass of white planes drifting above the distant streets, pride flags billowing atop several dozen buildings. As they watched the sun sink beyond the lines and spires, Gareth leaned over, resting his head on William's shoulder. The gesture was unfamiliar, uncharacteristic, even, and for the first time in weeks William relaxed.

This was it. They were home.

19.

When they were fifteen and sixteen years old, the two boys had only the gaps between routines, routines others had set for them: school, home, sports clubs, the Boy's Brigade. These blank spaces were all the more precious for the fact that they had no classes together and shared no extracurricular interests. Were it not for lunch breaks, walks home, and the occasional evening, William and Gareth might never have seen each other at all. They'd lived separate, fixed existences, and found themselves only in snatches of time spent together.

These moments had been the high point of each day, though neither ever knew how much it meant to the other. Each assumed the anticipation was for themselves alone, that they were the ordinary one, and the brevity of their time together meant that conversation never faltered, never dwindled. There were always stories about parents, or teachers, or how William's brother had tried to make a bong out of a spark plug and engine piston. And moments not spent conferring were spent exploring: hurriedly grasping one another, trembling so hard their hands shook.

Though they rarely had more than an hour or two, there was one night which had been different. One night which was special. Gareth's parents had left town, under strict instruction that he take care of the family cats and not invite anyone over. Of course, Gareth had immediately invited William, who'd begged and nagged his parents until they'd relented. He'd neglected to mention the absence of adult supervision.

Though they'd not done anything out of the ordinary—they'd kissed and fumbled, talked, listened to the radio—it had been a turning point in each boy's life. Firstly, because it was the weekend in which each had realised what they were. They'd used the word cautiously, like small children using forbidden swear words.

I'm gay, they'd said in turn, only for themselves, only for one another. They'd laughed, light-headed, dizzy with the relief of it. William had learned the word from the radio broadcasts and told Gareth what it meant. *I'm gay*, each confirmed. They'd kissed, as though sealing a vow.

Then they'd gone back to living their lives in the gaps between routines: snatching glances across the playground, eating lunch together, walking home from school. Yet each clung to the memory of that night, and their love grew in the space between classes and homework, sports practice and the Boy's Brigade. When they were older, each assumed, they'd have all the time in the world.

Now they'd made it all the way to Berlin. Together they unpacked their paltry belongings, which—considering each had arrived with just a single suitcase—didn't take long at all. Barring the small piles of books stacked upon the coffee table, the place looked much the same as when they'd entered.

But it was theirs.

Neither slept that first evening. Instead, they wallowed in one another, spending hours talking and caressing. They watched from the balcony as the sun came up, sharing a blanket and marvelling at the proud pink sky.

It was the weekend, and job applications would have to wait till Monday. The cupboards were stocked with abandoned cans of beans, peaches, and sweetcorn, which they slurped with their fingers. Once sated they slept, sweating through the warm September day, kicking the sheets to the floor. When they woke it was evening again. The sun had already slipped behind the towers, while the towers themselves shimmered, light spilling from a hundred thousand windows.

William had planned on buying a couple of bottles and toasting their new home, but as soon as they'd ridden the elevator down to the street Gareth began scouting for a bar. After all, they'd spent the past weeks almost entirely alone together, and didn't it make sense to see

131

how people lived? William agreed; that did make sense. Gareth had been recommended a place, back in Brighton, and so he led the way.

They did buy a couple of bottles, from a small, ad hoc corner shop at the edge of their block. Gareth readied his ID but wasn't asked for it. They drank the beer as they walked to the bus stop and waited for the bus, each a little dizzy as they binned their bottles and boarded.

The journey took them northward through the city. In Maytree they disembarked, took a lift up to the station, and rode the elevated rail north to Twinkstadt. The bar was located on a busy rooftop plaza by the light-rail station. William sighed at the sight of the price list posted by the door; their envelope of dinari wouldn't last long.

"Let's just have one drink each, get a feel for the place," Gareth suggested.

Despite the expense, the bar itself was warm and welcoming, the buzz of fifty conversations drifting from inside. It reminded William of the pubs back in England, only the clientele was brash and colourful, and the staff actually smiled. Gareth ordered for them, the two settling into a window booth with a view of the street far below. They downed the first half of their glasses and savoured the rest.

Each was lost in thought when the whole establishment fell silent. Gareth gazed over William's shoulder; William twisted around in his seat.

A woman stood still in shock; her back was soaking wet, suds drip-drip-dripping to the floor, rivulets running down her legs. The man next to her spun around, eyes wide, arms spread, fists clenched. He opened his mouth to shout and accuse, but his threats were interrupted.

"Fucking breeders," someone shouted.

The man's crimson face swung left to right, searching for the voice, for the one who'd thrown a nearly full pint of brown ale over his partner. But it was too busy. There were too many hostile faces.

The dripping woman still hadn't turned around. Instead, she gripped the edge of the bar, her knuckles white.

"I think it's disgusting," someone shouted.

The man's head swung again, but this voice came from a different direction. He gestured to the scowling barman, demanding to know who, *who* had soaked his wife? The man behind the bar—a handsome

132

albino with paper-white hair and skin—gave a shrug as the dripping woman brought one hand to her face, her damp shoulders heaving.

William hadn't seen who'd thrown the drink, but Gareth quietly gestured to a group of drunken young twinks. Most of them held back, uncertain what they should do. But a couple were watching the scene with barely concealed grins. One of them held an empty glass.

"Fuck off, het scum," someone bellowed.

For a moment the situation fascinated William. For years he'd received jabs and taunts for his sexuality, and there was a savage thrill to seeing a straight couple treated like—well, like gay people. They had the whole wide world to themselves, and it was gratifying to see the rules reversed, to see straights become the victims for once. But the feeling lasted only for a moment, ground to horror by the woman's tears, by the man's panicked defence, and he gripped Gareth's arm, searching his lover's expression for some distaste, some sympathy for the couple, some sign he wasn't enjoying this. But his face said nothing, revealed nothing.

The husband shouted again, angry and confused. *We're bi, we're bisexual, we're not heteros.*

One of the twinks laughed, a breathy guffaw. Another drink was thrown, red wine dripping down the man's reddened face. Finally, a doorman stepped in, taking the husband and wife by the upper arms and leading them out of the bar. The wife covered her face with her hands as she was dragged through the double doors, the back of her tights streaked with ale and her dress spotted with wine. A few patrons burst into a cheer; others returned to their conversations.

All except the two young men in a booth by the window. Each gazed into the murky remainder of their drinks, as though peering into tea leaves, or a glass ball; as though their future could be divined, if only they looked hard enough.

20.

Berlin's summer sprang anew that September, the smoke hazing beneath a heat wave which shimmered the skyline and baked the pavements. The residents spilled out onto any and all available green space, as parks, gardens, and even the central reservations of major boulevards flooded with bare skin and oversized parasols. The beaches of the many lakes surrounding the city were crowded further still; bevvies set on floating rafts cluttered the canals and rivers.

Q remained difficult to judge; all William could see was a fractured lack of uniformity, as chaotically colourful as light through stained glass. Whenever someone tried to make conversation—whether shopkeeper, passerby, or neighbour hanging laundry—William quickly hurried away, usually with an apologetic grunt or shrug. He flinched with the echoes of jeering classmates and surly mechanics. Yet the narrow lanes around their apartment block were full of all sorts, and when he saw men wearing makeup, he couldn't help but stare. Even though they never stayed in one place for long, such overt gender deviance contravening city law, they still wore their liberty on their very faces. Though William desperately wanted to express his admiration, to go up and compliment them, he was unable to work up the courage.

By contrast, Gareth lunged into conversation with anyone and everyone he could encounter, though he didn't even seem to notice the makeup-clad men and their illicit eyeshadow. With an uncanny ability to adopt the manner and even posture of anyone before him, it wasn't long before he found work: in the very bar they'd visited on their second night, on the rooftop plaza in Twinkstadt's south. He returned from his shifts late, clambering into their shared sofa bed and sinking into a thick and immediate sleep. William would hold him close, compensating for the evening's lonely hours, and feeling all the lonelier for it.

Of course, William needed work, too. Each day he scoured the newspaper listings, poring through positions for which he was unqualified. In fleeing his hometown he'd also fled school. Officially he'd dropped out. Before, he'd spent all his energy on getting through each day, planning when he could next see Gareth, avoiding being caught. There'd been little time to think about the future, and now that the future was here, he didn't know what to do with it.

When Gareth asked him how his employment hunt was going, he quickly changed the subject, and did his best to ignore his partner's quiet disapproval.

He learnt to cook. At first he bought frozen meals from the small, disorganised corner shop on the edge of their block, and even those had remained frozen at the centre. But as the nights stretched longer, he experimented, starting simple: bangers and mash. He read as he prepared food, paperbacks from a nearby library of Berlin authors: Isherwood, Bechdel, Maupin, Winterson. As he sliced and diced and steamed and boiled, his hands grew faster, firmer, more capable. Dishes which had been burned started coming out even, the bland became spicy. He was surprised by how much he enjoyed it, this conjuring of meals from nothing but ingredients. His mother had always huffed and puffed red-faced over the oven, making it clear how much she suffered for every bite they took. William did no such thing. Instead, he took quiet pride in Gareth's enjoyment of curries and quiches, hummus platters and kebab skewers.

One evening he clambered atop a rickety chair, reaching into the back of the highest kitchen cabinets in search of misplaced oregano, when his grasping palm came upon a small cylinder. A lipstick. A bright, fuchsia pink lipstick. His pumpmuscle pounded as he remembered his impromptu makeover in Brighton, thought of the colourful residents of his district. To change the colour of his lips on a whim was a forbidden kind of magic.

Still, it had been worn before, it probably wasn't hygienic, and besides, what would that make him—into the flouncing sissy his classmates saw? That his parents had so desperately feared? He pushed the tube back into the furthest reaches of the cupboard, back into the cobwebs and the shadows, and gently closed the door.

By October the heat lifted. One final, brutal thunderstorm declared an end to the summer, as residents watched forks of lightning strike the tips of skyscrapers, thundercracks drowning out street music and traffic. Once over, the climate was sedate: neither cool nor warm, with a featureless white sky peering between the ziggurat peaks of high buildings. The kind of weather which casts a blank unreality over everything.

Before, William's life had been structured. Now time opened before him, blank and endless, a wealth he couldn't spend. He no longer listened to the radio: it had once been his lifeline to a distant world, but now he was actually there.

One day he walked around the block. The next day, another. Raised in a country in which public transportation was comprised of little more than occasional buses, he was astounded by the complex mesh of underground, light-rail, tram, and overhead train lines. Even more than the towering structures, even more than the millions of same-sex couples, this was what he found most exotic, the most exhilarating. After buying a transit map from a nearby kiosk, he rode those lines while following them with his finger. He could ride a different route every day, and it would still be years before he'd seen it all. And always, new connections were being added: his increasingly dog-eared map boasted tracks which would be *complete by November 1999, complete by February 2000, complete by May 2001.*

When journeying on the trains, William was driven by impulse alone, as if the city itself were alive—a colossal organism, and he was a small but important part of its ordered chaos; the transport network was a conscious web of neurons. This was something he could grasp, and the interest became a hobby of sorts. And the further he rode the more the passengers changed: outside of Q there were no painted lips surrounded by silky beards; instead, the fashions were more upscale, the tastes more uniform. More controlled. Male passengers would run their gaze over his body as they feigned interest in newspapers or poster advertisements, and whether they did so in judgement or attraction, he couldn't tell.

Every other shift he travelled to Gareth's workplace, walking the two blocks north to the Harvey Milk Platz bus terminal, then taking the elevated rail to the rooftop bevvies of Twinkstadt. Once there, he'd drink soda and read in the dim light, finding excuses to avoid conversation with the other patrons. Occasionally he made eye contact with Gareth, and the two would share a secret grin; a flash of warmth.

One afternoon he arrived to find the bevvy packed with punters, all clad in white and green, all cheering in unison, building to a monstrous roar.

COME ON, BRUISERS! BRUISERS, COME ON!

Even Gareth's cheeks had been daubed in green and white. This was an acceptable, masculine kind of makeup, the kind worn openly, which marked you as part of a team. William was surprised. Why would the gay city have sports? His father used to drag him to local football games, as though the ardour of the crowd would chant away his "sensitivity," as though passive participation would make him a man. ("Salt of the earth," so his father described himself—but what could grow in salted earth?) He'd tried to enjoy these games, he'd even tried to feel the spirit of the crowd, but it just wasn't in him. He'd believed he was broken.

As the bar erupted into yet another cheer, he flinched, knocking over his cola. Gareth didn't seem to notice, serving drinks by the sixes and not stopping even for a moment.

Soon November rain battered the towers, from the penthouse garrets of Maytree to Gareth's high-perched bevvy. The remainder splattered the windscreens of elevated trains, ran in streams along the gutters of skyways, dribbling down to street level where it settled in roadside puddles and soaked shoes. The darkening sky stretched the shadows, casting a gloom which was broken by Twinkstadt's neon strips of commercial avenues, as well as Q's small stores, lit by strings of coloured lights.

Finally, William found a job listed in the back of the newspaper, and was hired after a brief, nondescript interview. He now worked in a sales office which occupied the lower stories of an ugly, sprawling building on the edge of his district. Thrown from the suburbs straight into the service sector economy, there were long hours, low pay, monitored toilet breaks, back-bruising chairs, angry voices, and quotas, quotas, quotas. Yet in spite of it all, he was proud. He was relieved he had some sort of place in the grand, chaotic scheme of things. He bought a tie and three starchy, matching shirts.

He sold health. In the papers he'd learnt that the state-run service of the epidemic days had been torn apart and fed to new health insurance companies. His role was to cold-call rich daddies and offer them premium packages, or destitute twinks for the budget call-if-you-get-cancer options. Who could complain? They were lucky to be here, his boss reminded. You could always be fighting for existence in the straight world.

His co-workers dressed conservatively, the men in ties like his own, the women in blouses and knee-length skirts, in all the colours between navy and charcoal. William kept getting the others confused, and there was little time for chatter. The day's labour took its toll. Potential customers weren't happy to be phoned from the blue and were perfectly prepared to take out their day's frustrations on a hapless salesperson. William wasn't allowed to hang up the phone, even when they shouted with such intensity that he had to hold the receiver at arm's length. He needed to make at least five sales per shift and had to work until he got them.

When he finally headed home, whether at six or eight or ten, he was too tired to cook anything other than oven-ready meals or instant pasta. Dust gathered in the corners of the small house, the kitchen sink was smeary and stained, and a persistent smell cloyed from the Tupperware at the back of the fridge. Now he seldom rode the train. There was just the short bus journey between home and work, work and home.

But he was employed. There was no longer any need for guilt now he was contributing to the rent, the bills, and the odd small luxuries. Every few weeks they'd ride the elevator down to the street and go to dinner, or else to the movie theatre, whichever they could afford.

One evening William came home to find the upper room of their home clouded with steam, pans clattering on the stove and the worktops stained with sauce. *Surprise,* Gareth announced, kissing William on the cheek and getting tomato on the collar of his work shirt. The gesture was sweet, but as they ate the rubbery pasta William couldn't help but notice that every cabinet had been flung wide open in the hunt for ingredients.

Later that night, with the dishes done and Gareth snoring from the sofa bed, William stood atop the rickety chair and reached for the forbidden lipstick. It was gone.

December was the strangest month. Whereas back in England the windows of stores and family homes would fill with greens and reds, baubles and bells, Berlin's December was fractured. Shards of Christmas mixed with Hannukah, the Fiesta of Our Lady, Omisoka, even Saturnalia. Snow flurried mid-month, smoothing architectural angles and freezing into icy sheets before devolving into grey slush. Icicles hanging from walkways were cleared each morning, lest they plummet into the unsuspecting skulls of those below.

William settled into his workplace. He kept his head down, ate lunch at his desk, and was sure not to complain. When the boss greeted him with an unreasonably cheerful smile, William smiled right back. He gave just enough, and just little enough, approaching each day with resigned pragmatism, and feeling older by the end of the shift. He even worked Christmas Day, and before he knew it the month was almost over.

New Year's Eve was a late shift, and once done William braved the cold sleet and trolled to Gareth's bevvie. Squeezing through the crowds at the rooftop plaza, he made his way in and stood near his usual spot at the end of the bar. Straining his ears, he caught snatches of his partner's voice. When had Gareth picked up so much Polari? William knew a few words—*smoke* for *city*, *bevvies* for *bars*, *nell* for both *listen* and *ear*—but he used them clumsily and self-consciously, when he used them at all.

Gareth, on the other hand, wove them into his sentences with effortless ease—*aris, bat, bagaga*—terms William had never heard. Once, Gareth had chastised him for using the gay tongue, had clamped his hand over William's lips to keep the words from spilling forth. Now he was well on his way to speaking it like a native.

"Bona evening, lover." Gareth leaned over the bar and kissed William on the cheek. He was swamped: the only ones working were him and his albino supervisor.

"And a happy new year," William responded.

"Nix for another twenty-five minutes. I can't help but varda the clock when I work." Summoned by a customer, Gareth darted over, served two drinks, and returned to William with a fresh soda.

"There's whiskey in this," William exclaimed.

"Sssssh," Gareth whispered. "I shushed it when no one was looking. Just drink it and say thank you."

"Well, thank you," William replied, trying not to pull a face as he sipped the bitter liquor. Gareth returned to serve the never-ending stream of customers, joking around with them and the white-haired bartender while covertly pocketing tips. He returned to William as the countdown began.

"We did it. We're here," he exclaimed, gesturing around himself as the year reached its final seconds. Though sober, the room's warmth and alcoholic haze made both young men feel tipsy, even celebratory. It was the first time they were welcoming the new year together. True, it wasn't what William had anticipated during those weeks in Brighton, but surely life was a slow process of learning that nothing turns out as expected. This, he assumed, was adulthood.

Excerpt from
The Honest Guide to Berlin

Trans Berliners.

Berlin does not recognise sex change procedures, nor does it acknowledge genders other than male or female. This may come as a surprise to many of those visiting the gay city-state—after all, aren't trans individuals just another maligned minority being persecuted for who they are? So far, the response from the government has been a resounding "no." Official state ideology favours a fixed view of sex and gender as the basis of same-sex relationships, with any deviation an unacceptable dilution of gay identity.

The situation was different in pre-war Berlin: Magnus Hirschfeld himself founded both the Scientific-Humanitarian Committee and the Institute for Sexual Research, each of which fought not only for homosexual rights, but for those of trans individuals as well. The city also saw the world's first sex change operation, when Dora Richter underwent vaginoplasty in 1931. When the Nazi government rose to power in 1933, trans residents were among the first to fight back, and the guerrilla warfare undertaken by trans partisans was central to the city's resistance.

However, the new government of the Gay Republic opposed trans rights. With a population shell-shocked from the horrors of the war, the first election was won by the nationalist-conservative Gay Patriotic League and its lesbian sister party, The Demetan Union, both of which listed trans identities as subversive. In challenging the gender binary on which male-male and female-female partnerships are formed, trans "ideology" was deemed hostile to the interests of the gay state.

This policy continued under the next administration,

headed by the left-leaning Gay Progress Party and the Party of Lesbian Socialists. Though later years saw calls for tolerance from radical parties such as the Green Lesbian Left and the Woodfolk Alliance, they have never come close to establishing trans rights in either the gay Senate or the lesbian Assembly. Civil unrest and public violence from other marginalised groups has done little to help the cause.

Today, trans residents in the city-state have congregated beneath the Tchaikovsky Transit Bridge on the border of Q and Hetcarsey, in a neighbourhood colloquially known as Remould. As trans people are considered default collaborators with the queer terrorist movement, Berlin authorities have surrounded this "transhood" with an eight-kilometre (five-mile) long wall. Though the wall has succeeded in discouraging residents and services from reaching Remould, it has also resulted in a thriving black market, and a "degenerate" culture which has been cut off from the rest of the city.

REMOULD

The Gay Republic

1999

21.

Of course, the morning Cissie returned from the trans town was every ounce the disaster she'd feared. She'd never stayed out the whole night before and arrived home to find Howard absolutely beside himself— his face flushed bright red, asking if Cissie had cheated on him. His voice was small with disbelief, like a child asking if there really is no Santa Claus. Soothing her husband, Cissie told small truths: that she hadn't had sex with anyone; that she'd merely gotten lost; that she'd spent the night, alone, in a bed provided by a kind stranger. Of course, she didn't tell him about the trans town itself. She doubted even Ms. Fortier would understand that.

After a while Howard calmed down, treating her gently, delicately. He could touch very softly when he wanted to. It was moments like that in which she felt most loved, and in which she was most in love with Howard.

Yet still the walls closed in, slowly and surely, as though they were sneaking up on her. This was her life, and it impacted no one outside of her apartment building. Outside of those ever-creeping walls, she simply didn't exist.

Her strange adventure was over, though her mind often wandered back to the town beneath the bridge. When she was loading the washing machine in the basement laundry, for example. Or doing the dishes. Soon those daydreams became urges, and by the time a week had passed she longed to return to its everlasting twilight. Just once. She hadn't seen the *whole* place, after all. Perhaps she was missing out on something.

So, she left the children with Ms. Fortier (telling her she'd joined a book club), bought a map from a small tourist kiosk, and set off down the skyway.

As she neared the bridge she began to worry. Was she intruding? Perhaps she was an annoyance. There was no way she really belonged down there, and if she didn't belong, well, she was surely just a lookie-loo. But she was also young and strong, and having two children had pushed her stamina to its limits. Surely, she could be of some use. There was clearly plenty of work needed doing, and she'd be an eager volunteer. All she wanted were answers.

Relieved to find the gate unguarded, she asked around for Fiorella, finding her in a tailoring shop. She was working at a noisy, pedal-powered sewing machine, surrounded by rolls of fabric packed into a space little larger than Cissie's bathroom. Flashlights were positioned all around, lighting her work.

Fiorella was not exactly delighted to see her.

"I'm sorry, cis palonie. I have nanti time to take you on a tour." She glanced at Cissie with narrowed eyes, suspicious of her return.

"I don't need a tour. I want to help."

"I don't need your help either."

Fiorella said nothing more for a minute or two, glaring at the rasping machine as she pushed fabric toward needle. Then she announced, "Someone might, though. Maybe."

With a hefty sigh she stood up, stretched, and walked Cissie through Remould to a quiet residential avenue which was brightly flooded by a construction lamp. Someone was on their knees filling a pothole, one of many in the pockmarked street.

"Samboy," Fiorella cried. "I have a bona chica for you." With that she left, a short cackle betraying her amusement.

The figure kept working, silhouetted by the harsh white light until Cissie walked closer. It was the Black Irish man who'd given that indecipherable speech in the gaffercarsey. He was wearing a white tank top with cream-coloured sweat stains seeping down from his neck and armpits. His wiry arms shimmered.

"Can I help?" Cissie asked.

The man didn't even turn to her. "We're perfectly capable of helping ourselves."

"Well, I'll be just here if you need me," she replied. Then she waited and watched as he transferred his trowel from bucket to pock. After an uncomfortably long time he gestured for Cissie to hand him another bucket of cement, which she lugged over to him. He said nothing more, and once done he departed without even a simple goodbye.

But she returned a few days later. There was always something in Remould crying out for repair, and Sam seemed to spend the majority of his days fixing and mending, replacing windows and doors, filling the breakout of potholes, reattaching cables and washing lines, even sealing creaky, leaky rooftops. Now and then Fiorella brought them lunch, a sandwich or a raggedly cut hunk of pie, each time seeming mildly surprised by the cis palonie's return.

Sometimes Cissie arrived to find Remould guarded by those women, the ones who'd harassed Fiorella, and though they warily glared at her as she passed by, they never spoke to her, and never stopped her. Even so, Cissie only relaxed once she was safely through the gate.

Once inside, she fetched a screwdriver here, a tile there, and though at first such help was mere obligation, as she returned over the next weeks, she started to enjoy it for its own sake. She liked feeling useful, of making an impact outside of her own family, and the secret visits even made her feel closer to Howard. She felt she understood him and his pride a little better, appreciating the sense of accomplishment from fixing things with your own two hands, the joy in working toward the public good, and the satisfying ache which followed.

They always worked in near total silence. So, when they'd been repainting the front door to the gaffercarsey—under that same blazing lamplight—and Sam asked, "Where are you from then?" she'd been caught entirely off guard.

"Oh. The States." She'd been so unused to conversation she struggled to get the words out. "And you?"

"Cork, originally. It's in Ireland."

"They have Black people in Ireland?"

And though she'd winced, and inwardly chastised herself—*Idiot! Of course there are Black Irish people, you're talking to one!*—he actually laughed at her ignorance, a deep, quaking guffaw. "Yes. Not many though. And one fewer now."

His amusement made Cissie less nervous, and a few minutes later she worked up the courage to enquire:

"What actually is *trans?*"

True, Fiorella had told her when they'd first met, but she'd not understood her answer. Thankfully Sam's response was less cryptic. He actually seemed to relish explaining it to someone so entirely ignorant on the matter, someone with no preconceived notions either way. Keeping his eyes on his paintbrush, he described how sometimes people are born into the wrong body, whether man or woman, and so needed to make changes to match how they were inside—switching clothes, taking hormones, and maybe having surgery. That was trans.

Then he'd explained that the world wasn't always so neatly divided into men and women, that there were people who considered themselves neither, or both, or even different things at different times. That was trans, too.

She could just about understand, particularly as she had seen examples all around her. But she'd wondered about Sam himself. After all, he looked like a man, he acted like a man. Was he even *trans?* Or was he, like Cissie, a visitor? She went over the question in her head, again and again, and by the time it came out it was mangled into:

"What are you?"

"What do you think I am?" he asked.

"A man."

"And that's what I am."

He told her that though he was a man, he'd been raised as a girl. Cissie had been shocked: she just couldn't imagine him as a someone's daughter, playing with dolls and wearing skirts. Drunk on such suddenly open talk, Cissie couldn't help herself; so many thoughts and questions welled in her, she couldn't keep them from spilling out.

"But . . . your beard!"

"Hormones," he said.

"And you're so strong!"

"All kinds of people are strong," he said.

"I'm sorry," Cissie said, flustered. "I just would never have guessed. I mean, why do you even need to live here? You look like a man, you sound like a man—" she stopped short of telling him he *smelled* like a man "—I mean, you could go wherever you want. No one would know, on the outside."

148

That was it; her clumsiness had finally crossed a line. A shadow passed over Sam's face—but not the storm clouds of anger, no. It was worse than that. He was overcast with misery. He told her that the reason he stayed in Remould was very simple: this was his home. The people there were his friends, his family. Yes, many trans people did live in other parts of the city, never telling anyone about their old lives, their old names.

"But what does it mean to live in silence?" he asked. "What does that do to you, in the end?"

His words echoed round her head whenever she rushed dinner because she'd come home too late from the trans town. They resounded whenever she left the children with Ms. Fortier, telling her she had another meeting of her fictitious book club. But she couldn't help herself. The more she went, the more she helped fix, the more she was wedded to the town of unending dusk.

22.

In this way months passed by, in excuses and secret visits. Cissie'd learned the trans town like the back of her hand—or *famble*, as Sam said. She became a fixture, just like the faraway hum from the bridge overhead, just like the countless tiny generators that worked relentlessly to light the streets and houses. She learned that there were only two modes for Remould's streets: comfortingly crowded, or eerily empty. The main street, for example, buzzed through all hours. There the endless evening was brightened by strings of year-round Christmas lights, sizzling neon signs, and red bulbs which glowed from upper windows while daring tourists waited in front of the doors below. Other streets, however, lay dim and chilly, with only the soft buzz of distant traffic and occasional clack of footsteps.

The street they were currently on was one of the eerie, dark, quiet ones. The muscles of Sam's arms were taut as he screwed in the bracket for a garbage can, grunting with each turn as Cissie held the can in place. Not for the first time she wondered if he was sexually interested in her (as a few of the boys from her church had once been), but he was so relaxed, so free of that awkward erotic tension.

Then again, what did she really know about men and their ways? The only male friend she'd ever had was Howard's old workmate, Rob. Kind, jovial Rob, who'd always taken her seriously, always had something to talk to her about. But he and Howard had fallen out over some nonsense, years ago, when they'd first gone to Berlin, and she'd not seen him since. Where was he now? Back in Ohio, she supposed. Besides, Rob didn't count, not really. He'd been Howard's friend, not hers.

"And how's the old bones?" Sam asked, his low, melodic voice echoing down the road. She still hadn't learned much about him, but, oddly, he was quite curious about her own rather unremarkable life. In Remould it was she who was the oddity.

"The old *what?*" she queried, arms trembling as she held the metal cylinder steady.

"The husband," he replied, reaching for another screw. "Homer. How's he doing?"

Sam was dryly teasing her, she knew that, but she corrected him, nonetheless. "It's Howard, I told you his name is Howard."

"Yes, that one."

"Well, he's been doing just fine," she answered, her fingers numbed by the growing cold. "Better than fine, actually. He's been . . . cheerful. Kind, attentive, playful with the kids. Maybe it's this study group he's got going."

Study group was the term she'd settled on, the label she'd slapped over Howard's gang of Bible-toting, middle-aged men. Yes, she'd been worried at first, but Howard no longer pushed his faith onto her—the family prayers had stopped, and she could come and go as she pleased. Ms. Fortier was right: he had set up a boys' club and it had relaxed him, made him feel better. Besides, they were quite harmless. When they'd finally met again in her apartment, she'd listened through the bedroom door, and found their attempts at manly talk comical, like listening to children learning how to swear. *It's God's duty to look after our families,* announced one man with a quavering, whining voice. *We have to be brave, like Lot in Sodom,* added another.

Yes, it was strange, and she'd have preferred he not vanish each Tuesday and Thursday, but she was in no position to criticise.

"We're almost done," Sam instructed. Cissie nodded. Every tendon of her forearms ached. "Now let go."

The can stayed up, proud on its fixture. Lowering herself to the cracked sidewalk, Cissie massaged her sore muscles as Sam tidied away his tools. Neither of them noticed Fiorella until she was directly behind them.

"Hey Samboy!" she greeted. "The trash can wait. We've urgent work needs doing."

Cissie had yet to figure out the exact relationship between Fiorella and Sam. She waved hello, only to receive a wan smile in return; in fact, the more Cissie came back, the more the Italian woman seemed to suspect her and her motives.

"Some ground floor windows need replacing," she told Sam. "A group of bevvied-up cis men slipped by the patrols last menge, trolled through the gate. It's light damage, mostly—they upturned some bins, cackled some nasty lavs—you know, to prove how big and brave they are. The windows are the worst of it."

With a wave of one lilac fingernail Fiorella led them down the glowing main street, past its stalls and shops, the bakery, a plus-sized shoe store, and an unlicensed pharmacy. Then they turned left off the commercial avenue and stopped at an apartment building.

Glass crystals twinkled from the sidewalk. The windows of the ground-floor apartment gaped wide, open mouths with ragged teeth. A group of burlier residents were unloading the last of the replacement panes, propping them up by the building's door. Two older people were thanking them in profuse Polari, while handing out mug after mug of cheap substitute coffee.

"I just don't get it." Cissie hadn't meant to speak her thoughts aloud.

"What don't you get, cis palonie?" Fiorella asked, folding her arms and finally looking directly at Cissie.

"Oh. I mean, I can't understand why they'd come here, why they'd smash things. Honestly, I don't get why anyone would cause trouble for people they don't even know."

Fiorella muttered something beneath her breath.

"In my experience," Sam answered, while already inspecting the damage, "it's far easier to hate folk you don't know. Most of the time, at least."

Cissie had nothing to say to that; she couldn't comprehend hating anyone in such a loose, abstract way. It wasn't that she hadn't known hatred, or anger—for a long time she'd hated her parents—but the emotion was something concentrated, a laser focus on a specific target, not some indiscriminate fog. And this blanket hate simply passed over her; she got to go home to Hetcarsey, after all.

All she could do was help. So, she donned a thick pair of gloves, and set to work clearing the street of broken shards.

That night, when the children were safely tucked up in bed and Howard's low snore made the thin walls tremble, she examined herself in the small bathroom mirror. She ran her fingertips over the tense lines of her hands. The sinews of her arms. The whitened clench of her knuckles. She had worked hard before—first as a waitress when she'd first moved in with Howard, and then as a mother—but this was new, satisfying in a way she couldn't fully articulate. Every muscle was sore, but she savoured the sensation as she clicked off the light, crept to the bedroom, and slipped beneath the covers. Already half asleep, she wrapped herself around Howard, spooning his body with her own, nuzzling his neck as she drifted.

23.

Late afternoon sunlight streamed through the tiny living room window, causing the smoke from Ms. Fortier's cigarette to glow like a magic cloud above the heads of Cissie and the boys. It was a quiet hour of the day, with only the odd burr of conversation wafting from the skyway below.

Cissie rattled the board game box before her two children. Little Jonah stared up, eyes wide with excitement, but Thomas was unimpressed.

"That game's for babies," he sneered, casting a cruel glance toward his younger brother. Jonah missed the jab, and automatically echoed the sentiments of his elder brother.

"I don't like that game either," he concurred, dismissing the joy which had welled in him just a moment earlier.

"Your mother plays this game," Ms. Fortier intervened. "Is your mother a baby?"

Jonah looked toward Cissie, shrieking with laughter at this blasphemy, while Thomas remained aloof. At almost nine years old, he was already distancing himself from his parents.

"What would you like to play, then?" Cissie magnanimously asked her older son.

"I don't care."

"Listen to me, miniature Howard." Ms. Fortier leaned toward Thomas as though sharing a conspiracy, prompting the curious boy to do the same. "You have an easy choice. Either you show respect to your mother, or I use your rude little mouth as an ashtray."

"Ms. Fortier!" Cissie exclaimed.

"He knows I'm kidding." Ms. Fortier smiled at Thomas as she leaned back, then muttered, "He knows I'm probably kidding."

"Let's play monopoly," Cissie declared, pulling a raggedy cardboard box from beneath the couch: an old pre-War British version she'd found in a charity store. Really, she couldn't stand the game, but it was the only one both children could agree upon.

"But I'll tell you what," she offered, hunting around the living room for a felt-tip pen. "Why don't we change it?"

"Change it?" She'd finally piqued Thomas' interest. Jonah looked to his brother for direction.

"Change it," Cissie confirmed, finding a marker on top of the television set. "We can alter the place names. Like this one, here. Does anyone know where 'Old Kent Road' actually is?"

"No," both boys chorused.

"Ms. Fortier?" Cissie asked.

"I don't have a clue, my dear. It probably doesn't exist anymore."

"Well then, why don't we make it—" she squeaked the felt-tip across the first square, crossing out the old name and saying the new words as she wrote them, "—*Chanting Chavvies Infant Academy*. There. What do you think?"

The two boys leaned in to read the defacement.

"That's where I go to school!" Jonah squealed, pointing at the board.

"Do mine too," Thomas insisted, prompting Cissie to write *Gildy Journo Middle School* over Whitechapel.

"That's my *old* school," he corrected, but seemed no less pleased by the result.

"Where else?" she asked, and the boys clamoured with suggestions, Thomas temporarily forgetting his age as they insisted Cissie add Britz Park, the toy store, and their street, Amity Boulevard, all the while making the same amendments to the corresponding cards. Only when they ran low with suggestions did Cissie scribble her own.

"What's *Remould?*" Thomas asked, peering at the new name. Ms. Fortier narrowed her eyes, watching Cissie from the other end of the sofa.

"Yes, Cissie sweet, I also don't know this place."

"Oh, just somewhere I heard of," Cissie lied, suddenly realising her mistake. "Let's get rid of that actually, it's a silly name."

"Now there's a big black smudge." Thomas pointed to the Monopoly board, once she'd done scrawling out the name.

"It doesn't matter. Look, let's put the skyway there, instead."

The only name they didn't alter was Mayfair, the last location. When Cissie held the marker to the cardboard, Jonah shrieked as though she were about to pierce his skin. Despite the combined attempts of both Cissie and Ms. Fortier to soothe him, he only calmed down once the marker pen was placed into a drawer.

Each of the boys bought their own schools, of course, refusing to part with them throughout the course of the game. As always, Cissie granted money to Jonah when he lost, ignoring Thomas' opposition to these "baby rules." The four played for hours, the boys fighting for ownership of the toy store as Cissie and Ms. Fortier competed for stations and utilities. Lost in the game, Cissie hadn't even begun making dinner by the time Howard returned from work.

The strangest part was that he wasn't upset at all. Instead, he trolled straight back out and returned with Chinese food, even including a portion for Ms. Fortier. The boys were overjoyed to have spent hours playing games only to be rewarded with takeout, a luxury usually reserved for birthdays.

"We've gotta treat the boys once in a while," he cheerfully proclaimed, before pressing his lips to Cissie's cheek.

She could have sworn she caught a sceptical glance from Ms. Fortier, though when she looked again her old neighbour was helping Jonah spoon fried rice onto his plate.

The trans town's next task was most perplexing: apparently, they were to repair the red-brick wall which surrounded Remould. The one which literally walled them in. The materials had already been delivered, waiting in a neat, trusting stack right out in the open as Sam and Cissie placed and lit the bright halogen work lamp.

"Why exactly are we doing this?" she asked Sam, staring up at the crumbled section of brickwork as he clambered up a small stepladder and began slathering mortar onto the topmost row.

"Because," he explained, the lamp throwing stark shadows across the bricks, "if this barrier goes tumbling they might build an even bigger one, one we can't just troll through whenever we like. Better the naff you know, and all that."

"That either makes total sense, or absolutely none," Cissie replied, passing him a fresh brick from the stack.

Slowly, slowly she was learning Berlin's way of things. She was even beginning to grasp the difference between the "gays" and the "queers." From what she understood, the gays were your run-of-the-mill homosexuals. They had their groupings—bears, twinks, daddies, she remembered those—their tribes, if you will. It was the same with the lesbians. But the queers, they were the ones who, for whatever reason, didn't fit in. The ones who couldn't be categorised.

She also knew there was violence brewing between the included and the excluded, though she still couldn't see why such hostility would arise in the first place. To the straight world, gays and queers were one and the same. Puzzled, she said as much to Sam.

"Then you savvy more than you realise," he told her, his voice even more melodic than usual, betraying his enthusiasm. "And you're right. It doesn't matter if you're gay or queer or bi or trans, we're all ogled as freaks by the outside world. So yeah, it would make sense for us to stand together. But sadly, that's nix how it works. A lot of gay people just want the world to ogle them as normal. We make them less normal by association, so they push us away. Think about it: if you want the playground bully to like you, you don't want to be seen with the other weird kids. That's what it boils down to."

Oh, she knew she didn't grasp it all, not just yet—she was straight-born and straight-raised, after all—but she was trying, and Sam's tolerance of her appeared to be slipping toward a sort of workplace camaraderie.

Despite the crisp chill to the air, Sam put down his mortar and pulled off his shirt. Cissie looked without looking, snatching glances at his floodlit torso. His sweat-sheened chest was firm and sinewy, a lean contrast to her husband's comforting, fleshy belly; a thin trail of dark hair ran down the plane of his stomach. His nipples hardened with the cold, and beneath were two faint scars, which were lighter than the rest of his skin. *A mastectomy,* she realised, before feeling guilty, as though she were invading his private history with her thoughts. But she couldn't help those stolen glances; she watched his muscles twist as he reached for the trowel. The only man's body she'd seen up close was Howard's; even her father had always hidden himself in thick undershirts and thermal underwear.

"Let me try," Cissie insisted, as much to distract herself as anything.

"Try what?"

"Laying the bricks," she answered.

"Are you sure, my fair palonie? If they're uneven, you'll be exiled from here forever."

Cissie stuck her tongue out, covering her physical curiosity with the childish gesture. With raised eyebrows, Sam stepped off the ladder and handed her the trowel.

"Be smooth, confident, and careful," he instructed. "As though you're spreading butter for royalty."

"Like this?"

"Exactly," he cackled. "Give me just a second—"

Sam sprinted away, a sudden movement which caused Cissie to jolt, and which ruined her smooth motion.

"Wait right there," he called back. So, she waited, masonry trowel in hand.

After a few minutes, Sam returned with a yellow hard hat, the kind construction workers wear. It immediately reminded Cissie of Howard.

"I don't need to wear that," she said, coming down from the ladder.

"Of course, you don't *need* to," Sam said. "But it's dolly, no? You'll varda a real workhomie in that."

"What?" Cissie asked. He often left her behind with his Polari.

"I mean you'll look like a real workman," he translated.

That was the problem. The hat was too much like the one Howard wore.

"If I wear that it's like I'm not taking this work seriously," she countered.

How could she wear Howard's hat?

It's not his hat, she corrected herself.

"If we took ourselves seriously, we'd all go meshiginer," Sam whispered, sliding the yellow headgear over her hair. With it firmly in place atop her head, he guided her to a nearby window, which was bathed in the violet neon glow of an old barbershop sign.

Cissie gazed at her faint, spectral reflection. She looked different. In charge, dominant. Though it was the same kind of hat worn by a hundred thousand construction workers, it swelled her with a sense of power. *Ridiculous*, she reminded herself. It was just a plastic yellow hat.

The two returned to their task, Sam passing the bricks, Cissie now laying them. With each stroke she felt masterful, even when she got it wrong and Sam corrected her with mocking jokes and gentle touches. By the time the repair was complete her arms had ached, then numbed, then ached again, but she stared at the obscene wall with abject fascination.

She had rebuilt that. Someday it would crumble or fall, but that could never take away the fact that she, herself, had actually rebuilt it.

Ms. Fortier was waiting in their building's skyway lobby when Cissie returned home that afternoon. The strip lights above cradled the silhouettes of dead insects, slowly decomposing shadows. Illuminated by this dim yellow glow and the fuggy light from the windows, the older palonie was seated on a metallic bench, a half-dead fern wilting to each side. In her hands she clutched a magazine, though her eyes were roving over each person entering and exiting the building through the equally filthy glass doors.

When she spotted Cissie coming in from the walkway, she lowered her gaze and pretended to read.

"Why hello, Ms. Fortier," Cissie greeted, a teasing edge to her voice. "I didn't know you sat here."

"Sweetness!" Ms. Fortier exclaimed in mock surprise. "Why, when you're my age you take the chance to sit where you can. Especially when you've been looking after two young children."

She fussily closed the magazine and placed it to her side, lancing Cissie with a pointed look. "Of course, I just don't have the energy to go skipping who-knows-where every single day."

"I don't go out every single—" Cissie caught herself. "I'm sorry, I don't know what you're talking about. I've been going to my book club."

"Of course, I could be wrong," Ms. Fortier replied. "I am just an old woman. A useless, silly old woman . . ."

Cissie knew her better than to believe this self-deprecation. It wasn't personal, not telling Ms. Fortier about Remould; she just couldn't risk it slipping out and reaching her husband's ears.

". . . but just in case I'm right, Cissie dear, let me give you one piece of advice. Just one, and I'll leave you alone."

Cissie nodded: she was already late making a start on the evening meal, and there was little chance of Howard going to fetch Chinese food two nights in a row.

"Now, there's no harm in dipping your toe into this city now and again." The older neighbour huffed as she stood, ready to leave. "But be careful when immersing yourself, my sweet. It's easier than you might think to be in over your head, and by that point it's too late—by then you're already submerged."

With that said, she left for the elevator.

Cissie fumed. She'd been in such a good mood, and now it was ruined; in fact, she felt as indignant as Thomas whenever she ordered him to make his bed or clean his teeth. How dare she? Ms. Fortier had no right to spy on her, no right at all. *I'm an adult,* she told herself as she walked over to the lobby's convenience store and purchased four overpriced frozen pizzas for dinner. *I know what I'm doing.*

When she got back Howard was already home, playing dominoes with the boys. But unlike with Ms. Fortier, there were no insinuations. He asked no questions and made no demands. He simply hugged her hello, his strong arms enveloping her shoulders, his comfortable belly pressed up against her.

24.

She could no longer leave the children with Ms. Fortier, that much was obvious. So, she took Thomas and Jonas to *Happy Lappers Daycare*, a cute, affordable little place just off the walkway to Q. Howard would question the expense, but she'd find some explanation. Somehow.

Of course, as soon as Thomas saw the colourful walls and bright cartoon murals, he announced that the place was for babies, though his complaints faded the moment he saw a video game machine. He wandered straight over, picked up the controller, and began living as a bright pink cat. Jonah waddled over to his side and watched. Cissie hesitated, but the daycare owner assured her that they wouldn't be playing all day. She even handed Cissie a programme, complete with crafts and educational activities. So Cissie paid up and left, kissing each child on the forehead. Thomas instantly wiped her kiss away.

Glancing back as she left, Cissie felt a stab of guilt. What, exactly, was she doing? She didn't know. All she savvied was that she needed this—this double life, this other self, whatever it was. It was the only thing that was all her own.

When she arrived at Remould Sam was seated at one of the tables in the gaffercarsey, already having breakfast. On her approach, he pulled up a chair and divided half his food onto a spare plate, as though he'd been expecting her.

And even though she'd longed for Sam's company, now she was here, she didn't know what to say. She ate in awkward, confused silence, with Ms. Fortier's scornful warning ringing through her head. *Dip your toe, don't get submerged.* Well, what if it was already too late? What if she was already underwater?

She loved Remould, in its menge, bizarre way. She loved the work, the time she spent with Sam. That all made sense: it had given her fresh purpose, a life she'd never expected. But there was more to it, and her motivations were murky even to herself. When she was with Sam a part of her felt at ease, more comfortable than she had ever been. Yet another part of her was ever giddy with nervous tension and felt a constant threat of nausea. She saw him as intoxicatingly male, yet also something more, something else, and she knew that in doing so she did him some vague wrong. And so her thoughts tangled like thick seaweed, dragging her down.

"Please, Cissie." Sam put down his croissant and interrupted her miserable reverie. "You look gloomy with guilt, and I think I know why."

Her very bones shot cold. Had she been so obvious? She would never betray Howard, not with anything more than stray thoughts. Bad stray thoughts.

"You don't need to worry so much," he comforted, putting his hand on her arm. "I think you're attractive, too. And I'll tell no flies, I've thought about it. More than a little, if I'm fully honest. But I also savvy how important your marriage is, and I want you to be happy. So relax: I'm not going to do anything, and neither are you. I'm only talking to you about this because sometimes—sometimes cackling our thoughts aloud can be helpful. It can help dispel tension, no?"

"I suppose so." She hated how easily she was read, how her thoughts played out in her expression, as though she deserved nothing private. Her mother always said it was important for a woman to carry an air of mystery.

"Cissie, despite being a homie—that's *a man* for you learners—I was raised as a palonie. I savvy how you're supposed to think, better than your average bloke will, at any rate. Just know that I spend time with you because I like you, and I think being here is probably bona for you, too. You varda a *grand nouveau palonie*. That's a whole new woman," he added. His grin was that of some friendly devil.

Surrendering to temptation and eager to change the subject, Cissie made a request which had played on her mind ever since her last visit.

"That reminds me, when we work today . . ." she spoke slowly, before grinding to a pause. Sam waited patiently, eyebrows raised. ". . . could I wear the hard hat again?"

Her companion burst out laughing, a naughty, throaty guffaw which caused people seated nearby to glance over.

"Of course, my fair homiepalonie. Just wait here."

He threw himself up from the table and darted from the door, his whole body a tight coil of kinetic energy. Cissie was still pondering the term "homiepalonie" when he returned with an armful of rags, which he gently, religiously, placed down upon the table. Clothes. The yellow construction worker hat was piled on top, hefty work boots beneath.

"Are you ready?" he asked.

"I stopped believing in 'ready,'" she responded. "What are those?"

"They're for you to wear while we work."

"They look—" she removed the hard hat from the top of the pile and picked up a rough flannel shirt, "—they look like men's clothes."

"Not *men's* clothes," her cove corrected. "Specifically, they're *my* clothes. And today they're *your* clothes."

"I don't think I—"

"Cissie," Sam interrupted. "They're just clobber, and they're much more appropriate for manual dickey than what you usually wear."

Cissie ogled down at her breezy skirt and soft blouse, then to the pile. The maroon flannel shirt, rough denim pants, scratchy woollen socks, and heavy boots. It was much, much more than a simple hat.

"I'll do it," she announced. We all need an escape from ourselves.

"You can go change in the back," Sam stated, pointing to the curtained doorway which led to the gaffercarsey's rear rooms and the upstairs dormitory she'd slept in her very first night in Remould. She dressed quickly in the dim hallway, pulling off her skirt and blouse, putting on the jeans and shirt. At least it all smelled clean.

Though she entered the main room hesitantly and with more than a little awkwardness, Sam applauded. The people at the next table were cheerfully ogling the scene.

"You make a bona manly," Sam praised. "It just needs detail. For your face—your *eke*."

He pulled a black marker from his pocket. "Don't worry, we can wash it off before you leave."

Cissie didn't even flinch as he brought it to her face in gentle flutters, giggling while adding a neat goatee, which she then admired in her pocket mirror.

"Now stand tall," Sam instructed. "No, no, not poised, not so elegant. You're a manly now, stop worrying about how you look. Manlies don't, or at least not the straight ones. There, that's it. That's great. Now you need a name."

"Howard," Cissie announced, without hesitation.

Sam raised an eyebrow. "Then we've work to do, Howard."

At first Cissie felt nothing, not even from wearing the hat. But as they set about hauling crates from the back of a truck—crates filled with smuggled hormones—she once again felt the strain of her arms, the pull on her legs and buttocks, that strange sense of power. Physical power. Soon the denim and flannel felt natural, as though she wore them every day.

With the truck empty they sat on the kerb and wolfed at sandwiches.

"You're getting stronger, *Howard*," Sam teased, taking a large bite and chewing thoughtfully. Cissie appreciated the fact that he swallowed before speaking again.

"All right. I have to ask. Why use your husband's name? I'm not judging. It's just a little bit kinky."

Truth was, she didn't have an answer. It had just felt right.

After leaving Remould she picked the children up from the daycare. The two boys giggled and pointed at her head—despite Sam's promises, faint traces of the marker-pen goatee remained even after she'd scrubbed her eke with soap in the gaffercarsey's bathroom.

"Mommy's face is dirty," Jonah chuckled, and the marks only vanished once she got back to the apartment and applied liberal layers of concealer. She then made a start on dinner, only for Howard to come home, turn off the stove, and say, "We're eating out tonight."

The very last thing Cissie expected was to be invited out to dinner. In all the time she and Howard had been married, they had never gone on a dinner date. Not unless you counted eating hot dogs down at the mall, back before Thomas was born.

She thought it was a joke, of course, but Howard had planned everything. A friend from his Bible study group had offered to take the kids for the evening.

"They live in the block opposite, and his wife is very nice. Isn't it time the kids made some friends?"

He'd even chosen a restaurant.

"Sudanese, just ten minutes' walk away. Sounds exotic, right?"

Of course, she said yes. To all of it. Howard waited patiently in the living room as she redid her makeup and hovered between clothes, revelling in a soft femininity which was quite the opposite of what she'd inhabited earlier that day. This, too, was an adventure. She chose a jade green dress she'd only worn twice before, for fear of ruining it with spills and tears. As the bedroom door swung open, Howard's eyes widened at the sight of her.

"Where's my wife?" he asked. It was a corny joke, but they laughed all the same. When had they last laughed together?

Howard didn't own a suit, but he put on a brand-new shirt and the trousers she'd ironed earlier that week. When they were both ready, he took her arm in his and escorted her down the hallway. It was only as they paraded themselves through the streets of Hetcarsey that Cissie began to worry. This wasn't Howard's usual behaviour. Perhaps the meal was the backdrop for bad news.

"Look how jealous people are," Howard smirked. In truth no one really noticed them, but she grinned back all the same, warm in the glow of shared conspiracy.

The restaurant was a chatty, colourful hole-in-the-wall, half the surfaces draped in bright blankets which were softly lit by wall-mounted lamps. The waiter placed a candle on the tablecloth and struck a match, as Howard took Cissie's coat and pulled out her chair. Slowly, she relaxed. Why did there have to be something wrong? Why not just enjoy a special evening together? They each had their own interests and diversions, and perhaps that was what they'd needed all along.

Howard took her hand. He held on to it as they read the menus. The waiter returned, and they even kept their fingers entwined as they ordered.

"I know we haven't done this a lot," Howard explained once the waiter was out of earshot. He spoke haltingly, as though he were measuring and approving every word.

"But you've been a champion to me and the boys. You moved across the world for me, and I need you to know how much I appreciate it. I really do, Cissie. It's not always been easy for you, I know that. Don't ever think I don't know that. You've made sacrifices I can never repay, but I'm going to try."

He stopped, just for a minute, as he stared down at the colourful tablecloth, his face burning red and his grip on her hand tightening. Cissie couldn't help herself. Her eyes welled; her throat clogged.

"I love you, Cissie. I don't always say it enough, I don't show it enough, but it's true." He looked her directly in the eyes. "You're the one person in my life who's always trusted me, who's always been there for me, who's supported me no matter what. I love you more than anything."

The waiter returned with their drinks, prompting Cissie to dab at her eyes with the napkin. She said nothing, having no idea what to say. She had never felt more special.

Excerpt from
The Honest Guide to Berlin

Culture.

Berlin is home to some of the largest and most prolific media companies on the planet, and despite frequent condemnation of the Republic's books, songs, radio broadcasts, television shows, and movies, they are nevertheless enjoyed throughout the straight world. Berlin-based music legends such as Freddie Mercury and Elton John have found diverse fan bases, while the all-gay sitcom *Coves and the Smoke* enjoys an audience in the tens of millions. The "homosexual lifestyle" may be frequently mocked and derided, but gay cultural exports have never been stronger. Whether this will lead to greater acceptance of homosexuality in the outside world—or whether this strange double standard continues—remains to be seen.

Though the gay content of Berlin's media has given it a reputation as an anarchic free-for-all, there are actually strict guidelines on what can be published, filmed, or broadcast within the Gay Republic. The Media Production Code (informally known as the Luvvie Code) was first created during a series of meetings between government officials and media representatives, most importantly the popular nationalist radio host Kenneth Luvvie.

Established in 1985 during the height of the DISS epidemic, the code is divided into two parts: the first focuses on adherence to established gay moral guidelines in general, so as not to "encourage deviant or subversive behaviour within the Gay Republic." The second is more specific, forbidding positive depictions of elements known to "undermine gay or lesbian identity." Media which fails to adhere to the Production Code will not be rated by any official body and is therefore barred from distribution. This has not stopped illicit material from circulating, finding its way from unsavoury studios into otherwise respectable homes and businesses (see *Dangers and Annoyances*, p. 80).

GUTLESS

The Gay Republic

1999

25.

Do not be mistaken, dear nellers. There are many reasons they give as to why our Republic cannot succeed: that we are sinners, that we are too selfish, too decadent. That fruits are wealthy capitalists. That fruits are militant socialists. But the principal reason—the one which always sticks—is that we can't have children.

You will all have nelled it before you moved here, and, dear listeners, you may even have wondered it yourself. How can the Gay Republic exist without little chavvies?

Yet we do have them. We have well-achieving schools, enterprising youth groups, playgrounds in the thousands. More than anything else, the existence of our great smoke has proven that we, too, have families.

And our families are nix accidental. Fruits and dykes can give the most bona of gifts to one another, in the most sacred and platonic of all conceptions. Every child is born by choice, and so our families last.

At the centre of all this is the loving couple, united in gay marriage, united in amor, united in duty for their land. I might be called old-fashioned. I might even be called conservative. Yet I call myself traditional. Marriage is a sacred duty in our smoke, more so here than anywhere else. Around the world we varda adultery, divorce, domestic violence. Nix here. The heterosexual may have invented the nuclear family, yet we have perfected it.

But what, you might ask, about choice? What about diversity, of freedom? What of the fruits and dykes who don't choose the nuclear family unit? These questions are asked by the journo, and it is our duty to answer them.

The truth is our only choice is between marriage and destruction. Diversity can only exist within the limits of survival. Bisexuality, adultery, gender-bending, free love, all of these flaws weaken the fragile fabric of our Republic. They aid the heterosexual world in its quest to wipe us from the

171

eke of the earth. They threaten our identity as gay men and women. After all, our Republic rests upon the shoulders of men marrying men, and women wedding women. Without those values, what distinguishes us? What holds us all together?

We've withstood centuries of oppression, and we finally have our freedom. We cannot allow radicals and terrorists to attack us from within, to collapse the strictures of our society. Not after everything we've worked for. Not after everything we've built. Rest assured, my nellers, we fight so our love can be protected. We have no other choice.

Gareth was seated at the table in the bevvie's back room, a car magazine open in front of him, the radio to one side. He stroked the pictures of vehicles with his finger, tracing the edges, trying not to savvy what could've been, the work he could've done if he'd had a chance to learn the trade.

"Boyno, homie," Björn called, dashing away Gareth's thoughts as he trolled into the break room. He was Swedish, but the guy cackled with a thick American accent. A snow-pale ghost with white hair—Gareth still had no idea whether Björn was a dyed or real albino, but he'd spent the past months watching for dark roots just the same. He'd seen nix so far.

"Enough nelling that," the supervisor said, pointing at the radio. "It's dead out there. I need company."

"Fine," Gareth relented, turning the radio off. No one wanted the afternoon shifts. The afternoon was a dead space, the gap between busy lunch hours and the night rush. Those in-between times moved slow as treacle: a couple of lazy flies buzzed around the bar taps; the rooftop plaza was empty but for a throng of auburn thrushes; the traffic below slugged by in sleepy crawl.

"Politics," Björn said once they were side by side behind the bar. "It's all meshiginer, if you ask me. I don't savvy why you bother with it."

"I don't," Gareth insisted. "It's just . . ." he paused for a moment. "William likes it. Besides, it's good for my Polari."

He wasn't sure why he'd lied to Björn. Maybe it was the way he'd said *politics*, maybe it was 'cause he wanted Björn to like him. But he'd told flies all the same—truth was, William'd stopped listening to the radio broadcasts not long after they'd arrived in Berlin. It was Gareth who couldn't let it go. No, more than that, Gareth actually liked the old auntie on the radio. See, back in England being a fruit'd been a burden, a deformity of sorts. But the old auntie said nix to that. Not only was he not deformed, he was actually bona.

"I prefer something with a beat," Björn said, rapping his fingers against the faux-wood bar, swinging his eke from side to side in a silly dance.

Gareth smiled despite himself. Of all the supervisors he could have had, he'd hit the jackpot with Björn, who did a good job while not taking it too seriously. Their friendship—if it was enough to be called a friendship—was mostly based on teasing each other and gossiping about customers. It was a relief to just laugh and joke around.

"I can see why all the dollies want you," Gareth taunted.

So Björn moved his lacoddy slower, switching to a sensual rhythm that poked fun at the twinks on subway adverts and in the clubs. He didn't notice the gruff daddy who'd just entered, and who didn't seem to find the dance the least bit funny.

"What'll it be, sir?" Gareth asked the annoyed homie. On varding the intruder, Björn turned away, covering his mouth to hide the giggles.

"Some decent service, for a start," the man spat back. "Failing that, a whiskey and soda."

Though Gareth couldn't be rude exactly, he got revenge by going as slow as possible. Björn joined in, and the two pretended to bump into each other, slowing the whole thing down even more.

"Here you go," Gareth offered, once the drink was finished. The daddy paid without saying another lav.

"Come out with me tonight," Björn cackled. "We'll go to The Oracle. It's just a few blocks south of here, over in Maytree."

"Can't. I need to get home to William. I've been on menge shifts all week, and this is the first night we can actually spend together."

"But you hardly ever come out," Björn replied. "It's all home and here, home and here. Do you ever troll anywhere else?"

Truth was that Gareth didn't know what to say. He'd asked William out a whole bunch of times, but William'd always said they didn't have the money, or he was too tired from work, or else he wanted to cook them a meal, or he'd some new book he was reading. It was like he was too afraid to actually enjoy the smoke around him. He'd tried to talk about it, but William was the one bona with language, and when he disagreed on something, he could run rings around Gareth, distract him with pretty-sounding words. Making him lose the point.

"Come on," Björn continued, clearly seeing a gap in Gareth's defences. "He won't mind just this once."

"He will," Gareth answered. "He'll miss me. He doesn't really know anyone else."

"You know what I savvy?" Björn asked.

"Nix," Gareth sighed. "But I'm sure you'll tell me."

"I savvy you're *letting* him be this way. You're enabling him with your behaviour."

"Get lost," Gareth replied. "Those aren't your words. Where'd you read that? Some new pop-trash relationship guide?"

"Doesn't matter where I read it," Björn said. "It's still true. *Come onnnnn*," he insisted like a chavvie, squeezing Gareth's arm. "Come on, come on, come on."

"Fine," Gareth relented. "*Fine*," he said again, shaking himself free from Björn's grip. Once again, he smiled, though he'd not meant to. It was nice to have a mate who was light and easy, without all the seriousness. Björn picked up the phone and handed it to Gareth, watching as he dialled.

"Hello, lover," William answered.

"Um, yes, hey." Gareth choked out the first words. He'd never enjoyed telephone conversations.

"Everything all right?" William asked.

"I just—Björn asked if I'd go with him to The Oracle this evening. It's a club bordering Twinkstadt and Maytree, and—"

"Oh." There was a lull before William continued. "Go, it'll be fun."

"You want to come with us? Just us boys?" Gareth'd asked, already savvying what the answer would be.

"I'm good, I've some reading I want to get on with."

Gareth gripped the phone tight, his anger sharp and sudden. Why couldn't William come out just once, actually share an experience with him?

"You don't want to go?" he asked.

"Not really. It's not my thing."

"You've never even been," Gareth found himself accusing. "We're young, we should be out enjoying ourselves—"

"I have been enjoying myself," William replied. He sounded defensive. "Are you not enjoying yourself?"

Gareth couldn't answer. He held the phone tight. After a painful silence he said, "I just thought we'd be doing more than this."

"More?"

Gareth gripped the phone harder and harder. It was as though William was trying to find the worst possible meaning in whatever he said. Well, if that was what William wanted, he wasn't going to fight it.

"More than spending all our time at home. You know what I mean," he said. "We're living like we're—"

"What, Gareth? Like we're what?"

"You're not savvying what I'm trying to say," Gareth replied. "Just nell me. I wanted you to come because I love you. I just wanted you there with me."

There was a pause before William said, "Fine, then I'll come."

"No, look, don't worry," Gareth answered. He'd swelled with anger, but it'd gone in an instant; he felt like the air'd been let out of him. His grip on the phone loosened. "Don't worry about it."

"I mean it," William insisted, his voice quiet. "I'll come with you."

"It's all right," Gareth said, suddenly exhausted. "Maybe next time."

"We'll do that."

He felt sick. That is, until he and Björn stepped out into the cool Twinkstadt night. The streets were waking up: music poured from open windows, flooding the air with possibility.

"I told you he wouldn't mind," Björn cackled.

Björn was lucky enough to live in the district. Twinkstadt and Maytree were much more exciting than Q, with trendy stores and hordes of tourists, the brightly sparkling lure of the bevvies, the cackling groups of homies on nights out, the street performers busking to the dawn. Part of Gareth hoped that someday William would agree to get married. Make themselves official. Maybe then they could live as a real couple, living in a real district—not the ramshackle shithole they lived in now, where the bevvies were too small, and the shops sold secondhand clothes. Living in Q he couldn't help but feel that life itself was passing him by, that his youth was trolling away.

They headed to Björn's first, and even the carsey he shared with his husband was better than what Gareth had. For a start, it was actually close to work, and though it was only a bijou bit bigger than his rooftop house, it came with a laundry facility, bona furniture, and big windows varding out over a sea of neon. The apartment showed Gareth what might've been.

Just as he was dwelling on the past, Björn rummaged through his wardrobe and fambled him a blood red button-up shirt.

"You can wear this," he offered. "Now put it on and let's get going. We've a long, long menge ahead."

26.

For the first time in weeks William had the chance to cook something that didn't come out of a box, carton, or can, and he was going to make the most of it. There'd been a terrorist scare at the office. His manager had stumbled in pale as china, and with a wavering, quavering voice told them that some bisexual activist group had called in a bomb threat. The employees all stayed seated, rooted in uncertainty, until the manager set off the fire alarms. Then came a mad scramble to the exits, all elbows and panic.

The scare was probably fake, but they'd got the afternoon off anyway. Seizing the opportunity, William trolled over to a makeshift community library a few streets away from his apartment and borrowed a recipe book, shyly avoiding both eye contact and idle chatter with the make-do librarian. Then he scoured the district's small shops for ingredients.

It wasn't fancy, but Gareth had always loved "toad in the hole," that peculiar British combination of egg batter and sausages, and this would be the first time he'd eaten it since they'd left England. Gareth had given up so much so they could be together, and William at least wanted to give him this.

First up, he needed a large mixing bowl. Precariously balanced on a wobbly chair, he reached into one of the high kitchen cabinets and found the large glass yellow one he'd bought at a basement flea market. As he carefully pulled it free his hand nudged something small and plastic, which rolled out and fell to the floor with a clatter.

It was the fuchsia pink lipstick.

It must have rolled away from where he'd left it. Gently setting the bowl down onto the work surface, he knelt to pick up the small plastic cylinder, took the cap off, and twisted it. Just to check it wasn't broken.

The colour was even brighter and more vivid than the label. His hand trembled as he took a sharp knife and carefully cut off the tip, then tested a little on the paper-white skin of his forearm. The pigment shone like neon, and, after making sure it washed off with soap and water, he trolled down to the bathroom mirror and slowly, gently applied it to his lips.

His smile was exotic and intoxicating. He'd no idea how long he stood in front of the toothpaste-dotted mirror, but when he returned to the kitchen and resumed cooking it was already dark outside. He snatched glances of himself in the window's reflection as he cracked the eggs and sifted flour, and he was just mixing the batter in the large yellow glass bowl when the phone rang.

"Hello, lover," William answered, knowing it would be Gareth. It was always Gareth.

"Um, yes, hey." Gareth sounded nervous. William put the bowl down, taking care not to smear lipstick on the receiver.

"Everything all right?" he asked.

"I just—Björn asked if I'd go with him to The Oracle this evening. It's a club bordering Twinkstadt and Maytree, and—"

"Oh." Standing there with a wooden spoon in hand and a bowl of batter before him, William's adolescent heart sank. He didn't know how to respond. The meal was to be a surprise, but if it meant Gareth had to cancel his plans, well, then it became an obligation. He didn't want that.

"Go, it'll be fun," he insisted.

"You want to come with us? Just us boys?"

You'd be less of a target if you acted more like a lad.

"I'm good," William answered. "I've some reading I want to get on with." He thought that would be it. But Gareth's voice was edged with annoyance.

"You don't want to go, do you?" he accused.

"Maybe next time." Why was this a problem?

"You've never even been. We're young, we should be out enjoying ourselves—"

"I have been enjoying myself," William interjected, his stomach churning. "Are you not enjoying yourself?"

"I just thought we'd be doing more than this."

"More?" William gripped the phone in both hands. The only couples he'd ever seen were his parents, Gareth's parents, and their parents' friends. What was it they did? What more was there?

"More than spending all our time at home. You know what I mean," Gareth said. William honestly didn't. "We're living like we're—"

"What, Gareth?" William interrupted. "Like we're what?"

"You're not savvying what I'm trying to say. Just nell me. I wanted you to come because I love you. I just wanted you there with me."

All right. All right, he could understand that. Glancing at himself in the window, the bright fuchsia lipstick was visible even in the pale reflection, the glistening city lights twinkling beyond. "Fine," he answered, "then I'll come."

"No, look, don't worry. Don't worry about it." Gareth replied. His voice was distant, and not because of a bad phone connection—when British people said, "don't worry about it," they always meant the exact opposite. Somehow William had done something wrong, but he'd no idea how to put it right again. He'd offered, he'd offered to go with him. He tried once more.

"I mean it. I'll come with you."

"Whatever," Gareth spat. "Maybe next time."

"I'd like that," William answered, before the line went dead.

First, he carefully placed the phone's receiver back onto its cradle. Then he swung his fist into the bowl of batter and watched it shatter against the floor.

27.

He felt ridiculous the moment the bowl broke. Bright shards gleamed in a pool of beige batter, sparkling under the ceiling lights and reflecting flashes of fuchsia pink as he knelt down toward them. Humiliation prickled him while he picked at the fragments of glass, as though an unseen audience had judged his life and found him wanting. Not his circumstances, not his orientation, but him, himself, whole.

All those long-held dreams of a life with Gareth, of their emigrating to a distant world, and he'd never planned beyond their arrival. He'd assumed a happily ever after—that once they had the space to be themselves, he and Gareth would spend their days contented, an ambition which now seemed as beige and formless as the gloop he was mopping up with toilet paper.

If anything, they'd grown less familiar. Sometimes, not always, but sometimes, they would scoot around one another while preparing lunch or brushing teeth, with all the formal discomfort of strangers. Sometimes, not always, but sometimes, they'd sit in silence as they ate.

He stayed on the floor once he'd finished cleaning up the remnants of their dinner, his back resting against the kitchen cabinets. He was tired. He closed his eyes, losing himself in memory, falling back years, finding himself seated on a different floor, leaning against a bed. Beneath him, the rich shag carpeting of Gareth's bedroom, on which he'd so often slid around, marvelling at his own footprints. Next to him was Gareth, both of them too young to shave. Between them lay an open pornographic magazine.

"She looks pretty," he'd tentatively declared, ogling the naked lady. It was like when Gareth had showed him the car magazines, and William savvied he should react to these naked women with passion.

"She does look pretty," Gareth concurred, and as William glanced up, he'd been surprised to find his friend watching him. Did Gareth know he'd had no reaction to the smooth, rounded bodies lying before him? That he was so fundamentally broken? He tried, he really tried, but the palonie's allure evaded him.

He turned the page, to a woman with brown hair. She was kneeling in front of the camera, presenting her buttocks. "She looks pretty." Realising he'd repeated himself, he added, "She has a nice bottom."

Gareth laughed. At first it was a giggle, but it swelled to a roar, him throwing his head back like a supervillain. William's face had burned. His best friend knew he was faking interest. Everybody knew.

Sensing William's humiliation, Gareth stopped. Carefully, almost tenderly, he leaned over and closed the magazine.

William held his breath, awaiting judgement.

He never expected to feel Gareth's lips on his own. He'd never anticipated his hand on his neck, his tongue clumsily lurching into his mouth. He'd been confused, but his body surged with excitement, a strange elated buzz coursing through him as his hands trembled uncontrollably against thick carpet. Gareth pulled away.

"Was that all right?"

William couldn't have spoken a word. But he nodded, his body trembling, his face flushed crimson. He was shocked by the soft warmth of Gareth's lips, his tongue, the feel of him. Now sparked with lust, he lunged at his friend, crushing the magazine as they pulled off each other's shirts, feeling skin against skin. He'd never imagined anything like it. It was he who clambered up onto the bed, it was he who'd pulled Gareth down on top of him.

Later would come the fear, the self-loathing, the worry that he'd broken the bond with the only friend he had—but in that moment it was only them, wrapped blissfully around one another.

He opened his eyes. The room was bare, the kitchen floor cold and still damp from where he'd cleaned up the batter. The sound of the neighbour's laughter grazed through the thin wall dividing their house from the one next door.

It would take work. If he wanted to keep his relationship from collapsing, it stood to reason that he would have to maintain it. That meant trolling all the way to Maytree, finding the nightclub they'd gone to, and proving to his partner that he would make the effort. He would drink, he would dance, he would show how much Gareth meant to him.

He exited the subway at Maytree, then rode the sweaty, crowded elevator fifteen floors upward, spilling out onto the elevated rail platform. Up here, the winter wind—which had been little more than a light breeze at street level—was an unforgiving torrent, forcing passengers to clutch their hats and huddle in bulky coats. In his hurry William had only thrown on a light jacket, and so he shivered amid the mass of bodies as they awaited the Maytree Circular.

Would Gareth be pleased to see him, or was William intruding on his territory? A small part of him hoped to find his partner in some dark corner of the club, enveloped in another homie, thrusting away his fidelity. At least that would be something they could deal with: something tangible, something solvable.

The hanging train arrived, coming to a stop with a gentle hiss. Once boarded, it pulled away from the station, gently rocking as it dangled from the overhead track. William had never seen this part of the city by night, and the illuminated windows of gildy apartments rolled by with a low electric hum, revealing living rooms, kitchens, libraries, and bedrooms, flashing thousands of private lives. He couldn't help but ogle them: at one window a pair of daddies were dancing, arms wrapped around each other's shoulders. At another a lone homie painted a self-portrait while wearing nothing at all. They passed a generous terrace bedecked with twinkling lights. Sky-high mansions complete with ornate gardens. Walkways lined with small cafés, warm glows spilling over outdoor tables.

Glancing around the carriage, he realised that several of the passengers were staring at him. Some in snatched glances. Some openly. He wondered what the matter could be, before remembering. He was still wearing the lipstick. Slyly pulling a handkerchief from his pocket, he rubbed at his lips until the bright pigment stopped smearing the plain white cloth.

That done, William avoided eye contact with the strangers around him, keeping his focus on the map by the doors. His destination was seven stops away, then five, then two. Rain pattered and then beat against the windows until finally the train hummed to a halt at Lorca Gate. As the doors opened William half expected to step out onto empty air, but his feet found the platform, and the train continued its glide.

The station was grand. High arched windows. Carved stone statues of ancient Greek glorias, a solemn semi-nude array of mythological figures, and though their bodies were rendered in intricate detail, their ogles looked empty. Behind them were the ornate high carseys of Maytree, capped with elaborate decals: some shimmered with crystal-coloured lights, others boasted ziggurats and spires, a few were plated bronze.

He made his way down a spiral iron staircase which wound around an iron elevator shaft, his legs already aching by the time he reached the street.

The rain fell, heavy and relentless. The wet pavement shimmered with the golden lights of Maytree, which danced as William's feet sploshed through the puddles. A male couple walked past, their posh raincoats crisp and their faces ascowl, and William wondered if anyone ever looked as unhappy as the rich; he'd seen such couples in the straight world, with their quiet, gilded resentment. Men with set jaws and women with stern eyes, with starched clothes and starched anger.

But after wandering for a minute or two he could no longer see much at all; his drenched hair stuck to his forehead, his eyes stung. Wiping his face with the clean side of his handkerchief, he glanced around, looking for some clue as to The Oracle's location. He'd imagined it would be immediately visible—maybe a huge neon sign, or gaping, mouth-like entrance—and he hadn't considered the fact that he might not be able to find it. He felt foolish, a feeling which was only made worse as the rain ran down his neck and into his collar, an icy trickle streaming down to his socks.

A group of daddies walked by beneath a cloud of umbrellas, salt-and-pepper hair over trim shirts and sharp suits. They gently jostled and prodded one another as they walked, wallowing in some group in-joke. One of them looked at William as he passed by, his ogles running up and down his body.

"Excuse me," William called out, unsure if he could be heard above the downpour.

"Yes?" The man stopped as his friends careened ahead. Without prompting, he held his umbrella over William, sheltering them both. "Tell me, how can I help you?"

His eyes were kind, and something about his voice was familiar. He was a good forty years William's senior, though the slate-grey stubble and the lines etched into his forehead gave him a handsome, solemn appearance.

"Could you tell me where The Oracle is?" William enquired, before adding a belated "Please?"

"Yes, I could tell you where that is," the older homie teased, his teeth brilliant white, his posture perfect. "Though I don't savvy if I should."

"Why?" William stammered. "I mean, whyever not?"

The man's face was only a kiss away from William's. Beneath the smell of spring rain, he could smell the distinct tang of aftershave, and was strangely, distantly attracted.

"Because people can lose themselves in places like that," the man declared with a warm smile. "Look, I understand you, I know what you're going through. I've been there myself."

"You have?"

"Of course! I might be an antique by now, but I remember being young. At least I think I do—you can tell me if I'm cod. That means *wrong* in Polari," he explained. "Here goes: I think you're a curious young manly. A boy finding his place in the world. You've been here less than a year, two at most, and you've probably only ever been with your husband. You want to savvy what you've been missing, yet you're worried about making mistakes. Berlin is a big, strange smoke when you're new to it, and you don't know where to start. So, you're nervous. You're uncertain. But part of you—at least part of you is excited."

William didn't pull away when the man took his hand and squeezed it. He was flattered, he was curious, and it was only in the moment of that small contact that he realised how lonely he'd been over the past months.

"Aren't your—" he paused for a moment, struggling to recall the Polari "—*coves* getting away?"

"Let them go," the daddy hushed, a whisper of shared conspiracy. "They're rich and pompous and dull. Besides, I see them all the time. And I've only just met you."

They huddled together as sheets of rain fell around the umbrella.

"This might sound silly," the man continued, "but you varda sweet, and you varda honest. Can I ask you a question?"

William could feel him trembling: the man was nervous too. Knowing that helped him relax. He nodded.

"Of course."

The stranger smiled again. "Where are you from, young manly?"

"Twinkstadt," William answered. He wasn't sure why he lied, but was surprised how natural it was, how true it felt in the moment.

The man's grin grew wider, baring dignified laughter lines at the corner of his eyes.

"Then let me be blunt, if you'll allow it. Will you troll home with me? It's not far, I live in this neighbourhood. We'll dry you off, warm up, and have a bevvie. You can tell me your story. Perhaps I can share mine in return. You might even find it useful."

William faltered. The only other homie who'd ever shown real interest in him had been Gareth.

Gareth.

He didn't want to be distracted from his evening's mission, but the older man was right: he had no idea what he was doing. Perhaps he could help—after all, he'd once been like William. Young. Anxious. Lonely. And now he was charming and sophisticated, a natural part of the urban landscape which surrounded them.

He ignored the faint stirrings of attraction, the giddy lilt to his stomach as the gentleman squeezed his hand once more.

"Just for a drink," he relented. "Then I'll take you straight to The Oracle."

"It's a deal."

The older man put his arm around William as they trolled away from the station, passing doormen and flowerpots, pristine boutiques and grand awnings over which antique gas lamps threw sweeping shadows. The only blemish in sight went unnoticed by both men: scarlet letters scrawled across a wall, *Nix Boxes Nix Boxes Nix Boxes*, veiled by the evening's dark. After a fifteen-minute walk the gildy towers fell away, replaced by vintage, five-storey apartment buildings; the streets so quiet it could have been anywhere else. Anywhere but Berlin.

28.

It was jarring to be confronted by a scene lifted straight from the nineteenth century, complete with cobbles and antique streetlamps. There was an austere Prussian elegance to everything, a reminder of the city's origins, of everything which had been smashed to smithereens and then paved over. Windows were furnished with all the flourishes of a wedding cake, fronted by balconies of fine, looping ironwork, and sloping rooftops were capped in terracotta tiles.

Yet for all its embellishments, the location didn't give the impression of a bygone era so much as its recreation: a movie-set, theme-park vision of old Europe, one too self-conscious to feel authentic, and too clean to feel sincere. The only hint that they were still in the city were the towering lights in the background.

"Welcome to Maytree Village," the daddy exclaimed, stopping outside an archway. Before them stood a gate, guarded by a young twink in prim uniform.

"Bona evening, sir," the doorman greeted, tipping his green cap with one hand and unlocking the gate with the other. All the while he maintained a fixed, polite smile, one only betrayed by the tiniest flicker, a flash of resentment that William may have imagined.

They entered a large courtyard, full of ornate masonry bathed in the gentle glow of yellow lamps. A large double door was set into each of the courtyard's walls, numbered one through three. The older man directed William to number three, before fumbling with an elaborate set of keys.

"Just this way," he directed.

Caught up in curiosity, William had focused on his ostentatious surroundings, daunted by a level of wealth he'd never encountered in person. The building's staff and fine flourishes had a hypnotising, inebriating effect, one which made it all the more dreamlike. He didn't question what he was doing or why, only that he was tumbling down some strange rabbit hole.

"We're here. Carsey sweet carsey," the older man announced, as he opened the door and pulled William inside.

A wide hallway surrounded them: painted cream, with high ceilings. The upper walls were adorned with carvings and sculptures: floral arrangements and handsome faces. Pushing open a door near twice his height, the daddy guided William into a lavish living room, all modern leather furniture and chrome finishings.

"Let me take that," he offered, reaching for William's damp coat.

Seating himself on a creaking sofa, William noticed the surrounding walls were lined with newspaper clippings, cradled in frames of all sizes.

"I'm a bit of a Duchess, if that isn't obvious enough already. That's a rich old homie to you," the older man said, explaining the obvious. He then fiddled with an antique record player, flooding the room with unfamiliar music, somewhere between classical and folk, some obscure old Berlin genre. "I make a decent income, made good investments, own a few carseys. You'll get no false modesty here: I like to enjoy my success, because what else is life for? I like to share it with young manlys such as yourself."

Before William could ask what that meant exactly, the man held up a finger and then disappeared into the hallway. He returned a few moments later with a pair of fluffy white towels, handing one to William before unbuttoning his own damp shirt. His chest was covered with a neatly rimmed mat of salt-and-pepper hair, which swirled around his nipples and plunged down his stomach. While he scrubbed himself dry, William undressed, removing his shirt and trousers and leaving only his underwear. The towel was warm and impossibly soft, but he felt exposed; he was danglier, skinnier than the homie before him, with a single strip of hair crawling up the middle of his chest. It was as though his own inexperience were written on his body.

Once done, they stood before one another, awkwardly half naked. William considered putting his wet clothes back on, but his host simply pulled two glasses from a cabinet set into the wall and filled each from a whiskey decanter. Not knowing what else to do, William ogled the framed clippings that lined the walls. Each story revolved around a man called Kenneth Luvvie. He was younger in many of the pictures, and his accolades bragged from faded print.

No. No, it wasn't possible.

William squinted at the dulled type to make sure. When he spoke, his voice was thin with surprise.

"You're the radio host?"

"*The* radio host!" Kenneth Luvvie roared with laughter, his chest heaving. "Alas, I'm not the only one."

"But it's you!" William's voice cracked like he was thirteen. It was true he hadn't listened to the broadcasts much since he'd arrived, but they'd meant so much to him, back in Britain. "I've listened to you."

"You and every other homie with a wireless," Luvvie replied, guiding them both back to the sofa, one hand on William's shoulder as he handed him a glass and then picked up his own. "Cheers."

After the toast, he leant forward and brought his mouth to William's. His lips were soft, his breath bittersweet from the liquor. A few pounding heartbeats later, and William pulled away. He sipped at the liquid which burned his lips and tongue, wiping away the imprint of Kenneth Luvvie's kiss, feeling the warmth of his body as their bare thighs touched.

"Do you have a husband?" William enquired.

"I'm afraid . . . no . . ." the radio host stammered, his authority slipping for just a moment. "I did, once. You'll be too young to remember the worst of the blood plague, that a transfusion could end your life."

Luvvie gazed into the caramel-coloured depths of his drink. A deep, old sorrow echoed from his stiffened body, yawning dark and vast; an ancient chasm.

"I'm sorry," William said. It wasn't enough, but it was all he had.

"Don't be sorry, chicken," Luvvie replied, turning his gaze toward William. A smile faltered across his face. "Just kiss me."

"I want to," William confessed, a part-truth.

"But . . ." the radio manly left the word hanging, turning it into a question.

"But I don't understand."

"It's simple enough," the manly joked, his despair covered once more by his broad, affable confidence. "You just put your lips against mine."

William sipped at his drink.

"Look," Luvvie continued, "I can read your thoughts. They're written across your face. You wonder how I, an advocate for marriage, the family, and gay values, could encourage you to cheat. How I could flaunt the rules so brazenly."

He leaned forward before William could reply.

"I've lived here a very long time, my chicken. And believe me when I say that things aren't what they once were. You see, in the early journos it was different. In the early journos we had the luxury to be ourselves. Split off from the straight world, we were free to build something bona and beautiful. To make our own rules. Of course, the straight world couldn't understand. They envied and detested us."

William nodded, already dizzied from drink. The radio manly was working himself up, his face tinged pink, his thigh parting from William's as he leant forward, losing himself.

"They ogled our glittering city, they ogled our success, and they wanted to claim it for themselves. Remember, they had all the rest of planet Earth to spoil, but no, no, they couldn't let us have this one smoke. So they trolled here by the thousands. They cackled that it wasn't enough for us to be homies loving homies, or palonies loving palonies. Nix, no. They wanted to unpick our identity, to blur the lines of gender, to make us couple with homies, palonies, and whatever's in between. Of course, most of them were heteros in disguise. They still are. They don't understand Berlin, because they could never understand Berlin. They just want our city for themselves."

He paused.

"But where were they when the plague hit? When we were dying by the millions?"

"I don't know," William answered, his voice wavering. Not only did he live in Q, but just an hour ago he'd trolled around with painted lips; he'd been one of those blurring the boundaries Luvvie held dear. "But I don't understand what this has to do with us, now," he stammered.

"Ogle it this way, beancove," Luvvie replied, softening just a little at William's apprehension. "This is the only place in the world where it's safe to be a homosexual. Our values, they keep us secure. Part of that is thanks to gay marriage, the official love between two men, or two women. It's that which helps us determine who is a fruit, and who is a hettie saboteur. It keeps them from infiltrating too deeply, from taking over our great smoke and forcing us back to the margins."

He refreshed their drinks, spilling a little over his thumb, which he then licked clean. "But among ourselves, my chicken, we need to be a little more flexible. Quietly, and in private. Homies have urges, we're all wise enough to savvy that."

"And what about those fruits that don't fit in?" William asked. As if to quench his growing unease he downed the rest of his drink in a single swig, feeling the warmth burn down his throat and into his belly.

"If they don't fit in, they're not a fruit," Luvvie replied. It was obvious he enjoyed such banter. "That's just how it is."

The room fuzzed warm with liquor as William blurted, "But isn't it all based in lies? Us, this, the secrecy?"

Confronted by his host's pragmatism and the finery of his home, William felt like he was being ungrateful. That he was young and petulant. Yet Luvvie seemed to take his outburst with good humour, as though he'd heard this objection a thousand times before.

"The real world's messier than it is on the radio. Besides, did you troll here just to cackle about morals and politics?" Without waiting for a response, he filled William's glass once again, then pulled him up from the sofa. "Come on. We don't need to cackle over useless things."

When William hesitated, he softened again, stroking the younger man's cheek.

"I am sorry. I savvy you mean what you say, and that this is important for you. You are young, you are idealistic. I recognise my younger self in that. Understand that I don't mean to insult or dismiss you. Perhaps the way we do things is nix perfect, but we have to survive. You have ogled the world outside Berlin. You savvy what is at stake."

William heard the distant chants of his schoolmates, felt the slaps and kicks; saw his father's purpled face, dripping crimson droplets.

This time when Luvvie kissed him, William kissed him back.

191

When Luvvie directed him toward a staircase, William followed. Once at the bottom they stopped before another locked door, this one with a small number panel to one side, upon which Luvvie tapped out a code.

"Aha," he exclaimed as it swung open.

The basement room was lit by two small bare bulbs, one red, one white. It was a dark playground of leather straps and harnesses. At the centre hung a large swing, complete with four cuffs. William tentatively stepped up to it, touching it, the smell of leather curling its way into his nostrils. As he touched it, it swung away, then toward him. The music, which had been loud upstairs, was soft in the darkness.

"I'll savvy you've not played with any of this before, my chicken," Luvvie stated. "Allow me to open your mind a little."

He kissed William once more, deeply, urgently, before stepping back and removing his underwear, carefully folding it over the back of a rigid metal chair. By the chair stood a trolley, which cradled an array of colourful latex objects of various sizes and shapes, as well as some kind of gas mask. William hesitated. He'd never been naked in front of any man other than Gareth.

"If you're unsure, I can pay," Luvvie offered, as though he'd done so many times before. "Don't worry, it doesn't make you a rent boy. Just a chicken in need of a little dinari—as I say, I like to share my success."

Without knowing exactly what he planned on doing, William pulled off his underwear and dropped it to the concrete floor. He was relieved when it was Luvvie who clambered into the swing. Not just relieved: a woozy arousal coursed through his body.

"Let's start easy," the radio manly ordered. "First, strap me in."

William did as he was told, securing the buckles and tugging at the straps, deftly securing Luvvie in place, wrists and then ankles alluringly bound. Trussed up before him, the radio manly was handsome and helpless.

"Touch me, bijou chicken. Don't be strange."

"I want to talk some more first," William demanded, still stark naked.

"You want to torture me for information?" Luvvie grinned. "Go right ahead."

William brought his hand to the manly's chest fur, gently stroking his nipples. Luvvie groaned, his head tilted back.

"What would you say," William began, his voice slow and soft, "to those you shove away and exclude, in order to 'survive'? What would you say to the fruits who don't fit in?"

Luvvie's face crumpled in irritation. Gone was the paternal tolerance, that indulgent smile. Instead, he spoke hurriedly, eager to get this tedious verbal foreplay over with.

"As I said, this is our city. No one forced them to troll here. Now touch me. Touch me however you want."

Yes, William was attracted to him. But he halted, his hand hovering over Luvvie's bare body. For so long he'd listened to this man's voice, naively dreaming of that distant republic, of a mythical place where people could live as themselves. Instead, he'd found this: a land governed by small hypocrisies; a world so unlike the one he'd grown up in, but so much the same.

"I can't." He bent down and scooped up his underwear. "I'm sorry, I just can't."

"You can't what?" the helpless manly asked, craning his neck toward William. "Wait, where are you trolling?"

Luvvie's voice followed him from the room as William fled up the stairs, into the lounge with its rows of framed articles, and snatched up the remainder of his damp clothes.

"Let me down, at least. *Fuck!* Let me down. I said, let me down!"

William dressed by the front door as the distant cries mingled with the music. If the trussed-up homie had known more about him, he would never have let him into his carsey. Yet whether due to vanity, or simple lust, he'd mistaken William for one of his own. And maybe William had no idea who he truly was, but he was certain it had nix to do with this.

Clothed once more, he practically fell into the well-tended courtyard, hurrying past the doorman. He stumbled down the gildy street until he was out of sight, then ran all the way to the station, slipping and sliding on the wet pavement.

29.

He didn't know if he shivered from fear or his still-wet clothes, but William only relaxed upon reaching the narrow twists and curves of Pogey Street. The rain had stopped, and it was a relief to return to his neighbourhood. Though most of the small stores were shuttered, a thousand rectangles of light gazed down from above: warm yellows, cold blues, and musty pinks, together forming a bright patchwork of interlocking lives. It was a very human miracle, to see millions of people living cheek-by-jowl, stacked atop one another, and still getting by.

As he passed beneath a string of lights draped between opposite windows, his thoughts returned to the man he'd left hanging, helpless in his sling.

Someone will find him. He'll have staff.

Though he privately consoled himself (as he'd done on the hanging train of the Maytree Circular, as he'd done on the subway back to Q) he couldn't quite shake his concern for the awful manly who was trapped, alone, in his basement.

On reaching his building, he saw a woman waiting for the rooftop elevator. She was older than William—somewhere in her late twenties—and clad in an oversized coat, with a shocked mop of yellow-blonde hair fraying beneath a woollen cap. She had the strong jawline of a comic book hero, and when he caught her eye, she didn't seem surprised. She just stared back.

"Evening," he greeted, a little too English, a little too formal. The woman nodded in response, then turned to greet the opening elevator doors. William followed her inside.

It was the first word he'd spoken to any of the neighbours. They stood side by side as they rose to meet the glowing windows, as the ground fell away beneath them.

"You look dreadful." The woman finally spoke. Her accent was German, her tone low and gruff.

"I feel dreadful," William confessed. Expensive whiskey still coated his teeth, bitter and strangely herbal. "I wish I'd stayed home."

"Bad dates will do that to you," she stated, a tinge of reproach to her voice. She gazed out at the city beyond, a gesture which called for an end to their brief interaction.

"It wasn't a date," William replied, feeling a strong urge to correct the stranger.

"What was it then?"

"I—I don't know," he admitted. And though he hadn't meant to confess the evening's excitement to someone he didn't even know, he also had no one else to tell.

"I met a rich old daddy on the street. I sort of . . . tied him up."

The stranger seemed unimpressed. "How nice."

"I left him there."

To William's astonishment, the strong-jawed woman actually smiled—and then laughed, a robust guffaw which seemed to come straight from her belly. "Tell me you're nix kidding."

"I swear, it's the truth."

The laughter had warmed her face, flushing it with colour. "*Danke,*" she huffed. "Thank you. I think I needed that."

The elevator reached the rooftop, and the two trudged out over the damp flagstones toward the row of cottages, bracing against the icy breeze.

"You live here, too?" William asked the obvious.

"You could say so." Out in the cold she'd frozen again, her ogles fixed straight ahead. She stopped at the cottage next to William's and pulled a key from her pocket.

"Do you think he'll be all right?" William blurted. "With me leaving him there, I mean. You don't think he'll dehydrate or have a stroke or something?"

The stranger laughed once more and disappeared into the house without another word.

It was good to be home. It might not have been as grand as the dwelling he'd just fled, but he was comforted by the personal touches which surrounded him: the wonky standing lamp drunkenly leaning in the corner; the rickety bookcase which had been lying, unclaimed, outside their building; the musty linens Gareth found at a flea market, and which William had washed and hung on the walls.

Once upstairs, he unfolded the sofa bed and laid out the sheets. Still fully clothed, he climbed beneath the covers and listened for the door, waiting for Gareth to return.

"Some young troublemakers caused a right palaver for that old Mr. Luvvie."

His boss announced the news as he approached William's desk, giddy as a child and holding up a roll of newspaper. "Take a look at this." He unfurled the newspaper in front of William.

LUVVIE CAUGHT IN A BIND.

"It's been too long since we've had a good scandal." The boss grinned. Below the headline was a grainy photograph of Luvvie, naked and aloft in his swing. The picture had been taken by some vengeful witness who'd stumbled upon the scene: perhaps the doorman, perhaps a cleaner, perhaps someone else entirely. William melted with relief; he hadn't left Luvvie to starve to death, after all.

Then his boss yanked the newspaper away, off to deliver the news to some other favourite.

That lunchtime, beneath the unending fluorescent sparkle of the employee canteen, William listened, passively, to the clamour of his co-workers. Luvvie was on everyone's lips: some guffawed at the news, swapping bawdy jokes. Others ranted, red-eked with fury. Not toward Luvvie, nor his indiscretions, but toward the villain who'd tied up and disgraced a hero of the city. They didn't *want* to know the sins of their idols, and, judging by their spit-flecked fury, were perfectly prepared to shoot the messenger. There was no obvious division between these two sides—their tables were scattered throughout the canteen, together forming a strange cacophony of humour and indignance.

Stopping by a bodega on the way home, William found that this same divide split the newspapers, some of which mocked with bawdy headlines, some railing against the disrespect shown to a pillar of the community. He returned home feeling strangely naff.

Gareth had nelled nothing of the netters; or else he didn't care. Either way, he didn't mention it to William that evening as they sat down to dinner. They spoke in small talk, of work and chores, until the dwindling conversation prompted Gareth to turn on the radio. It was time for Luvvie's broadcast, but there was nix way William could ask Gareth to turn it off, not without alerting him to his indiscretions. So, he steeled himself for the radio manly's voice, only to nell a radio opera from the San Francisco ghetto. Carefully setting down his fork, Gareth brushed through the stations, his cheek almost pressed against the speaker until he gave up.

Neither mentioned Luvvie's absence. They ate the rest of the meal in silence, the latest sugary pop from Twinkstadt blasting between them.

30.

The following journo was a Saturday. Gareth was working, and William took the opportunity to clean their increasingly shabby little house. The bathroom was lined with dark mould, the fixtures dull with grime, so he bleached and scrubbed, shining the taps and showerhead, brushing the tiles until they gleamed. Upstairs was also in a state, the living room-cum-sleeping area strewn with William's books and Gareth's clutter, the floor streaked with mud. So, he gathered and swept and mopped and wiped, restoring the carsey to a condition his parents would almost have considered presentable.

The muscles of his lacoddy ached with exertion. The work was satisfying, particularly when William stopped and surveyed the pristine carsey—the neatly stacked books, the whiff of lemon—but isolation covered him, dark and thick as February clouds. Taking the chair and reaching into the usual spot, William grasped the lipstick. No one was home, so what did it matter if he tried it on? Who would see?

All he was doing was changing the colour of his lips, but he would never dare let Gareth savvy what he'd been up to. There was no way he'd understand, not the lipstick, not his going home with Luvvie, nor his abandoning him in a sling. William could picture his inevitable confusion, the distance that would yawn between them, widened by his inexplicable acts. He'd want to know why William couldn't just be normal, and William wouldn't have an answer. Gareth had been transparent in his desire to fit in, had even repeatedly hinted at matrimony. There'd been an edge to his voice, letting William know that this future came with a deadline. They'd known each other long enough to read the lilts and intonations, to nell what lay beneath words.

With lipstick carefully applied, he opened the front door just ajar, and peered out. The rooftop was devoid of people; it was safe.

So, he picked up a basket of dripping laundry and carried it out to the clotheslines, scattering tiny sparrows as they took off into the sky. The late winter's wind howled across the roof, whipping in from the east as William hung sheets and trousers, shirts and underpants, pegging each item securely as he could—but still the gale caught one of Gareth's socks.

William reached out to grasp it, but it spiralled away, up and above the city, lost among the rooftops.

"What the fuck is wrong with you?"

The gruff German voice shocked him still. It was so sudden, so angry, coming from beyond one of the billowing bedsheets.

"I said, *what the fuck is wrong with you?*"

Its owner now stepped into view: freed from the constraints of her woollen cap, her shock of yellow-blond hair batted about in the breeze. It was the young woman he'd met in the elevator, the one who lived next door. Only now William could varda she wasn't angry at all. Her grin was wide and sincere. He did his best to cover the lower half of his face with his hand, shielding the bright makeup from view.

"I thought you'd screwed with some random old manly," the woman exclaimed. "You didn't say the manly in question was *Kenneth fucking Luvvie.*"

"You didn't ask," William shot back, shouting above the wind, his palm still hiding his mouth.

"I have to tell you, I'm impressed," the woman replied. She said something more, but her voice was caught and carried away by the breeze.

"What's that?" William called back, struggling to hear.

"I'm Henna," she shouted. "Hen-na."

"William," he replied. "As in Shakespeare."

Henna nodded, then stooped to help him hang the remaining clothes. A small, foolish part of him was pleased someone knew what had happened. They worked side by side, William keeping his face angled away from her, hot with shame; he wasn't a real man. He'd never be a real man.

"Hey." William flinched as Henna cackled right into his ear. "You nix need to hide your mouth. I ogled you leaving your carsey. It's a nice colour, but too dark for you."

199

William laughed—it came as a retch, but he couldn't help it. He was relieved; someone had seen him and didn't consider him a freak.

"That's us done," she announced, hanging the last of the washing. "I have to troll off now. Meet me out here tomorrow. Same time. Keep your lips naked."

The next journo he left Gareth snoring and went out to find Henna. She was in the far corner of the rooftop, lying atop a blanket, though she sat up as William approached. She had two small pouches with her, one pink, one green. Motioning William to sit with her, she pulled a small tin from the green pouch, and began rolling a cigarette with verdant herbs. It took a few seconds for William to recognise the same substance he'd once smelled behind the school bike sheds, where the unruliest students made their hideout.

"That's marijuana!" he exclaimed.

"*Echt?* What planet are you from?" asked Henna, her attention still on the paper between her fingers.

"I've never smoked it," William admitted, feeling as naive and provincial as when he'd first arrived in Berlin.

"Well, now's your chance, if you want." She placed the joint between her lips and lit a match, carefully sheltering the flame with her palms. As she exhaled, the wind swept the smoke above their heads and away.

She then held it out to William.

"Thank you."

He'd have liked to say he hadn't coughed, that he'd imbibed the weed with cool sophistication. But he hacked and wheezed as Henna slapped him on the back.

Once he'd regained his breath, the world was softer, mellower. He noticed things he usually overlooked: the textured brickwork of the cottages. The cracks in the flagstones, weaving and winding like a thousand streams and deltas. The funny little sparrows that bobbed about the rooftop. His own fingers, and the strange way his skin bunched about the knuckles.

"I think I like this," he declared, his mouth sticky and dry.

"Why wouldn't you?" Henna asked, as she handed him a flask full of water. William didn't know what to think of his new neighbour. He'd not met someone so cold and friendly, warm and abrasive, all at once. Then again, with the exception of small talk with his co-workers, flirtations with his boss, and the encounter with Luvvie, William hadn't spoken much to anyone since he arrived in Berlin.

Henna seemed to remember something, heaving herself up and rummaging through the pink pouch. "I almost forgot," she cackled, pulling out a handful of small tubes. "We've got plenty spare at my carsey."

William wanted to ask who *we* referred to, but Henna was already piling them into his open palm: peach and ochre, rose, dusty quartz. From the ogle of things, she didn't even wear lipstick.

"Here." She took one, popped off the lid, and traced it along his wrist, considering it a moment before fambling another and drawing a darker line below the first. When there were five pink lines echoing down his arm, she asked which he liked best.

He pointed.

"Bona choice. And don't worry," she added, running it over his lips. "They're barely used. Kara gets tired of them so quickly."

"Kara?" William asked, but Henna ignored the implicit question, placing the lipstick into his famble, curling his fingers around the tube. He thanked her, placing it into his pocket. The two sat in silence for a while, as William admired a knot of weeds at the edge of the rooftop, the complex formations of clouds high above.

"I don't know what I'm doing here," he finally said. He didn't know why he said it.

"Can I ask you a question?" Henna said, by way of reply. "I need you to be honest. No flies. Can you do that?"

William nodded, though he wasn't certain he could.

"Why did you leave Luvvie in that swing?" she asked. "I'm sure he could have offered you dinari. Or connections. But you left him."

"I don't know," was his honest answer.

"But I think you do know, and William, you promised me nanti flies. Did you dislike the manly? Did you find him objectionable?"

"I was just embarrassed. I didn't even know him." He clasped his sweaty hands together, entwining his fingers. Perhaps it was her Teutonic accent, or the intent way she focused on him, but something about Henna demanded plain, spoken truth.

Confession.

"*Hör mal*," she said. "If it wasn't personal, then it was political. I think you didn't hate him. You hated what he did, and what he represented. Am I wrong?"

"You're not wrong," he admitted. "But it wasn't really a decision. I didn't plan it."

"William, savvy this. Very few of our actions are truly planned. We make them into decisions with hindsight, no?"

He sipped at the cold water and watched the ruffles and billows of his laundry as it danced with the wind.

"You had an opportunity, and you took it," Henna stated. "Even though it could have ruined your life. I savvy you did that for a reason. So, face it."

She stood and placed the tin back into the green pouch, and the remaining lipsticks into the pink.

"On Wednesday I'm going littering. That means I'll be giving out leaflets. Flyers," she clarified. "I will be out here at six sharp."

Holding out her hand, Henna helped pull him to his feet.

"I hope I was nix wrong about you, William."

William had no idea what she could be wrong about, but Henna had already scooped up the blanket and trolled to her carsey, opening the door just a crack and slipping through; maybe, William thought, she was hiding something inside. Or maybe he was just stoned. Either way, she carefully closed the door behind her.

Back in his own cottage, William found Gareth still sleeping. Slipping down to the bathroom, he carefully, quietly closed the door, just as Henna had done. Taking the gift from his pocket, he gently recoated his lips. It was a calmer tone than the one he'd tried before, a softer, more genial shade better suited to his pale complexion. It was the colour of ballet slippers and the instant strawberry puddings he'd loved as a child. It was the shade he turned when he blushed.

William stood in the bathroom for who knew how long, examining his own image until he heard the rustling of the bedsheets upstairs, then the double thump of Gareth's feet hitting the floor. Without stopping to think, he turned on the hot tap and stuck his face beneath the fierce burning stream, scrubbing at his mouth with his hands until the water ran clear.

Excerpt from
The Honest Guide to Berlin

Same-Sex Marriage.

Berlin is well known for its extravagant wedding ceremonies, not least due to the fact that it is the first (and so far, only) administration to legalise same-sex marriage. Celebrities the world over have spent many millions on widely broadcast and opulent ceremonies. Though no other state currently recognises Berlin-tendered marriage certificates, this has done nothing to stop gay couples flocking from every corner of the world for their very own.

Though monogamous adherence to a same-sex marriage is a requirement for full citizenship of the Gay Republic (see *Visa Requirements*, p. 70), a great number of Berlin's citizens opt for second, and even third ceremonies to reaffirm their partnership. If you're interested in attending one of these ceremonies, be sure to check the local listings.

Do take care to ensure that the service you're visiting is legal. Some more unscrupulous establishments have been known to assist bigamy, and even to perform ceremonies for three or four individuals in a "trio" or "quad"—a practice which remains highly illegal. Tourists are not exempt from the legal consequences of attending one of these "weddings," and you should contact your local embassy should you encounter any difficulties (see *Important Contacts*, p. 2).

A WHOLE NEW CARSEY

The Gay Republic

1999

31.

It was Cissie's first time in Sam's carsey, and she hadn't even been invited. It was Fiorella who'd grudgingly led her there, guiding her by the hand down Remould's colorful main street to a doorway beside the bakery, a door she'd passed many times without even noticing, and one to which Fiorella had her own key.

At the top of a dark set of stairs Fiorella had unlocked a second door, which swung out into a large living room dominated by used mugs, old tools, dog-eared leatherette sofas, and packed bookshelves. The place smelled earthy and sharp—cedar and wood polish—and was nothing like she'd expected: windows stretched from floor to ceiling, and though there was no natural daylight falling through, they shimmered with the colours of the street below: neon pinks, blues, and purples; red glimmers from the buildings opposite; hot orange-yellow flickers from a hundred naked flames. As they trolled into the room, they cast a dozen shadows in as many hues.

In between the windows was a door to a large balcony. The place held both grandeur and decay, as though squatters had occupied the abandoned quarters of a ruined aristocracy. Did Fiorella live here? Did she and Sam live here together? Cissie realised there was an awful lot she still didn't know about the manly.

"Sam," she called. Fiorella immediately shushed her.

"He's been sick."

"Sick?"

On one of the sofas, a pile of clothes shifted—or what Cissie had thought was a pile of clothes, but which was apparently a mass of blankets. Sam peered out from underneath.

"Cissie," he greeted her, with what was either a wince or a momentary smile.

"Hey." She paced over to his nest of comforters. "You're sick? Are you all right?"

"Has Fiorella been offloading her melodrama again?" Sam accused, his voice thick and heavy. "Don't let her worry you."

"I'll give you melodrama," Fiorella gently threatened, before slinking off to another room.

"What's wrong with you?" Cissie pressed her palm to Sam's clammy forehead.

"Nix. Just a cold," he replied, hacking a low, rumbling cough as though to confirm the diagnosis. "It's rare for me to get sick, so when I do she tells everyone I'm at death's doorway."

"And she's . . ."

"She's my roommate. We met before we ever trolled to Remould. We even met before she was Fiorella and I was Sam."

He released a long sigh, which turned into another hacking cough.

Cissie wanted to ask why he'd never told her about this living arrangement, and in particular why she'd never been invited to his apartment. But then, she still knew little about either of them; however often she visited, however much she revealed of herself, their personal lives remained politely off-limits.

"Let me get you a hot drink," she offered, picking up two discarded mugs from the collection surrounding the sofa.

By the time she'd fumbled about the kitchen and returned with the two steaming drinks, Sam was already asleep, with one arm slung above the blankets. Soft mauve light spread across his skin, highlighting the contours of his shoulder, his collarbone. His lips fell apart, as though—

"How kind of you." Fiorella strode over and took a beverage from Cissie's hands. "Come on, I want to zhoosh you something."

Cissie followed her out onto the balcony, into the dark, warm air. The street below was busy with bodies trolling this way and that, as a clamour of voices called from the stalls lining the road. Their vantage point allowed them to witness every kind of activity: an old man staggered down the street clutching a sack of oranges. In an alleyway opposite, a group of teenagers shared a spliff in hurried puffs. In a quiet corner, an amorous couple embraced by makeshift lamplight.

It was different from the walkway below Cissie's window. From her own carsey, she could ogle people as they came and went, always hurrying, always on their way somewhere. It was a place where no one really lingered. In contrast, the main street below was a meeting point, a hub for every kind of exchange. Here she could view a vast web of life, one which stretched not only across the street, but over the streets surrounding, and into the city beyond. Wall or no wall.

"I love it," she confessed after several minutes had passed.

"It is pretty good, isn't it?" Fiorella agreed. "Samboy doesn't appreciate the view—he says he'd rather be among people than perched up above them. But I say he's missing out; he's missing out on more than he realises. But for some reason I savvied *you* might appreciate it."

"And why is that?" Cissie asked. Fiorella had surprised her: the Italian palonie had never shared a kind or intimate word. "I thought you didn't like me."

"I don't like you," Fiorella confirmed. "But that's because I don't know you. It's nix personal, we just have good reason to be wary of cis folks."

"Then why—"

"Because even though I don't really know you, Cissie, I do *see* you." Fiorella gripped the railing, leaning forward so she could better varda the street beneath.

"I see how you watch people, cis palonie. It's a woman thing, if you ask me—smart women survive by reading the scene around them, so they can savvy who to trust, or when to fucking run. Women have to be observant, but there's also pleasure in watching, in just seeing the world without having to be part of every little thing. That's what Samboy doesn't get. I do, that's all. We have that in common."

"But you still don't trust me," Cissie stated, surprised by her own boldness.

"*Trust* is a strong word," Fiorella replied, taking a bijou step back from the railing. "I don't have the best record with trust. But I appreciate everything you've done, and I accept that Sam mostly trusts you."

An argument broke out below: two homies hollering at one other, one gesturing in the other's eke. Nearby stallholders quickly trolled over, trying to keep the peace their businesses depended upon.

"He's exhausting himself," Fiorella confessed, as if from nowhere.

"With work. With worry. It's all too much right now."

Cissie didn't understand. Before getting sick, Sam had seemed as cheery as usual. If anything, she'd have said his biggest flaw was in not taking things seriously, or not as seriously as he should. There was a lack of gravity with Sam; though it dawned on Cissie that this was merely the eke he presented to *her*.

"Come with me," Fiorella stated, breaking in on Cissie's thoughts. Together they crept through the living room, past the nest of blankets, and down the stairs. They'd only trolled a block down the main street before Fiorella held out a sharp-nailed finger.

"There."

She pointed to a charred storefront, a lone pigeon skulking about outside. The storefront's window was a dark, yawning mouth with scorched lips, and within Cissie could varda the counters and shelves reduced to brittle charcoal.

"Oh my God."

She didn't need to ask what had happened, and Fiorella didn't need to explain. Instead, she led Cissie another two blocks, to a street which was close to pitch-dark. A jumble of metal parts were heaped by the gloomy roadside, as though a robot had spontaneously fallen apart.

"One of our generators," Fiorella explained. "They're cowards. They slip in when no one's watching."

She showed Cissie a small lamppost Sam had installed, the bulb smashed to smithereens. Then she zhooshed another broken window. In between each location Cissie ogled scrawls of graffiti, some half-scrubbed away, some intact. All of it was hostile. She winced at each garish hatred.

"I can see why Sam's been exhausted," Cissie weakly admitted. "But why is it so much worse now?"

"The protests, cis palonie. The riots. The more chaos the radicals cause, the worse they make things for us. We're the most vulnerable and the most visible. We're the ones who eke the consequences."

Cissie thought of Ramona Palomar, the mystery protester who'd helped her and the children. She thought of everything Sam had told her over the past months.

"But aren't they fighting for trans rights, too? Aren't they just

212

trying to make things better?"

"Better," Fiorella repeated, as though the word was new to her. "Better for whom?"

32.

At the doorway leading up to their apartment, Fiorella waved Cissie goodbye then trolled off toward the gaffercarsey.

"Be gentle with Samboy," she cackled, calling over one shoulder.

Cissie wavered in front of the door, her fist hovering an inch from its peeling paint, before she turned back to Remould's bustling main street. It was astonishing, how quickly the exotic became the usual, how the meshiginer became mundane. When she'd first ogled the avenue, it had seemed like a carnival, but now its stalls and stores were marked on her memory. She recognised people. Her father always said that familiarity breeds contempt, but she savvied how wrong he was; familiarity doesn't breed contempt, far from it—when push comes to shove, we'll defend the familiar with our lives.

She turned away from Sam's door. For the moment, he would rest. She would not.

Instead, she hovered around the stores and stalls, clumsily asking after anyone with two fambles and a little free time. Her question raised some eyebrows at first, but she slowly gathered volunteers, volunteers who followed her in an ever-lengthening snake, until she'd collected half a dozen. The regular maintenance crew were still sleeping off a long night's work, and Cissie's group included the baker, a lingo teacher, sex worker, courier, hair stylist, and—she was most surprised to learn—a model.

The train then made its way to one of the town's storehouses, gathering welding equipment and spare bulbs, a plate of glass and a window frame. Though few of the group she'd gathered had done maintenance dickey before, Cissie had watched and assisted Sam long enough to guide and direct (admittedly with one or two guesses, and one mistake with the generator which resulted in a shocking shower of sparks). She had never done this without Sam before, and there was something liberating about working with these strangers, in watching their confidence grow with each step.

In part, the task felt pointless—tonight there would doubtless be another bunch of thugs, another spate of targeted vandalism—and Cissie worked from a sense of duty. But, as the hours passed, she realised that their work wasn't pointless at all: it was vital to keep going in the face of aggression; to put things back together when others wanted you to fall apart. As she guided a new window into its frame, she could see how undoing damage was itself an act of defiance.

Months ago, back when she'd started, such work had made her feel closer to Howard. She'd felt an affinity in the act of creation, in making something from nothing. But she'd not been making; this was never an act of creation. She'd been repairing. It was a distinction she hadn't noticed before, but now the difference was clear as journo and menge. To build was bona, but to *rebuild*, well, that was something else entirely. Something precious.

They worked for hours—which was fine, seeing as the daycare centre was closed, and the children were once again in the care of Ms. Fortier (grateful for the company, her old cove had asked few questions). When they'd finally finished sealing the last window into its frame, the group parted, subdued and satisfied. And though Cissie herself felt proud, it wasn't the pride of egotism, but of having done her share as part of a team, of having worked together to make things just a bijou bit better.

She found her way back to the main street, and this time she didn't stall in front of Sam's door, but knocked. He opened it while bundled in a deep red blanket; with very little beneath, Cissie caught glimpses of taut skin as he guided her up the stairs and toward the sofa. A television blared.

"What's on?" she asked, pulling a violet blanket around her shoulders.

"Just a silly soap opera, but it's oddly compelling." His voche was still thick with sickness.

"What's it called?"

"*The Straights.*"

"Sounds exotic."

"Ssh. We're about to find out if Caroline chooses Richard or Dominic."

"Can't she have both?"

"Hush now."

So, she settled into the soft cushions, her head resting on Sam's shoulder in ambiguous intimacy. Exhausted from the journo's hard labour, she was barely able to hold her ogles open in the warm and cozy space. It was just a minute or two before she nelled the gentle buzz of Sam's snore, and though she tried to watch, the actors onscreen blurred, re-formed, and blurred again, their voices fuzzing in and out of clarity. After just half an episode she sank into a deep, thick sleep, and only woke up late the next morning.

33.

"Ms. Fortier, I am so sorry. I am so, so very sorry."

Ms. Fortier stood in her doorway, still as a statue as the children cackled and squawked from the other room. Was she furious or relieved? Her marble expression gave no clues, and there was no choice but to tell her friend the truth, or at least part of it. That was fine. Cissie had grown used to telling partial truths.

"I was so exhausted I fell asleep. I woke up less than an hour ago."

Still, Ms. Fortier neither moved nor spoke. Cissie's armpits prickled with apprehension.

"I promise you: this absolutely will not happen again. I can't thank you enough for taking care of them all night."

As Cissie shifted from one foot to the other Ms. Fortier waited in silence a few more moments, before she finally spoke.

"We need to talk."

First Cissie greeted the boys, kissing each on the forehead. Thomas wiped his kiss away and returned to the obscure game they'd created with two toy dump trucks and a mass of plastic soldiers. Cissie followed Ms. Fortier into her spare room.

Inside, the walls were papered with cowboys, a background of navy blue. A wooden toy box squatted in the corner; a stack of old comic books rested on a small desk. It was a boy's bedroom, but one frozen in time, a capsule from decades ago.

Ms. Fortier held out a lighter, clicked it into flame, and lit a cigarette.

"I really am sorry," Cissie began, cursing herself: not only had she been a bad mother, she'd been a bad friend.

The older woman regarded her with an intense, analytical look, one which made Cissie deeply uncomfortable, as though she were being ogled under a microscope.

"Your husband is right, you know," Ms. Fortier stated.

"Right about what?" Cissie had no idea what she was referring to.

"I know what Howard says about me. And it's true. I am a whore. Or, at least, I was. A prostitute. Oh," she exhaled, spilling blue-grey smoke. "Such ugly, ugly words they name us." She took another drag on the cigarette before adding, "Close your mouth, dear. It makes you look stupid, gaping like that. Always remember how you look, because trust me, men never forget it."

Cissie savvied nix what to say. In lieu of an answer, Ms. Fortier trolled over to an ancient record player—blue as the walls—and began the soft hum of music. It was a children's record, but the melody was oddly comforting. When she spoke again her voice was softer, fuzzed with the notes which floated around the two palonies.

"Yes, I know what Howard says. I keep an eye on the both of you, you see. This might sound silly, but I always considered you all my family, even if your husband is a horse's ass."

"We *are* family," Cissie implored. Ms. Fortier continued as though she'd said nothing.

"He was an accident. My boy. But my sweet, what a happy accident! Such a beautiful child, with so many smiles for his mother. I used to fantasise about what he'd be when he grew up. What his wife would be like. The grandchildren he would give me. Oh, he was free to make his own choices, but I wanted him to have a nice family."

She paused a moment.

"But a careless moment, and it was all gone. Poof. Just like that. I've spent years thinking about that day, about how different it all could have been."

The glow of the cigarette reached the filter. She immediately reached for another. Her hands shook. Cissie took the lighter and sparked it for her.

"My heart never mended. I knew it wouldn't. It never will. But I was so pleased to meet you and your children. You all seemed so happy, and you let me share in that. Cissie dear! I can't tell you what it meant. Ever since I've considered myself a grandmother to those boys."

"Me too," Cissie confessed.

"So, don't you complain about leaving them with me—it is a joy to care for them. But I see your family falling apart, even if you do not. Understand that I am not blaming you, Cissie, and I'm sorry if I did before. It's every woman's right to explore, to seize life and see the world around her. But your husband . . ."

Cissie swallowed. Hadn't Ms. Fortier told her not to worry herself over Howard? What had changed?

Her friend and neighbour exhaled, smoke billowing through her nostrils.

"You weren't the only one who was gone all night. You need to keep an eye on him, Cissie. I don't know what is going on, exactly, and I wish to God I did, if only to help you. But I have been watching him, and I've known enough men to know when they're planning something. Something stupid. *Merde*—" she dropped cigarette ash onto herself. "You must understand. You need to start watching him too."

That evening Cissie vardad Howard as he read bedtime stories to the children. The tales were generic ones from back in the States, bland and homogeneous, but Howard transformed them, crackling with the passion and ardour of a firebrand priest. The children listened, enraptured, until each fell asleep, but Howard didn't stop until he'd reached the end.

Closing the book, he then gazed upon his offspring as though he'd forgotten Cissie were even there. He jumped when she touched his shoulder.

"Would you join me in the living room, hon?"

He nodded, taking her famble as they quietly left the boys' room and sank into the sofa.

There was so much Cissie needed to ask, and so few ways she could.

Howard brought her hand to his lips and kissed her fingers.

"Is everything all right?" he asked, his voice soft with concern. Cissie thought she could see fear in that caring expression, but what did she know?

"You've been so kind and attentive lately—" she began.

Howard cut her off. Not aggressively, but with a certain cushioned force.

"I know. And it's sudden. The truth is simple. I realised how much you and the boys mean to me. It was like an epiphany, but there wasn't anything that triggered it. I just realised how much I take for granted, and I don't want to take anything for granted."

Before, this would have swayed her. But the fear she had seen in Ms. Fortier was real. She had noticed things Cissie hadn't.

"And the Bible group? I just wondered—"

Once more Howard cut her off, in that soft but immovable tone. He squeezed her hand.

"You were eighteen when we met. I was only twenty-three. I'd barely had a chance to live my own life, and you hadn't at all. We were young, Cissie. We were *so* young—" he shifted closer to her, carefully stroking her hair, "—and I don't regret anything, so please don't think that. I hope you don't have cause for regrets either. Do you?"

It was a genuine question. His eyes searched hers, imploring her to tell the truth.

"Not at all."

At her reply, Howard seemed to relax a little. His fingers withdrew from her hair. He leaned back into the cushions.

"I'm not very good at it, talking like this. What I'm trying to say is that we were all each other had. Every minute of it has been wonderful, but we had no time to discover who we really were. Thomas came straight away, and then you were *Mom*, and I was *Dad*."

He stopped.

"Would you like a drink?" he asked.

"A drink?"

Howard sprang from the couch and delved into one of the upper kitchen cabinets, returning with a dusty bottle of scotch. He then fetched two mismatched glasses.

"How long has it been since we just had a drink together?" he asked as he poured the liquor.

Cissie couldn't recall. They clanked their glasses together. The scotch burned, then warmed, a hearth in Cissie's stomach. Howard continued.

"We were parents. Not Howard anymore. Not Cecilia."

Cissie stared into the laps of brown liquid as she rolled it around in her glass. It had been a long time since she'd heard her whole first name.

"You're right."

"Cissie, this group gives me something else. It gives me purpose. I love you and the kids, but I also enjoy being part of this community—this *straight* community. A place where I can be one of the boys."

He took another swig of his drink.

"And yes, I'm worried. This city isn't a safe place for us, and we need protection. The group gives us that. But if I'm honest—completely, totally, no-holds-barred honest with you, Cissie—it makes me feel important."

"But what *do* you do?" Cissie finally asked, setting her glass down on the coffee table. "I need to know, Howard."

"And I need to keep it to myself," he replied, setting his own tumbler down. "I need something private. I need something for *me*. All you need to know is that everything is fine. I would never do anything to hurt you and the kids."

He had a gallant look about him. A brave, defiant look. It made Cissie feel sick.

"Howard, if you just told me—"

Again, he interrupted.

"We were both young. Neither of us had the chance to keep something for ourselves. We both need a little privacy. And we've both found it."

Cissie faltered. "What do you mean?"

"I mean," he replied, his tone stern, "I'm not the only one with secrets. I know you've been going off by yourself almost every day . . ."

She avoided his gaze. One of his new friends must have seen her. Or more than one. They'd been watching her, just as Ms. Fortier had been watching Howard.

". . .and I'm not going to ask you where you've been going. Because I trust you, Cissie. We need to trust each other more. You have your own space, and I know that you'd never do anything to hurt me or the boys."

He picked up his glass again and took a sip before continuing.

"I'm going to trust you, and you're going to trust me." He raised his glass, gesturing for her to do the same. "Do we have a deal?"

What could she do? Tell her husband about Remould, about dressing as a manly, using his name? Was she supposed to tell him about Sam?

She picked up her glass and they toasted once again. They finished their drinks and cemented the fragile agreement by creeping into their bedroom, by kissing and stroking each other. She only paused to reach over and flick off the bedside lamp. To lose herself in darkness. To bury herself in his arms.

34.

Things were getting worse. They were getting worse, and Howard knew it. He followed the news, he could see the war that was coming. And who would protect them, when the time came? Who would make that sacrifice?

He would do anything for his children. Anything.

Even so, his hands were shaking as he placed the letter into the envelope. His knees near-buckled as he left the apartment and descended the stairs. He was afraid, he didn't mind admitting that. Of course he was afraid.

When he got to the postbox, he shoved the letter in. Hard and fast, so he couldn't change his mind.

He felt guilt.

Guilt was his companion these days. He felt guilt for the sake of Cissie, because his secret was worse than hers could possibly be. It was always lingering by him, always whispering to him. Heavy and smothering. Guilt so thick he couldn't breathe.

He wasn't lying to her, of course he wasn't. He just hadn't told her everything. And it was necessary, because he was protecting her. Protecting her from the darker side of it all. Saving her from the dirty planning, all the stuff that stuck to you. That clung to you, week after week, every minute of the day. It was there whenever he kissed his wife, whenever he hugged his children. The ugly knowledge of what lay ahead.

At night he'd watch Cissie, beautiful in sleep, ignorant and serene. He'd cry, quietly, into his pillow.

Such ugly, ugly knowledge.

He needed to know that his family would be cared for, when the time came, should the worst happen. So he'd mailed a letter. Just in case, that was all. Just in case. He'd mailed it and now it was gone. Gone, with no going back.

Just in case.

He hoped she could forgive him.

Excerpt from
The Honest Guide to Berlin

Pride Month.

Though Berlin is an exciting destination at any time of year, the city really shines during the Pride Month festivities. Taking place each August, Pride Month involves a series of festivals, conferences, parades, and parties. There really is no way to sum up this thrilling time, and each district has its own way of celebrating: from Flora's lakeside raves and Maytree's celebrity banquets, to the grand art sales in Delos and the many sports tournaments of Adonis. This diversity of entertainment means there really are activities for every visitor, and a list of local events can be found at the nearest Tourist Information Carsey. Just be sure to drink plenty of water—and try not to be overwhelmed!

The first Pride Month was celebrated the year following Berlin's independence, in August of 1949. In contrast to the spectacle we see today, these first celebrations were modest in size, with public events comprised of small street parties and poetry readings—it wasn't until over a decade later that public funds were directed toward the festivities and the city recognised the potential for tourism. Similar, if smaller, pride events are also held in the Gay Republic's overseas territories and dependencies (see *Shared Administrative Zones, Overseas Territories, and Enclaves*, p. 18).

Though August in Berlin is primarily a month of fun and frolicking, visitors must remain aware that Pride Month is also a politically sensitive time. Berlin's political parties generally use this period for informal campaigning, with large crowds and public speeches turning many of the city's gatherings into impromptu rallies. In addition, certain pride events can attract protests and demonstrations, and police intervention is not unheard of. If an event seems particularly rowdy, just turn and "troll" the other way.

None of this should detract from one of the planet's most creative, enlightening, and exhilarating celebrations. Just be sensible, take precautions, and most of all—have fun!

FAMBLED

The Gay Republic

1999

35.

"So how did you get into this?" William asked, reclining back into the old sofaletty and taking a sip of wine.

He and Henna had tried several kinds of activism over the past several journos, starting with flyers. *Don't be scared*, she'd cackled, as though that would help, as William stood on some street corner with leaflets in his famble. He knew them by memory, having read them over and over—the call for queer rights, for the end to Berlin's social segregation—and all he had to do was hand them out. But every time someone approached, he'd held back. When they ogled him, catching sight of his blush-pink lipstick, he'd lost his nerve and averted his gaze.

I'm sorry, he'd apologised to Henna, every time someone had passed by empty-handed.

Later that sedder, they'd trolled to a vigil for those who'd been deported back to dangerous lands. A small square in Q was lit by a thousand candles. This was, in fact, easier—but he was careless with his candle, and almost lit a palonie's coat aflame.

Then there was the time Henna had pulled out a spray can and motioned to a blank patch of wall. It had to be something short; he'd never spray-painted before. So, he'd chosen two words he'd read in the leaflets: *Nix Boxes*. His fambles were shaky, and it came out more like *Mlx Bpxos*, but when he'd stood back and vardad his trembly work, he'd felt a faint flutter of pride.

Now they were taking the evening off and spending it at William's carsey. Gareth was on shift at the bevvie so wouldn't be back till late, and after rooting around the cupboards William had found half a bottle of red wine, which he'd sloppily decanted into mugs.

"*How did I get into this?*" Henna said, repeating his question with a mock English accent. "That's a whole story." She paused, taking a swig from a mug emblazoned with the name of his workplace, as he motioned for her to continue.

"Well, you may not believe this, *liebe* William. But I was actually born into wealth."

She glanced his way. There was a mischievous delight in her voice, and William gathered that she relished her fall from social grace.

"I was raised by my grandfathers, who wanted me to be the perfect lesbian princess. Imagine! Of course, it worked when I was a little chavvie, but once I became a teenager—"

"You rebelled," William filled in.

Henna ogled him sharply—no one likes their life story preempted.

"It was because of him, your radio manly. Kenneth Luvvie. For as long as I remember we would all sit down by the big marble fireplace and we'd nell his show together. But over time . . . see, it changed. Nix the words that were said, but the way they sounded. The way they sounded *to me*. When I was smaller, I'd hear him speak of family and feel like he was talking about us all, myself included.

"But what I wanted and what my grandfathers wanted were very different. They planned for me to gain a good degree and then marry some rich society palonie. I nix savvied what I wanted, but I savvied it wasn't that. So, I did the teenage thing. I stayed out, I got drunk and high, I made coves my grandfathers hated.

"I realised that when Luvvie talked of family, he didn't mean me. I wasn't included. And that was the whole point: they need some of us to be on the outside, because people like Luvvie—and like my grandfathers—they can only understand themselves by what they're *not*."

On that last lav she slammed her mug down onto the coffee table.

"Eventually they threw me out. So, I left. I nix knew where I was going, but I was angry. The first thing I did was take a brick and throw it through the window of a BonaMarkt."

"The supermarket?" William asked. "Why?"

"My grandfathers own the company."

William choked on red wine. Henna slapped his back. When he regained control of his breath, he asked, "So what made them throw you out? There must have been some final straw."

Immediately, Henna's eke set stern as stone. "Nothing," she insisted, picking up her mug and staring down into it. "It wasn't anything."

To William, Henna was a force of nature, and it was an impression which had formed the first time he'd nelled her manic, boisterous laugh. He envied her uncompromising conviction—indeed it was what drew him to her: the idle hope that he might gain some of her clarity and confidence.

Now she wouldn't even hold his gaze.

"I'm sorry," he whispered.

"William," Henna snapped. "Stop saying sorry. You can't be sorry, because you haven't done anything wrong. You apologise for your own existence, but it's no defence. It won't make people like you. It won't make them accept you."

"Do you think I'm an idiot?" William asked, as he rose to take his mug to the kitchen sink.

"Nix, *warte mal*—" Henna stood and grasped his arm. "I'm sorry. And I mean that." She paused for a moment, caught in some decision, before adding, "Come with me."

"Come with you where?" He wrenched his arm free of her grip.

"To my carsey."

He was still annoyed by her outburst, but he followed her out of curiosity, out onto the rooftop and into the warm breeze. They stopped outside Henna's peeling mauve door. A grey outline was all that remained of the knocker which had once taken pride of place at the very centre. It was the kind of unkempt touch which used to make his mother *tut* with irritation, before declaring that *The Neighbourhood Is Going to Pieces.*

Henna hesitated.

"Look, we don't have to—"

But the key was already scratching its way into the lock; the door was already opening. The small house had the same layout as his own, the bathroom on the lower floor, the stairs leading up toward the living quarters. Yet while the stairway was bare in William's home, here it was covered with shoes and stacks of leaflets. He was careful not to step on anything as they made their way upwards.

"Is that you, Henna?" a voice called from above. It sounded Spanish, thick and warm as gravy. "Sweetie, I found some macaroni. The supermarket was just going to throw it all out! What a waste of perfectly good carnish! I've half a mind—"

She stopped as soon as they reached the top of the stairs, Henna in front, William hovering behind her. The upstairs room was alive and plush, covered with cushions and drapes in a myriad of conflicting colours and textures, surrounding a bed large enough for three grown adults. The space was both humble and ostentatious, and William's first instinct was one of profound comfort, as though he could sink into the soft furnishings and be enveloped, warm and cocooned. On the other side of the room was the kitchen, as white and sparse as the living-sleeping area was bright and crowded. It was gartered with more stacks of leaflets.

"William, this is Ramona," Henna introduced. "Ramona, this is the neighbour I was talking about."

The palonie—Ramona—was short, and stout, with smooth, richly tanned skin. She remained motionless, as solid and inscrutable as a religious idol, with the only sign of life radiating through her eyes: framed by dark, thick liner, they shone with duelling thoughts. Though clearly older than Henna, her rounded form smoothed out her age; she could have been anywhere between thirty-five and sixty. Standing there before her, William felt like a child.

"Honeys," another voice called. This one came from the front door, and carried a sharp, Canadian twang. "I'm home. Did you know the suspension railway broke down? We were left hanging like a—"

On reaching the top of the stairs, she too stopped short. Unlike Ramona, she was not silent.

"Henna, who is this?"

The palonie folded her lean arms, elbows jutting out at sharp angles. Around forty years old, she was slender and of Asian heritage, with hair cropped close to her scalp. Her whole body was strained as she regarded William, and her obvious discomfort even sharpened her features: her eyebrows, her nose, her lips. It was as if

232

she'd stolen Ramona's edges.

"This is William," Henna repeated. "William, this is Kara."

Were this latest entrant not blocking the stairs, William would have fled the carsey. He was acutely embarrassed for invading their private space and felt as though he'd trolled upon an active crime scene.

"William, these are my wives," Henna announced.

"Henna!" Kara exploded.

"*Mi vida*—" Ramona implored.

"Or I should say 'our' wives," Henna clarified. "The three of us are together. There," she added, turning to each palonie in turn, "I said it. I told him. The world didn't end."

"Look, I should go—" William stepped toward Kara, whose face was now plum-pink. But she didn't move from her position, instead remaining firmly in place.

"Please." Ramona addressed William, drawing out the word in a low, warm rumble. "Now you're here, you should take a seat. We don't mean to offend; we're simply not used to . . . to visitors."

"I can't believe this," Kara snapped, the crack in her voice betraying how close she was to tears. "Henna, we made a promise to each other—"

"We can't hide forever," Henna burst back.

"I really, really should go," William attempted once more.

"Everyone," Ramona boomed, her voice suddenly thunderous as she took charge of the room. "Take a seat. We have a guest, and I will make us some tea." She turned to William. "You English like tea, no?"

William nodded. He perched at the edge of a cushioned stool as Kara drew up a wooden chair, and Henna flopped down onto the large, three-person letty. They waited as Ramona clanked about the kitchen, trolling between cabinets until the kettle began to wail.

"Thank you," William replied as Ramona handed him a steaming mug, then one to each of her wives. Finally, she lowered herself onto the edge of the bed.

"Well William, allow me to introduce ourselves in a more civilised manner. My handle is Ramona Palomar. This is my wife, Kara Koh. You already know my other wife."

"Ogle him," Kara fretted. "He could be a spy, he could be Lilly Law, he could be anything."

"And he knows now," Ramona replied, slow and calm. "There's nothing we can do about it. Henna made the decision for us."

She looked over at Henna, giving her an ogle of reproach.

"I told you," Henna protested, fambling her mug to the floor. "He's bona. William's the one who strung up Kenneth Luvvie, who exposed him for all the world to varda."

It wasn't quite true: William wasn't the one to ultimately expose Luvvie. Even so, he nix contradicted her. A small smile curved the edge of Ramona's lips.

"So he says," Kara interjected.

"Kara." Ramona placed a hand on her tense wife's knee. "Now that William is here, we have nanti choice but to trust him. What does rudeness accomplish?"

"I'm sorry," Kara dryly cackled. "Next week let's put an advert in the newspaper. We'll tell the whole city, have ourselves a celebration." She sarcastically raised her arms in mock jubilee. "Polyamory pride!"

"Kara's anxious because you could get us in a lot of trouble," Henna explained to William.

"Kara isn't the only one," Ramona corrected. "Henna has put us— how do you say it?—on the spot."

"I'm sor—" William almost apologised, before stopping himself. "Look, I wouldn't have come here if I'd known it would be a problem. Really. But I can promise you I won't tell anyone. Honestly, I've nobody to tell.

"Besides," he continued, suddenly realising something. "You know it was me who left Luvvie in that swing. He's powerful, he has money, he's connected. If you let out my secret, well, I'd be in just as much trouble."

There was a slight, almost imperceptible shift in Kara: she relaxed. Just the tiniest fraction, but there it was.

Ramona nodded slowly, then roared with laughter.

"That's certainly true. Listen, William—do you live alone?"

"I live with my . . ." he paused over the word, "boyfriend."

"Do us a favour, *chico*. Don't tell him about us. Don't tell anyone."

William hadn't even thought about telling Gareth. How would he even begin? He'd dropped hints about his activities with Henna, hoping it would spark some interest, that Gareth might even join them. But it hadn't worked. There was no way he would understand this.

"Don't worry, I won't."

"Well then," Ramona concluded, setting her own mug on the floor. "It's bona to meet you, William. It might have been under better circumstances, but let's start afresh. Could you perhaps join us for dinner, tomorrow night? You ogle like you need a good meal."

36.

The week leading up to Pride Month saw a mess of construction: rickety scaffolding climbed up walls, stages spread over intersections, flagpoles were erected on each corner. Soon rainbow bunting hung between the carseys and platforms were readied for popular performers. Piece by piece, the streets were transformed, the whole smoke converted into a carnival.

Take the rooftop bar in which Gareth dickeyed. Rather than merely sport posters and tinsel, the staff had worked for journos constructing papier-mâché butterflies, covering the entire ceiling in purples, blues, greens, yellows, oranges, and reds; the sparkle of overhead bulbs shone straight through, bathing the entire establishment in vivid colour.

Even William's workplace had been altered—within budget, at least. Each desk had been provided with its own economical, celebratory decor: which meant a multicoloured wreath up on the wall and a rainbow feather boa stretching across the back. It was the same for every desk on his floor, with the exception of the manager's office, which was transformed into a spectacle of crepe and banners, at the centre of which hung the republic's flag.

Up on the rooftop, the journo was still. The summer air sweltered over the flagstones, thick as shame. Beyond the ever-present white noise of distant traffic, the only sound was the clack of dice, and the soft crackle of burning marijuana.

The game was called *Charpering Pots*. William had nix played it before, whereas Henna had played since she was a chavvie.

"You don't need to know the game well," she insisted. "It's more chance than skill, that's why adults don't play so much. But I love that about it. It's more like real life."

"That's a pretty bleak viewpoint," William replied.

"Then tell me, filly William—was it skill brought you to Berlin, or was it chance?" She leaned over and fambled him the spliff. He managed to inhale without coughing, the back of his throat burning, the world fuzzing a little bit softer.

"You're being selective in your example," he cackled. "Let's try another. Tell me, dear Henna—was it skill brought you two wives, or was it chance?"

"You're nix making sense." She reached for the spliff, dragging a long toke.

"I mean," William began, trying to gather his increasingly stray thoughts, "was it really just luck formed your relationship? Or was it your skills? Your charm, your passion, your intellect?"

"You do flatter me, William." She fambled the herb back to him.

"I don't mean to." This time he lay back as he inhaled, luxuriating in the warm journo, the mellow smoke. The sky above was a brilliant, endless blue. An ocean he could dive into. A place in which he could lose himself.

"They were already together when I met them," Henna explained. "Ramona and Kara."

William liked Ramona. With her no-nonsense pragmatism and earthy warmth, she reminded him of a favourite aunt—an impression which had only grown over time, particularly as she took ample opportunity to feed him. No matter how much he ate, she was always concerned he was starving to death.

Kara, on the other famble, remained cold as fear. No matter how many times he visited their carsey, she always regarded him as a stranger. Not rude, exactly, but not welcoming. In fact, she treated him like his mother treated plumbers and electricians: always keeping a watchful ogle on them in case they stole the silverware.

"They were living in an apartment in Flora," Henna continued, "and I was working odd jobs in their neighbourhood. We all became friends before I kissed Ramona. Then one thing led to another, and the three of us fell in love. Kara freaked out at first, but believe it or not, she's the one who suggested I move in with them.

"Anyway, it worked. We were happy. But then the neighbours got weird and suspicious, you savvy, varding through the windows, gossiping about us, that sort of thing. When we found our mail was being opened, we trolled here, to Q, where we wouldn't be ogled or cackled about. If that's luck, or if that's charm, I can't tell you. Besides, it's your turn," she prompted, scooping up the dice.

"I am *way* beyond being able to play. Even a game of chance." William lifted his arm, the spliff between his fingers, prompting Henna to take it.

"Then am I to presume we're not off littering later?"

William savoured the sunlight on his skin. "I'm useless when I'm stoned."

"Well then, we'll have to be sober for what I've planned ne—"

She fell silent at the whine of the elevator, at the pad of footsteps across the rooftop, approaching them. William sat up.

"Gareth," he greeted him.

Yet Gareth gave nothing more than the briefest glance at William, before trolling straight past and unlocking their front door. It was then that William noticed the pink smudges on the end of the joint, and realised he was still wearing lipstick.

37.

"Come on Gareth. Talk to me."

Gareth was angry. Really fucking angry. But he wasn't like William. He wasn't bona with words, he couldn't twist and shape them like William could. When it came to talk, William always had the advantage. So, for the time being he cackled nix. Instead, he leaned into the refrigerator, taking a moment to enjoy the cool air on his eke. Then he reached in and cracked open a beer, taking a long, satisfying schlumph of the lager.

"Nanti that," he finally said. "I'm not talking to you when you're stoned."

Tonight, like so many nights, Gareth'd hoped to take William out, go to a bevvy together so he could finally, finally meet his coves. His supervisor Björn'd taken to calling William *the imaginary homie affair*, and though Gareth always laughed along, the truth was it stung. He'd hoped tonight would be different, but of course William was high.

It wasn't even a surprise to varda him wearing makeup. Gareth'd expected it; or if not this, exactly, then something like it. Something deviant. Something that would cause trouble, that would drive a wedge between them. The whole reason Gareth was even in the city was because he was attracted to men, and now here William was, making himself into less of one.

"It's my day off," William whined through a woman's lips. "I was just hanging out with Henna."

Henna. Gareth'd taken an instant dislike to the militant lesbian, and no flies. With her tattered "zhoosh me" protest clothes she screamed *troublemaker*, and worse, she encouraged William's angry loner side. She must have put the lipstick on him. William'd never fit in with her around, and what's more, he'd never be happy. Neither of them would be.

"Henna." He spat her name like a curse.

"I know you don't like her," William replied, "but can't you just get along for my sake? She's really not so bad—"

As William talked, Gareth took another long swig of his bevvy, trolled over to the kitchen cabinets, and pulled a leaflet from a drawer.

"What's this?" he interrupted. He unfolded the paper and began reading aloud. "*Nix Boxes: Our Demands for an Equal Republic. Step one: Desegregation. For too long our fair smoke has been divided, forcing lesbians into one area, gays into another, queers into yet another—*"

"I know what it says," William cackled.

"Or what about this?" Gareth continued. "*Step two: The legal right to a sex change. All of us deserve autonomy over our own bodies, and trans people are no exception—*"

"I know, I've read it."

"*Step three: Political rights. Q remains an unrecognised district, robbing queer, bisexual, and trans residents of representation in the Senate and the Assembly—*"

"Gareth. I get it."

"Apparently you don't," Gareth spat. "Apparently you don't get it at all. Where can we go if not here? Where are we supposed to live if we get kicked out of the gay smoke?"

"We're not . . ." William began, before trailing off. Whether he had no argument back, or whether he was just too stoned, Gareth had no idea. It nix mattered.

"This was our plan, William. We don't have another one. This was what we wanted, this was where we needed to be."

He tipped the rest of the can down his haldz and threw it into the rubbish bin.

Truth was, William'd got Gareth thinking about the future. He'd never dared before. Back in school he'd just gone from from journo to journo, never really planning, never dreaming. There was no *how things could be*, there was only *how things are*. So, he'd focused on the things he liked: cars, magazines, the odd moment with William. It was the bijou joys that got him through. The small bits of happiness. The distractions.

Sure, there were things he looked forward to. Quitting school, for one. Maybe he could've had a job in the Dovetree family garage. If William worked in the office, he could have ogled him all the time. But it wasn't a plan, and it wasn't a dream. It would just've been nice.

The first time he'd really thought about the future was when William'd run to his door. Gareth's face had been throbbing from where William's dad'd hit him, and he was in the middle of cackling with his parents. He'd been making up some story about a mugging.

But then William was there. It was the middle of the night, and William was asking him to run away together.

Suddenly there'd been a future. It was big and uncertain. It was terrifying. He'd had to choose: stay with his parents, or run away with William. Those were two completely different lives, and he'd only had a few moments to decide which one he'd wanted.

So he'd chosen the future with William. He'd leapt into the unknown, but at least there was a soft landing—the gay city, a thousand miles away. William'd been obsessed with it, nelling the radio broadcasts for years and years. It was William who'd been dreaming, but Gareth'd let himself get excited. He'd fantasised about a smoke full of people like him, where he'd be understood. Where he was nix alone. Where he could actually fit in, finally, properly. And yeah, he'd been looking forward to it, even when William wouldn't marry him. Even when they were sent to Q. See, William's dream had become his own.

And now William didn't want it. After all this, after everything, he was throwing away their only plan. And had he asked Gareth? Had William thought, even for a moment, about what *he* actually wanted?

Had he, hell.

But when he tried to say all that, it came out wrong. Gareth savvied that he was nix good at talking about his feelings, and William took advantage of it. Because if Gareth couldn't talk about his feelings, well, then they just didn't exist.

He thought about grabbing another bevvie from the fridge, but he wanted to get out. To get out and troll around, to enjoy this beautiful place! For all they'd been through, at least one of them should. If only William could see the glamour, the sparkle—if only he could varda Berlin through his ogles.

But he wouldn't. He wouldn't even try.

"Where are you going?" William yelled, as Gareth grabbed his coat and trolled down the stairs. He couldn't be around those lurid pink lips for a second more. He slammed the door behind himself.

But for a moment he paused, gazing out across the rooftops and out over the smoke, covered in Pride decorations. A single thrush landed on a rooftop aerial and then took off again.

Even through his anger, Gareth could still marvel at Berlin; he could still be struck by its beauty and thrilled by the promise of an evening in the city. Here was where he belonged. Here, he had a million futures, and any of them felt possible.

Excerpt from
The Schwul Zeitung

MAYTREE, Berlin—You would think being caught bound to a sling would be enough to cause anyone to slink away from public life. But not Kenneth Luvvie. Not only does the radio star still host his popular show, but this week he let slip a particularly astonishing surprise: the 59-year-old is running for political office.

"Let me be absolutely clear," Luvvie insisted. "It was a politically motivated act. The intention wasn't just to humiliate me, but to humiliate anyone who cares about the future of our smoke, and anyone who cares about the future of gay people. Well, I will nix let them. Nix! So, I'm running for leadership of the Gay Patriot League. Because we've let them get away with too much, and for far too long."

Though Luvvie's fans will doubtless be buoyed by the netters, he faces considerable hurdles if he hopes for leadership of the nationalist party. The Gay Patriotic League has thrived under the auspices of its current chairman, Heiner Baldwin-Schmidt, and it's unlikely the party membership will change course in the upcoming leadership elections. Luvvie, however, is undeterred.

"I've not even started yet," the radio host told *The Schwul Zeitung*, shortly after his announcement. "This smoke has suffered under the influence of weak fambles: disruption, riots, vandalism, they've all become a part of our daily life. Well, I say nix! I will show the party, indeed all Berliners, how serious I am. And I will do so before the vote."

Speculation has been rife as to exactly what, if anything, Luvvie has planned—but if the star lives up to his aggressive and unapologetic persona, he's sure to grab our attention.

HETTIE AND LADY

The Gay Republic

August 1999

38.

Where was Howard? Cissie knew he was with his group, but she hadn't a clue where they were, nor what they were doing. No matter how much she told herself she was being silly, that she was worrying over nothing, still the same questions circled. Where was he? And what in God's name was he getting himself into?

She was scaring herself, she savvied that. After all, she hadn't told Howard what she had been doing in Remould, and that wasn't so bad. But there was no relief. Her jaw clenched with stress as she cooked the children fish sticks and peas. Her shoulders hunched as she served dinner. She scolded Thomas when he threw food at his little brother.

"But he was making faces!" Thomas protested, with all the gravity children gave such things. Such silly, stupid, pointless things.

"I don't care," Cissie snapped. "Eat your damn food."

"Mommy said a naughty word!" Jonah chuckled, though neither Cissie nor Thomas paid him any attention.

"*He was making faces!*" Thomas repeated, as though Cissie hadn't nelled him the first time.

"And whose job is it to punish him if he's naughty?" she asked, her voice razor-edged.

"Yours," he sulked.

"Yours *who?*"

"Yours, *Mom*," he replied. There was a sarcastic undertone to his reply, one he'd never used before. Once again, she saw Howard in him, in the way his face was set in stone, in the way he showed his displeasure by aimlessly jabbing at his food.

"Go to your room," she ordered.

"What?" Thomas asked. Jonah's pale blue eyes darted between the two, taking in the conflict. Cissie set down her knife and fork.

"I said, go to your room, Thomas."

"But I didn't finish dinner." His tone was pure defiance.

"*I said go to your fucking room, right now!*" she screamed.

Thomas pushed his plate away, slowly stood, and trolled to his bedroom. If he was shaken by Cissie's outburst, he didn't show it in the slightest. The door slammed, and the room was quiet.

"Why are you crying, Mommy?" Jonah asked, wandering over to his mother and giving her a hug.

They sat together on the sofa, Jonah in Cissie's arms as they ogled television. It was later than she usually let him watch, and she kept one hand on the remote control in case of inappropriate programming. There was no noise from Thomas, and Howard still wasn't home.

"Mommy, look," Jonah pointed at the TV set, bouncing up and down with excitement; an array of rainbow-coloured balloons surrounded a stage. "Balloons!" he squealed.

Cissie leaned forward, taking in the scene. Some politician or other was making a speech for the opening of Pride Month. The mayor of Twinkstadt, the narration revealed.

But then something landed on the mayor's shoulder.

"What was that Mommy?"

She shook her head. "I don't know, sweetie."

Then another fell: a thin rectangle. And another, blown offstage by the breeze. Soon a cascade of paper fluttered down from above, a blizzard of falling flyers. Then the camera panned upward, to the walkway above, where two youths were emptying sacks of them down onto the assembly below. They ran as Lilly Law approached.

"It looks like a party," Jonah said.

Cissie kissed him on the forehead. To him this was a ticker-tape parade, not a political stunt; she envied his simplicity, the easy joy he found in all the colours and nonsense. Had the world ever been so charming?

The moment was interrupted by the doorbell. "Daddy's home," Jonah exclaimed, but when Cissie opened the door it wasn't Howard who faced her. The stranger had a beard and a shaved head. It took her several seconds to recognise who it was: a face she hadn't ogled since before Jonah was born, not since Howard first went to work in Berlin.

"Rob!"

"Cissie. It's been a while."

It certainly had been. He and Howard had fallen out while in Berlin, but Howard had never told her why, exactly, and she hadn't pushed the issue. She'd assumed Rob was back in Ohio.

"Come here," he greeted, opening his arms for a hug—he was still the same old Rob. Her nose met his denim jacket as he wrapped his arms around her. He smelled of faded sweat and stale clothes. "I came straight here," he explained. "From the airport."

"Well, come in, come in," Cissie offered, the situation strange and dreamily unreal. What was he doing here?

"This must be Thomas," Rob declared, bending down toward Jonah.

"Thomas is in his room," Cissie explained.

"He's being punished," Jonah cackled. "I'm Jonah."

"Well, hello there, Jonah." Rob pulled out two bright red lollipops. "This one's for you, and this one's for your brother." He turned to Cissie. "If that's all right."

"Sure," she agreed, still staggered by his presence. "But brush your teeth afterwards, Jonah. And then it's straight to bed."

"Thank you," Jonah hollered, running off to share his bounty with his brother.

"Would you like a drink?" Cissie offered her guest.

"I'd kill for a coffee," Rob replied. "It's been a long day."

With the children tucked into bed, Cissie gently closed the door and trolled over to the kitchen. She set a pan of water on the stove to boil and located the coffee granules as Rob seated himself on a high stool. The silence swelled between them, and the water was already starting to bubble by the time Cissie spoke.

"Why are you here, Rob? You didn't fly thousands of miles for a social call."

She was being rude, she knew that. In any other circumstance she would be pleased to ogle him, but now the unreality was giving way to lurching dread.

"No. You're right. I didn't," he responded, legs dangling like an overgrown child. "You always were perceptive."

"Perceptive? One of the children could see through you." The pan of water began to rattle against the stovetop. In all the years she'd been in Berlin, she'd never had a visitor. Whatever reason he had for coming, it wouldn't be bona. Him being here meant bad news.

"You do yourself down, Cissie. You were always too hard on yourself. You're an intelligent woman."

"Why in God's name are you here, Rob?"

Poor, gentle Rob. He looked taken aback, and then hurt. How many years had it been since she last saw him? Her fears over Howard were making her ungracious, and she never wished to be an ungracious host.

Rob shifted on his stool, ogling the floor. "I know it's been years, but I'm still your friend, Cissie. I'm still Howard's friend, even if he doesn't know it. I care about you both. I worry about you both."

That word was like a cold blade running down her spine. "Worry? But why would you worry about us?"

"He's in danger, Cissie." He pulled a crumpled piece of paper from his jacket pocket and handed it to her. "I got this in the mail the other day. I got the first flight here because I thought you should know. I thought there might be something I can do to help."

Cissie's blood thudded through her veins. She read the words over and over, as though they were written in an obscure language, and if she only kept reading and rereading then some new meaning might appear. But there it was, trembling in her hands.

Robert.

I know how long it's been. I know you probably don't want to hear from me. But we were friends, once. That might be over, but I need your help. I need you to do this one thing for me. Because I trust you. I still trust you.

If I'm dead, I need you to take care of Cissie and the boys. And if that happens, you'll get a letter. Then I want you to take my family back to Ohio. Where things make sense. Where it's safe.

Please don't throw this out. I know we should have spoken before, but life gets in the way. If you can't do this for me, then do it for Cissie. For the boys.

– Howard

39.

William woke. It was dark. The bed was empty.

There was a pounding at the front door. Pulling himself up, he slipped on a pair of trousers and stumbled across his menge carsey, almost tripping over a pair of Gareth's trainers.

"I'm coming," he called, his throat still thick with sleep. "Hold on."

He'd banked on an early night, slipping into bed with a paperback copy of *Rika Duka*, and had fallen asleep with the book on his chest. Glancing at the radio's blinking LED sparkle, he saw that it wasn't yet midnight.

The pounding continued.

"All right, all right." Barefoot and shirtless, he pulled the door open, only to find Henna in a state of agitation.

"He's on," she cackled, grabbing at his wrist. "He's on, come look."

"What?" William mumbled. "Who's on what?"

"Your boyfriend! Just come and varda. Hurry!"

Bare feet slapping rough flagstones, William followed Henna to her mauve front door, which had been left ajar. A television blared inside, a familiar voche growing as they ascended the stairs.

In front of the set were Ramona and Kara, snuggled together beneath a worn blanket. On varding the visitor, Ramona offered William a box of Spanish almond cookies, while Kara nodded her gruff hello. William perched on the bed alongside them as Luvvie appeared on the screen.

"That's not my boyfriend!" he objected.

"Shh," Kara hushed him as Luvvie spoke. Subtitles in five different languages crowded beneath his face.

"*. . . are making a mockery of everything our smoke stands for. All the suffering it took to get here. Pride is for everyone, and yet they seek to*

252

end it. Picketing in Diesel, disrupting the supply of Pride merchandise. Protest boats on Flora Lake, ruining the fireworks display. Even in Twinkstadt, they terrorised a mayoral speech, literally dropping nihilistic propaganda . . ."

"We got his attention," Henna cackled, prompting Kara to shush her. She paced back and forth as the camera edged toward Luvvie's eke, tinged purple with righteous affront.

"It's a city-wide sharda, and I'm taking a stand. All decent fruits should be taking a stand. We have a fifth column in our society, one which won't be happy until they've battyfanged everything we've built, and everything that keeps us safe. We've tolerated them, and they've shown us no tolerance in return."

At that moment the image switched to the underside of a colossal bridge, an intricate array of cables and pipes weaving and winding around one another in dull grey confusion. It then panned downward to a series of ramshackle carseys beneath, a neighbourhood shadowed by the bridge's bulk. In front of the carseys was a brick wall, with the words *beware! trannies* scrawled across its surface in lurid pink letters. William had never ogled the place before.

A narrator's voche took over from Luvvie.

"At the centre of the controversy is the slum called 'Remould,' a lawless area which has become a haven for criminal activities—including prostitution and gender deviancy. Many say it has also become the headquarters of the city's political dissidents. Now, Luvvie says he has found a solution."

The camera returned to Luvvie's face. The purple tinge was gone. Now he ogled pale, and eerily calm.

"If we're going to deal with the corruption in our city, we need to get right to its core. So we have a choice. It's unfortunate, but there it is. Either this pit of perversion goes, or our way of life does. If the residents of this oglesore wish to be a part of Berlin, they need to troll away from Remould and find real homes, real jobs, and pay the taxes which keep our city functioning.

"And to those residents, please, let me be the first to tell you: if you stay, you will be removed. I call upon all gay patriots to join me in a week's time, here, at the western entrance of this blight. This year we'll celebrate Pride the

253

way our forefathers did: with action, not words. With virtue rather than parties. Together we will finally, completely, and thoroughly clean out this rot. Perhaps then we can return to normal. Then we will be safe."

"Oh my God," Kara murmured.

Henna was already at the phone.

Once more the image shifted away from Luvvie, now zhooshing a bustling street within Remould, focusing first on the entrance to what looked like a brothel, then on an overturned trash can. The newscaster's voice resumed.

"Critics say Luvvie doesn't have the legal authority to force mass evictions, particularly using vigilante methods. But Luvvie's supporters claim that the neighbourhood's illegal status makes it fair game for a community clear-up. With Lilly Law refusing to make a statement either way, Remould's future..."

"Those poor people," Kara exclaimed.

Ramona stared at the screen.

William said nothing. Ogling Luvvie again had frozen him with shock, as though he'd been confronted by the radio manly in person. Disgust coursed through him: a physical revulsion at the manly who'd charmed him on a lonely, rainy night. He shuddered. Ramona reached over and put a warm famble on his.

"If they clear out Remould, then we're next," said Kara, her voice flat and ogles on the screen. "They won't stop there."

"Clearing out Remould is enough reason to stop him," Ramona reminded her wife. "We have coves there."

Henna returned the phone to its cradle.

"We're gathering," she announced. "All the groups. We're meeting at Remould."

"When?" Kara gasped.

"Now."

40.

Cissie's hair was loose, her makeup unmade. She ran like a child, slipping and sliding along the wet walkway. People were ogling, and she didn't care. She didn't! All her life she'd worried about what people thought of her, had wanted her family to appear presentable, to hide beneath a veneer of suburban respectability.

Where had it got her? Where?

Let people think what they like. Let them think she was crazed, fleeing through the evening in a nightgown and overcoat like some copper-headed demon, scaring away the pigeons. Well, fuck it. That's right fuck it. All the dignity in the world couldn't save her family. She shoved one famble into her coat pocket, feeling the crumpled paper, checking it was still there. That he'd still asked Rob to take her back to Ohio. That it was still real.

She'd always told herself that she'd chosen this life. Yes, she was a wife and mother, but that was what she had wanted, ever since Howard had leered at her from a ladder. A life that was her own.

Now, he'd stolen it from her. No, not stolen—it had never been hers in the first place. All these years and he'd varded her as some sort of accessory, a dependent to be passed along. He'd never asked what she wanted. That wasn't a factor.

Had it always been this way? She'd ogled her life as a series of choices, but had Howard?

Almost colliding with a woman who clutched bundles of bunting, she didn't even apologise. Howard had been her soulmate, but now she saw Cissie Parker through his eyes, and she didn't even recognise herself.

The elevator; the street. She passed a group of people singing and bevvying in a ramshackle cafe, and for a brutal moment longed to trade places with them. Any of them. It didn't matter.

She trolled on.

The bridge loomed overhead. She reached the gates of Remould, and was shaking as she arrived at Sam's carsey, but if she wanted to make her own choices, she had to do it now. His face widened to a smile when he ogled his late-night visitor.

Without saying a word Cissie grasped his wrist and pulled him toward her, feeling his lips with her own.

41.

They stood at an impasse, each varding the other from across the small kitchen.

"Gareth, I *have* to go to Remould."

"Do you?" Gareth asked. William hadn't savvied if the question was rhetorical or not, so he explained. He described the situation in the trans town and the danger its residents were in. But Gareth's ogles were glazed. Not because he wasn't listening, nor, for once, because he didn't understand. As he described the situation, William realised that Gareth, in fact, knew already. He knew exactly what was going on.

Idiot! Of course, he did. He turned the radio on every morning. It was always drifting through the bar where he worked.

"I can't just ignore this," William pleaded, his voice less certain than he'd intended.

Gareth barked a hard, sarcastic laugh.

"So, go," he replied, his voice a granite whisper. "I won't stop you."

William hesitated. His worst fear was that his relationship would simply fall apart, entropy weaving its way between them. Slowly, because destruction doesn't need to be fast. It can be so gradual it goes unnoticed. A weed grows, spreads a crack in the foundation. The crack gradually winds its way along a wall, sprouting new ones with each season, and the weed could be long dead by the time the structure collapses. William didn't know who he was without Gareth.

But they were different now, so far removed from their flighty adolescence: a sprout of hair peeked over Gareth's collar, while William's dangly body had filled out, just a little, and his eke was framed with a short beard. When had they transformed so, and how hadn't he noticed?

"Gareth, I want you to come to Remould with me," he implored. "I

257

need you to do this with me."

Gareth stared at the floor, his jaw clenching, before he finally spoke.

"You need me. But you don't listen to me. You *need* me," he repeated, stressing the word, "but you won't troll out with me. You don't wanna know about my life, or what's important to me. See, I know how you ogle things. You think I'm good with my hands, but not so smart. Come on, don't deny it. You're the brainy one, the one who loves to read, and I'm the dumb one. The one who doesn't really understand, the one who needs things explained.

"But the funny thing is, I've figured things out that you haven't. For instance, you think you savvy me, you think that you *need* me, but I'm just something you can hold on to. Something to stop you from blowing away."

"Gareth, please."

"Because you will blow away, William. If it wasn't this, it'd be something else. I savvy you better than anyone. And let me tell you, you can't fit in anywhere. You won't. Things were shit back home, sure, and at first, I thought things'd be different in Brighton. But they weren't. Then I thought things'd be different in Berlin. *But they weren't.*"

He hissed the last lavs, and a fleck of spittle hit William below the eye.

"The moment we were safe to love each other you started making yourself up like a woman. And then I realised—we could live anywhere, and things would be the same. Because the problem isn't where we live. The problem is you."

There were so many things William wanted to say in return. He wanted to shout back at him, to tell Gareth that he was being himself, that was all he ever wanted, to be true to himself, even when he wasn't sure what that was. He wanted to lay out all Gareth's faults in payment for his own, to force his partner to stare at his own reflection for once. At the same time, he wanted to soothe and reconcile, to not lose the most important thing in his world. He wanted to beg.

But with so much to say, he could say nix. Each reply crowded out the others. All he could do was slowly troll over to the sofa, sit down, and place his head in his hands.

Gareth continued. His voice was softer, but no less brutal.

"And you're crying. What do you want me to say? *Don't cry, William?* Well, I won't. You need to get it together. You're not thirteen anymore, and I'm nix gonna comfort you."

When William raised his head, he could ogle that Gareth looked stricken. He could ogle all the months of hurt, every small rejection. He'd never seen Gareth like that before—but it was just for a moment, before anger hardened his eke.

"There's the difference between us, William. I nix need sympathy, and I'm damn well not going to cry. I can look after myself. I've built a life here, and honestly, I've built it without you."

William opened his mouth to speak, yet nothing came out. It was true: their relationship had collapsed, and he didn't even know when it had happened. All that was left was crumbled mortar and broken bricks.

"I'm going to troll out for an hour," Gareth said, pulling on his shoes. "Gather up your stuff. Go to Remould."

And it was over. It was really over. The silence between them was the heaviest William had ever felt and was only broken when Gareth turned back and muttered his parting words. Words which would forever echo through William's mind, maddening and frustrating and ambiguous in all the worst ways.

"This could have been different."

PRIDE

The Gay Republic

August 1999

42.

Sparrows soared about the bridge above Remould, spiralling around one another as they swept downward, seeking the distant ground. Thirty storeys below, the bijou brown birds flitted into rubbish bins and blagged flecks of croissant from outdoor tables, thrusting their ekes back to swallow crumbs whole. With stomachs full, they rolled about the dusty paving before shooting upward, back toward the underbelly of concrete roadway and its never-ending rumble of traffic. They flitted about the crooks, eaves, and crevasses beneath the bridge, where they nestled in hollows and bickered with one another.

Then lumbered in the pigeons, hulking silver-purple lacoddies charging as they too sank toward the ground—seeking the same scraps, their heads bobbing as they trolled the streets for precious scavenge like tanks rolling through occupied territory. Then up, up, up again, to their nests about the undercarriage and great grey pillars of the grand flyover, bucking and cooing into position.

Yellow-bellied starlings, chanting thrushes, blood-red robins. These swarms of birds formed whole ecosystems, an entire world invardible to both the roaring tires above and the bustling population below. Gradually night descended, though it made bijou difference to the dusk beneath the bridge. The small hours were quiet, yet restless.

In the moments before dawn, a woman slipped out from a gate. Her auburn hair was dishevelled and her coat askew as she hurried away through the waning dark. There was no one to notice the look on her eke, a strange expression mixing fear and guilt, yet underlain with a deep satisfaction: as though she had just finished her last meal, as though it were the best she'd ever had. Then she vanished, stepping into an elevator and riding up toward the skyway.

Only a few minutes passed before a small band of people reached the same gate. Shuffling in the opposite direction to the distracted palonie, this wary cabal bore backpacks and parcels. In the middle of this huddle was a young man, his ogles red-lined. His world was on his back, everything he could cram into a frayed rucksack, everything he owned. Though sober, his gaze was that of a drunk in the moments before passing out: an unseeing, empty stare. He barely seemed to notice as a blonde woman in an old olive-toned army jacket took his arm. Then the group too was gone, in through the gate.

There was no one for a while. The sky above the bridge shifted ever so slightly, from a dark, blackish blue to deep purple.

From the distant streets then came a roar. A chanting crowd weaving and winding its way down narrow roads, glistening orange with the sparkle of a thousand lit torches. The noise of this glittering snake brought curious, bleary ekes to surrounding windows. At the head of this throng paced an older homie, his handsome salt-and-pepper face stern and unmoving, the lines etched into his forehead set with iron resolution.

Slowly, the journo began, a cacophony of squawks and chirps as sunrays shone with August force. But they wouldn't touch the world beneath the bridge. There no luppers of golden light fell; only torches lit the marching mob as they reached that gate. A crew in uniform clobber began assembling a wooden platform, hammering nails into boards, boards into place. The rest of the crowd massed about the growing stage until there was no further room; then they swept through the surrounding streets. With nix to do but wait, the crowd jostled and chattered and ate snacks, as the birds swept down from their high perch and scooped up the small remains.

Everywhere fluttered rainbows, their bright colours lost to the dark.

43.

There were a lot of them, volunteers who'd trolled across the city to defend Remould: most were from Q, but there were a few young homies from Twinkstadt, a pair of lesbians from Flora, and even a lone, grouchy bear in a tank top that revealed thickly furred shoulders. But it was the residents of Remould who captured William's attention. Even in the dark he could varda all sorts of gender combinations; they trolled openly and unselfconsciously, as though they, too, were part of this world, and they weren't going anywhere.

With too few beds in the "gaffercarsey"—which William discovered was a sort of dormitory-cum-community centre—the wooden floorboards were blanketed with pillows and twisted sheets, and it was nix long before snores echoed about the room. Loudest of all was Henna, who snorted a gravelly rumble louder than her two wives combined.

William thought he'd never sleep. He lay waiting as the constant twilight sank through the window, streetlamps glowing through the flimsy curtains. He ogled the mould-streaked ceiling.

Then he was sitting on the stairs. In his old house. He clutched the balustrade with tiny hands as he listened to the argument below. His mother's voice, sharp as nails. His father's thunderous boom.

And his little hands were trembling, but there were no tears. William just listened. They were angry, they were both so angry. Then his mother stormed from the front door. It slammed closed.

She was gone.

William's small heart broke. His mother was gone, and she wasn't coming back. Never. Never never never. His dad appeared, soothing, *She'll be back, William. She'll be back, William. She'll be back, William.* But it was no good. He was inconsolable; he cried out in pain.

"William. Stop that, William. Stop it, William!"

A mould-streaked ceiling. Henna was shaking him awake.

"I'm sorry," was all he could manage, his tongue sticky from sleep. "I'm sorry."

With a shake of her head, Henna rose from the mass of blankets and beckoned him to follow her. Together they traipsed down to the main room of the gaffercarsey.

He'd expected the place to be busy, but he wasn't ready for the varda before him: people—men, women, both, neither—were painting placards and buried in furious discussions. The odd few embraced, their ekes white with fear. Together, he and Henna found a free table in the far corner. Compared to all this, his own problems seemed petty. Yet they were all he could think about.

He loved Gareth. He still loved him. Not out of familiarity, not out of necessity, but for who he was. It didn't matter that they were different. He was nix perfect, but the truth was that William admired him, for being someone that he could never be.

"Do you think I'm a bad person?" he asked out loud.

For a moment Henna regarded him with a critical ogle.

"Yes."

William was taken aback.

"I mean—" she continued, "—well. Look at what people do. There are thousands of them gathered outside the walls here, wanting to tear other people from their homes. Fifty years ago this smoke was bombed to nix because people chose to follow the Nazis. The whole history of people has been *kill, suffer, kill again*. So perhaps you are a bad person. But I don't want to meet anyone who's a *good* person."

"That isn't what I meant," William countered.

"I savvy that. But perhaps it's more important than what you meant. William, I like you because you're different. You won't follow a crowd just because it's the easier thing to do."

It was the closest thing she would ever give him to a compliment, but even so he replied, "But Gareth said—"

"William. I will say this to you just once. What someone thinks about you—even someone as close to you as Gareth—is no reflection of who you are. In fact, there is no *who you are*. We're different with each person, we change with each circumstance. Maybe to Gareth you're a bad person. But to me, you're not. Isn't that enough?"

A palonie cackling in Italian came around with a tray of steaming mugs, dropping two off at their table. William cradled the hot ceramic in his fambles.

"Thank you for saying that," he cackled, as soon as they were alone again.

"Maybe you and Gareth just aren't suited to each other," Henna said. "Maybe you once were, and now you're not. Maybe when you finally had the freedom to find that out, you were just too different. Maybe it's that simple."

"Maybe you're right," William replied.

"Either way," Henna responded, rising to her feet. "There's nanti time for that now. I promise you, William, that if the people of Remould are still in their homes by this evening, then we'll talk about your relationship for a thousand years. But now, right now, we need to get busy."

44.

The past hours ran through Cissie's head as she trolled out Remould's gate; she practically floated through the streets as the sun rose. Moments came back to her one by one, like treasured snapshots.

Sam's lips on hers.

The desperate, sweeping passion as his body clung to her.

Each piece of clobber as it fell floorwards.

Stumbling over to the sofa.

His firm, sinewy body; dark curls of chest hair pressed against her skin.

His breath on her cheek.

Her tongue on his stomach.

Her tongue trailing downward.

Parting his legs.

For a moment she'd pulled back. She saw his naked body whole; his eyes caught hers. Then she dove forward, into the unknown. Her mouth between the valley of his legs. He was rough and soft; it was new. It was new and it was warm, and she'd needed it. She explored him with light flicks and then deep lunges, as though she could bury herself within him. There, she'd found herself. There, she could stay.

He gasped and cried out, thighs trembling against her cheeks.

Inside, there was no hatred. No secrets. Only the flow of bodies in easy rhythm, the heady scent of sweat, the craving, the need. All those ebbs and flows, their desire a story with no beginning nor end. His hands on every blazing inch of her.

Then his lips on hers once more.

Her breath mingling with his.

Finally, his gaze drifted. Sweaty and unfocused, he'd fallen into sleep. He'd snored softly, as Cissie held him close.

In the dark, the hard world whispered: *Howard, the kids.* So, she eased herself away from the glistening, exhausted man. She'd gathered up her clothes, and floated home.

"He's gone, Cissie."

Cissie had been drifting through her post-pleasure haze. Ms. Fortier's words didn't make any sense. Her eke was too taut, her tone too hurried, too harsh.

"What?" Cissie asked, sobering up at her old friend's panic.

"Howard," the older palonie hissed. "He's gone. He left last night with a group of men." Her voice quivered. "They were angry. I thought something had happened. I thought something had happened to you both."

"The children," Cissie gasped.

"The children are sleeping, my sweet. You don't need to worry about them."

Cissie could have collapsed with relief. Ms. Fortier guided her to the sofa and sat down, more for herself than for Cissie. Tears gleamed in the corners of her ogles, catching the dawn's light.

There was nothing else for it. Cissie told her friend everything: the trans town, the men's clothes, the odd jobs, the pleasure. As she told Ms. Fortier all she could remember, she realised that sex was the smallest way in which she'd betrayed Howard. For months she'd been leaving him, building up a life of her own, practising a version of herself which was all hers.

Yet Ms. Fortier remained composed, nodding along as she absorbed each new reality. There was no trace of shock, nor hint of judgement. Her eyes didn't so much as widen.

"That place, Cissie dear," Ms. Fortier informed her, as soon as she had finished. "Remould. It's been on the news."

She switched on the television set.

Cissie watched the flickering images with mounting, lurching horror. The threats. The speeches. The army of torch-wielding marchers, spilling around the wall which surrounded Remould. She'd known none of this—the place had been deserted when she slipped out before dawn, and there simply hadn't been time to read the news.

Worse, Sam had told her nothing.

Nausea churned her stomach. She leaned forward, her head between her legs.

"Cissie, are you all right?"

He did it to protect you, she realised. *He knew you'd insist on staying. He wanted to keep you away.*

Suddenly furious, she took a deep breath and sat up. Did he really varda her as so fragile, so weak?

"Cissie?"

"I'm fine. I'll be fine."

She stood. Light blazed outside, and the hoots and hollers of the skyway drifted in through the window.

"It's time to wake the children," she decided. "We're having a day out."

45.

They trolled together through Remould's perpetual twilight. The procession was led by a handsome Black homie, and as they reached the main street they were joined by pairs and groups from every doorway. A people ready to repel invasion, however futile it might be.

"Come out, come out, defend your town!" the leading homie called, over and over, as though entrancing people from their homes. As they emerged, some had banners, some had cameras, some even played instruments.

William marched alongside Henna, Ramona, and Kara, William's lips a striking red. Before they'd left the gaffercarsey Kara had approached, the tube held out like an offering—and in a sense, it was. William's eke burned as she carefully applied the lipstick to his moey, and varding the impromptu makeover, one of Remould's residents had then proffered dark liquid ogleliner. With a nod William consented, admiring the work in a compact mirror once the fatcha was applied. Finally, a young homiepalonie asked if they could switch shirts, and once more William relented—nix, accepted—because, despite everything, this bijou joy was something to celebrate. A pink, partially transparent blouse.

But it wasn't about the clothes. It wasn't about the makeup. They were nix more than symbols for what William felt inside. The fluid, confusing, wonderful absence where maleness would be. As they'd left the gaffercarsey, William finally savvied that acting like one of the lads had always been impossible.

They had never been a lad.

Now they trolled in a huddled mass through Remould. It was a strange, fractured occasion; part furious protest, part carnival. Neither homie nor palonie, William was nix different here—they were simply part of the crowd, even if that crowd stood out from the rest of the world.

271

Even so, they marvelled at how shabby Remould was: how pocked the streets, how scarred the buildings. For a moment they wondered why anyone would defend something so ramshackle, a place which seemed so fragile, where a grand concrete overpass blocked out the light. But it nix mattered. They could *feel* the love held for these streets with the stomping of feet; they could nell it screamed from a thousand lungs.

There was power in that sense of belonging—they could finally see it.

"Slow down! Slow down!"

The reverie lifted as the crowd neared the gate. They could ogle the mob beyond the wall, the elated, furious ekes of the enemy. William half expected to see Gareth, but there wasn't a familiar face among them. The opposing throng chanted with religious passion, waving torches high above their heads, alongside signs reading *GAYS FOR GAYS* and *LESBIAN NOT QUEER!*

Henna took one famble, a stranger the other. The group of men and women and neithers and everythings took each other's hands, forming chain after chain, a human barrier.

Then they waited.

46.

Cissie hurried along the skyway: Thomas' famble in her left, Jonah's in her right, Ms. Fortier just behind. The sunlight stung her tired eyes and clung to her skin. She kept walking. She didn't know what her plan was, but she needed to be there. She needed to be in Remould.

They were only briefly stalled: the boys were hungry, so Cissie stopped to buy brightly coloured ice creams, with two miniature rainbow flags for them to wave with sticky fingers. Otherwise, they didn't slow until the morning sun's glare was dimmed by the huge bridge above Remould.

They found themselves at the edge of a mob. The air was soaked with guilty tension, like a crowd before an execution.

"Excuse me." Clasping her children's hands tightly, Cissie tried to press her way through the gaps between the bodies, but it was no use. The mass blocked the way.

"Oh!" Ms. Fortier cried, delicately clutching her chest with one famble, a low moan wafting from her throat.

"Ohhhhhh."

For a moment Cissie panicked, until she caught the glint of mischief in her neighbour's ogle. Bellowing with authority, Cissie cried out, "Let us through! This woman needs medical help, let us through!"

The crowd parted with biblical force as the old palonie stumbled forward. Cissie grasped the boys to her sides.

"We need to get her to a doctor! Let us through!"

"I'm a nurse!" a voice called. Cissie ignored it. Bodies pressed in around them, with chanted words thundering from all sides, the energy building with the tension of a summer storm. The crowd was packed tighter and tighter, and still Cissie pushed forward, onward, until suddenly she, Ms. Fortier, and the children were at the front of the mob.

A huge wooden stage loomed, with Remould's gate behind. Beyond the gate she glimpsed the other group, the familiar faces of Remould's residents. But she couldn't see Sam.

Both crowds roared as a smartly dressed man approached the platform. He was too assured, too confident. Cissie took an instant dislike to his swagger, to the melodramatic way he cleared his throat.

Her children squealed and waved their little flags. Then the audience hushed.

"Homies and palonies," the man onstage began, his voice booming through the microphone.

47.

"We are gathered here because we are family. We are kin. We are fellow fruits. Yes, fruits!"

Howard peered from the window. Kenneth Luvvie.

He had a clear view of the degenerate.

His hands shook. Hell, his whole body shook.

But bravery isn't the absence of fear; bravery is acting in spite of it.

"See, fruit is the point. Fruit allows trees, plants, and bushes to propagate and thrive. It could even be cackled that the production of fruit is the pinnacle of the plant's existence—its most important, most precious commodity."

An image flashed through his mind: he was up a ladder, the moment he'd met Cissie.

The most beautiful girl he'd ever seen.

His family. His boys. He would do anything to protect them. Did they know how much he loved them?

His heart was full.

"So what? you might cackle in return. The fruits of arborage are hardly the same thing spat at us in hettie streets, or printed about us in hettie newspapers. But you see, there you'd be wrong once again. For like fruit, we are the pinnacle of our species' existence, proud among drab leaves."

It was almost time.

The cold steel in his hands calmed him.

His brothers were in place, just the same.

He was ready. He was ready he was ready he was ready.

"Perhaps you don't believe me. Then consider some of the best minds of the 20th century: Walt Whitman, Alan Turing, Andy Warhol. Sally Ride, James Baldwin, Marcel Proust, Gertrude Stein, Christopher Isherwood, George Ives—bear with me while I catch my breath—Virginia Woolf,

Tennessee Williams, Gore Vidal, Clay Aiken, Alan Ginsberg, John Maynard Keynes, Susan B. Anthony. Who savvies how many we could list, were we not attacked and battyfanged, if we'd been given full reign to be ourselves?"

Howard peered through the scope at the man onstage, felt his finger on the trigger.

It was so sure, so certain.

Too little in life is.

"Open your ogles! We can even troll back to the ancient world: Alexander of Macedon, Hatshepsut of Egypt, Socrates, Sappho, Aristotle. It doesn't matter when or where we charper. Hadrian, Caligula, Nero, Caesar!"

He checked his watch.

A few more moments.

"Gloria! It doesn't even matter if you call us fruits or not. Whether ladies, homos, fairies, queens, punks, or faggots, it doesn't matter! The hettie world pushes us down, because otherwise we rise above, high above them. Because the sweet truth is . . ."

No more thinking. Howard raised the gun, as he had a hundred times in practice. Only this time, he squeezed the trigger—

—and fired.

48.

Even at midday, the bar was jammed. Guys spilled out onto the rooftop—some in T-shirts, some in bijou glittery shorts, most of them drunk. It was bona, because the last thing Gareth wanted was to think. This way he could keep busy, stick to his work. And he did, darting about the butterfly-decorated bevvie serving ales, Maytree Mules, G&Ts, red wine spritzers. He ducked and dove 'round Björn as they served the mass of drunken homies. Now and then his friend caught his ogle, pulling a silly eke to cheer him up.

He was bona, was Björn. A real cove. He accepted what was, and what wasn't. He never asked too many questions.

Whiskey sodas, pink lemonade, a Palm Springs iced tea. There was so much chatter he couldn't nell the music. He was just mixing a Raw Paw Slinger when Björn nuzzled his neck with his nose.

Gareth laughed. Björn'd said something, but now the guests were singing, the melody spreading one by one through the whole bar. It was just some old track by some old diva, but it was hard not to get in the mood. So, Gareth sang too, though normally he wouldn't, and he only did 'cause no one would hear him above all the rest.

It felt good. For a moment it felt bona just to be lost in the words. To be singing as one.

Tequila, champagne, a Flora Fog. The song ended and once again the sadness spread. He ached for William. Constantly. He missed his friend and lover with a sting that wouldn't leave.

Cosmopolitans, raspberry daiquiris, a fuzzy navel. As he poured out shots of schnapps, he let himself think of William once again, just for a second, 'cause after all—

Gareth didn't see the flash. He didn't hear the blast as it burst through the packed bar, nor the roar of charring flame. He didn't see the bathroom mirrors shatter as the outer walls crumbled. He didn't feel the skin torn from his flesh, nor the flesh from his bones. He was gone by the time the roof collapsed, as concrete rained down upon the bodies, burying them all.

49.

The man onstage tumbled to the ground.

There were screams. Everywhere, screams and stomping feet. Cissie scooped Jonah up and grabbed Thomas' hand. They had to run. But where?

Shots rang from the sky; a man fell down. She fled the other way, clutching the children. Every second meant danger, each second could be the last. People fled everywhere.

Which way?

Which way?

Pick one!

"It's all right," she said, maybe whispering, maybe screaming, her words muted in all the chaos. "It's going to be all right."

She watched her feet; *don't fall, don't get trampled.*

They passed the stage, its boards glistening. Someone collided with her, nearly knocking Jonah from her arms. Cissie turned to push the stranger away, but the stranger sank to her knees, blood spilling over her clothes.

"It's all right," Cissie repeated, the words meaningless but more important than any she'd ever said. "I swear to God, it's going to be all right." She elbowed on, away, away.

Up above, birds spiraled.

Where was Ms. Fortier? Where was Sam? She pushed onward, onward, through Remould's gates. People fled down the streets, but she found the familiar lanes, she knew where to go.

"It's going to be all right."

Down the main street. Past the door to Sam's apartment. She couldn't feel her body as she staggered on, her arms and legs light as air.

There was only the will. Her will. On, on, on.

She reached the gaffercarsey. The doors wide open. She plunged inside.

"Cissie!"

Sam took Jonah from her arms. Only now she heard his screaming. Exhausted, her legs buckled. She fell to the floor.

50.

They saw Luvvie die;
a crimson flower blooming
from his salt-and-pepper head.
Gareth.
William had to reach Gareth.
They'd always rescued each other.
But: a woman.
Sprawled over the ground.
Grey hair across her face.
Arms shaking as she tried, tried, to push herself up.
They grasped her by the armpits; dragged her from the churning crowd.
They hid behind the stage.
My sweet! she cried. *The children!*
Sssssssssh, William hushed. *Sssssssssh*.
Their ogles met; she was quiet.
Gareth!
But as William rose,
she yanked their sleeve,
and pulled them down.
No! she spat. *Wait. Wait.*
So they took each other's hands
and listened to the screams
and shots
until,
finally,
finally,
there was quiet.
William let the woman go, and ran.

51.

Cissie woke knowing her life had changed for good.

"The children! Thomas, Jonah, where are they? Where are they?"

"Hush," a familiar voice soothed. Sam's eke. "They're all right. You're all right."

Her head throbbed. Her skin was tight with dried tears. Soon the blurry world shifted into focus.

The gaffercarsey. The tables had all been shunted to the walls, freeing space for injured bodies. Some people dashed to and fro, splinting legs broken in the stampede, calming those in shock. Others simply stared into space.

"Thomas," Cissie croaked. "Jonah."

Then she saw them—at the far end of the bar, Fiorella held one on each knee, softly reading a storybook to them. It was a miracle, but Jonah was engrossed, reading the words along with her. Thomas stared at the ground. Gone was his boyish bravado. He looked small and lost.

Cissie staggered to her feet; Sam caught her arm and helped her up. Slowly, they trolled across the room toward Fiorella and the boys. Cissie wrapped her chavvies in her arms, holding on as tight as she could. Usually they'd squirm to get away, but not that day, not at all.

She had no idea how long they cuddled together, but the room was a little darker by the time they pulled apart.

"Where's Dad?" Thomas asked.

It was then a sickening suspicion swelled, deep in her stomach.

"Sam. This might sound strange, but I have to go. I need you to watch the children, just for a couple hours. Can you do that for me? Please?"

"Anything."

His grin was wide as ever, but it was all for show. His ogles mirrored her own, reflecting her horror.

It was unreal, how normal the apartment looked. There were still toys about the floor and dishes in the sink. It could have been any night. Any normal, boring night.

There was no sign of Howard.

She could still be imagining things, she told herself. Trolling over to the kitchen, she set out a pan and started preparing cocoa. Then she abandoned it sitting cold on the stove and reached for Howard's scotch. She swigged straight from the bottle, carried it to the sofa, turned on the TV.

The attack was all over the news. Nothing was censored; they showed the bloodied bodies scattered outside Remould. She relived the shooting. People fleeing everywhere. Two opposing crowds became a single terrified mass.

There had been bombs. Eight of them, one for each gay and lesbian and queer district, detonated all at once. The screen showed piles of rubble, crimson soaking through the gaps. Emergency crews hauling broken bricks.

She couldn't take it; she turned off the set. Her gaze unfocused and thoughts scattered everywhere. The scotch grew warm between her fingers.

There she waited until she heard the key in the front door. For a single moment she clung to one last fragment of hope: perhaps he had gone out and got drunk. Perhaps he'd cheated on her. Anything. Anything but this.

There stood Howard, haggard and hunched, a large holdall in his hands. The moment she saw him, she knew. She knew.

"Howard." He barely seemed to register her. "Howard," she implored.

He dropped the holdall and glanced up at her, eyes shining with—what was it? Fear? Guilt?

Then it was gone. He was striding toward the bathroom. The door clicked and locked behind him. Cissie listened to the rush of water, the sloshing as he cleaned himself, before she trolled over to the bag. Unzipped it. Saw the dark metal.

The bathroom door opened once more. Howard was naked, a towel wrapped around his waist. The empty shape of the man who'd shot at people. Who'd shot at her children.

"Howard," she tried again.

He walked past her and into the bedroom, closing the door behind him. He hadn't acknowledged her because he couldn't. He couldn't face her.

Cissie had already made her decision. She walked over to the telephone, picked up the receiver, and dialled the three-digit number. Her hands shook.

She knew Howard would never surrender to the police. When they came, he would fight. He would die.

Once the call was done, she started making breakfast. It was past midnight, but she wanted him to wake to the smell of coffee and the sizzling of bacon. She didn't even flinch as the police burst through the door, shards of wood falling to the carpet, a mess she would never clean up.

One held a gun on her. She simply raised her hands and said, calmly as she could,

"He's in the room on the right."

The man with the gun nodded. Yet he kept his weapon trained on her. He motioned to the others. They kicked open the bedroom door, the room she'd shared for so many years, screaming at Howard to stay still.

He hollered back, a cornered animal. Cissie ogled nothing, but knew he was lunging at them, a last desperate act.

Then, gunshots.

On the stove, the bacon burned. So too the eggs. Just out of sight, her husband bled onto the bedroom carpet.

The handcuffs were cold and tight, but she didn't care. Though she knew she'd never see the apartment again, she didn't look back. She couldn't see the point.

INTO THE FAR VARDA

The Gay Republic

September 1999

52.

"Do you need us to go in with you?"

The offer was bona. The offer was kind. But William savvied this was best done alone. Alone was something they were getting used to.

"No. Thank you, but no."

Even so, Henna, Ramona, and Kara waited on the doorstep as William stepped inside the cottage. The place which had been the young homiepalonie's home just weeks before.

William had run toward the bar, once the shooting had stopped. The transit networks were down, and few roads were open to traffic. Everywhere, Lilly Law had swarmed the streets, erecting cordons and barriers, telling people to troll home. Yet William ran on. Would Gareth be pleased to see them? By that point they simply hadn't cared. If Gareth was safe, that would be enough. That was all they needed.

William had run to the bar, but the bar wasn't there. At first, they thought they'd got the address wrong. There was only a police line, the ambulances and fire engines, and beyond those, a mass of crumbled concrete and twisted steel. Rubble flowed, like foam from beer.

Cut short, the elevated rail line dangled midair, pointing toward the wreckage.

Across the city, a thousand hearts were crushed; debris was cleared, and shattered lives swept away. What could be done with so much pain?

William hadn't wept, not then nor in the following days, when they'd stayed in the gaffercarsey with Henna and her wives. The loss was too big to varda. They felt nix as they identified Gareth's charred wallet, his mangled keys—then signed a form confirming the death. Even then, they couldn't grasp it.

Only the rooftop carsey was real. The one the two had shared together, the one William now entered.

There, everything was the same. The wonky standing lamp drunkenly leaning in the corner. The rickety bookcase which had been lying, unclaimed, outside their building. The musty linens Gareth had found at a flea market, and which William had washed and hung on the walls. Even the sofa bed was still pulled out, strewn with twisted sheets.

This was all that was left. This was all they'd made together.

"I thought I'd see you again," William said out loud, their lone voice echoing through the room.

They spoke without meaning to. They spoke with no one to hear.

"I just assumed there'd be another time. That there was always later."

They drew a deep breath, long and slow, inhaling the musty and familiar. They sat down, perching on the edge of the sofa bed.

"I didn't say everything I wanted to, that last time I vardad you. When you shouted. When I left. I'm so naff at speaking up—it's just easier to run away, and let the running speak for itself. See, I savvy how to run. But I don't savvy how to say difficult, painful things. Especially not to you, Gareth."

William's head was between their hands. They growled, anger swelling from their stomach.

"Fuck. *Fuck.* I'm never going to see you again; I'm never going to say the things I wanted to say. But you did, didn't you? You had your chance, you got it all out of your system."

They didn't know where this rage came from, nor how much of it they held inside.

"Well here's what I wanted to say, for all the good it'll do. You thought I was never happy anywhere, that I never would be. But for all my faults, at least I was always *me*. You changed yourself so much that I've no idea who you really were. Oh, I know, I know, you had to survive. We all do. Tell me, Gareth—was it a success? Was it all worth it?"

Now, they were shouting, their throat raw.

"Where did it get you, Gareth? Where the fuck are you now?"

William didn't even notice the door open, not until Henna touched his shoulder.

···

They'd wanted to fuss over him, particularly Ramona, who remained convinced she could feed away any pain. But William couldn't. Not just now. Instead, they rode the hanging train for hours at a time, alone, in circles, the seats plastered with newspapers which bore all the aftershocks of the attack.

Beneath the huge concrete bridge, Remould was in mourning; the dusk was that bijou bit darker, the clothes and lanterns held less sparkle. The trans town was safe, for now, but the cost had been paid in friends, neighbours, lovers. Everybody had lost somebody. But as always life went on, pausing only for an afternoon's memorial.

The gaffercarsey was crowded by the time William and the three wives arrived. They stood near the back as the room hushed for a moment's silence. Then a tired-varding manly introduced as Sam took the stage, fresh lines creasing around his ogles.

"Does anyone here have anything to say? About someone they knew, someone they cared about?"

William felt Henna's famble on the bijou of their back. They nodded, and Sam beckoned them up onto the stage.

There William stood, facing a hundred grieving people. Reaching into their pocket, they took out a small photograph. It had been taken back in Brighton, them and Gareth cheek to cheek, dazzled by the flash. They vardad happy together. William gently stroked the image of their friend and lover.

They tried to keep calm. They tried not to cry.

Breathe, William. Breathe.

But it was no use. William choked on grief, their whole body shaking. They couldn't keep it together. It was all broken, and though they could carry on and the pain would fade, it would still always be there, a part of them that would never be fixed. They brought a trembling wrist to their cheek, smearing the tears rather than wiping them away.

Sam placed a famble on William's shoulder.

"I'm sorry," William choked.

But Sam just shook his head, drawing William into a hug, sharing their sorrow. It only made them sob harder, echoing across the room as their chest burned, as their nose streamed.

There was the nell of chairs scraping, of feet ascending the stage. Henna spread an arm around William's quaking shoulders, and she, too, held them as they heaved. A stranger reached out: their hand found William's left, squeezing gently. Another found their right.

William squeezed back as more and more lacoddies wrapped themselves around them. In the embrace of strangers, they let grief overwhelm.

All fruits are family.

And so they cried. There were no sneers. There was no laughter. Only simple gestures to soothe the pain, the outrage, all the hurt they couldn't hold in.

For once, William felt at home.

They belonged.

53.

She gave them the names and described their ekes, everything she could remember, even the Bibles and the cardigans. It wasn't like in the movies; no bright sparkle shined in her ogles, there were no funny mind games. The police just seemed tired and ordinary, and Cissie grew used to the bland white room with its cheap plastic chairs.

Time floated by without recollection. They assured her the children were fine, but for now they needed the bona facts. No flies.

The bed in her cell was hard and cold. She never slept. She simply ate and talked, ate and talked, moving from small room to small room. How could anything be real in such a place? They never alluded to Howard's death.

Then all of a sudden, it was over. She was to wait in the reception area for the children. They would be brought to her. She drank cheap coffee and waited.

"Mommy!" Jonah squealed, scampering down the corridor, hurling himself into her lap. Thomas trailed behind—a little slower, but no less pleased. Behind them were the adults. Sam. Ms. Fortier. Rob. Exhaustion lined their ekes, but they brightened at the sight of her.

Cissie buried her face in Jonah's hair, inhaling the scent of his scalp as she had when he was a baby. She kissed Thomas' cheek, and he didn't wipe it away.

"Were you really in jail, Mom?" he asked, his voice tinged with awe.

"Just for a little bit."

She held them close. They would have questions, ones she didn't know how to answer, but for now there was bliss.

• • •

"It's *charming*," Ms. Fortier ambiguously declared, once they reached Remould. Her face shifted with the lights: neon and gas lamps, the red sparkle above an ordinary doorway. "Though to be honest, my sweet, it reminds me of places I'd rather forget."

Cissie nodded. Ahead strode Rob and Sam, the children riding their shoulders.

"I don't want to forget anything," Cissie admitted. "I hate Howard. And I miss him. To be honest, I don't really know what to feel, but I know I don't want to forget. I don't want to forget any of it."

"And you shouldn't," Ms. Fortier declared. For a while they cackled nothing, watching the children as they waved their warms and screeched *giddyup!* while treating the men like horses.

"The police asked again and again what I knew. What I saw. I mean, you noticed something, but I just . . ." Cissie trailed off, stopping entirely as the children and their mounts rode on. "Do you think I'm naïve?" she asked.

The older palonie took a moment to light a cigarette.

"You know," she began, spilling a cloud of pale grey smoke from her lips, "before I met you, I was comfortable with myself, with my apartment, letting the world do what it wants."

She paused.

"But I really believe that these days I am a little wiser, that I have a little more courage. And that is because of you, Cissie dear. Your curiosity provoked me, it made me less complacent, and less afraid. Always, I hope we are friends. I want you to know that any time you need me, I am with you."

Cissie reached out and embraced her.

"Be careful, my dear," Ms. Fortier gasped, as she wheezed out another cloud of smoke. "I'm held together with stubbornness and tar."

Somehow, they laughed. After glancing all around to see no one was watching, Cissie stole a drag of her cigarette, the smoke spiralling into the warm fall breeze.

"They're getting away," she motioned to the others as they shrank ever smaller.

"Just one more moment," Ms. Fortier fambled Cissie's sleeve. "You know, they both spoke to me, when you were with the police. The American wants to take you back to—"

"Ohio," Cissie prompted.

"Wherever that is. He says he can arrange a place for you and the boys to stay, set up a new life. Yet the other one thinks you should remain here, in this very neighbourhood. They each want to know what you will do. But I am selfish, my sweet. I need to know first."

"I have to go away." She wasn't certain until she saw the disappointment on Sam's eke. It was small compensation, but she leaned across the couch and kissed his lips. Soft and warm. "I just can't stay here."

"Because of what your husband did?" Sam asked, taking her hand. "Cissie, you could change your name, no one would know, no one who mattered."

"It's not that. I mean, someone would find out, sooner or later, and the poor children . . . What I mean is, it's not *just* that."

"What else is there?" His famble tightened around hers.

Cissie gazed from his window as it shimmered with the lights of the street below. Water sprinkled down from above—a leaky pipe, perhaps, or a neighbour spraying plants. Bright droplets formed against the glass, smearing the colours as they danced down the pane, forming new patterns with each trail.

"It's that, for once, I want to run. I want to run away. And not straight into a lover's arms, but somewhere there's no one to catch me. Whatever happens, I want to know that I made my own decision. That the life I'm living is one I built for myself."

"And where might that be?"

"I've no idea. But Ms. Fortier has already agreed to go with me."

Sam nodded as a cheeky grin grew across his eke.

"I'm sure that'll be interesting."

He kissed her cheek; his way of showing that she was his cove, first and foremost.

A friend.

...

When she was a little girl, Cissie had read picture books all about dishy princes and dolly princesses—but nix fantasy had ever prepared her for the fruit smoke. For the last time she trolled the towering crisscross streets of Hetcarsey, soaking in the shabby grandeur. She still marvelled at the nells, at the dizzying array of lives above and around her.

The balconies and their rows of dripping laundry; the cackles and catcalls in a hundred Polaris; the neon and printed and famble-painted signs, coating every blank surface as they zhooshed burlesque shows and suicide hotlines and international phone cards.

She saw it all through new ogles.

It wasn't only her who'd been altered: in all the chaos the outcasts had been front and centre, and a few tentative voices had spoken in sympathy. She trolled past two men, a bear and twink strolling famble-in-famble without a care in the world. One or two shopkeepers ogled, but nix was said. They could read the changing times.

Curries and kebabs, won ton soups and matzoh balls, scents spilled from greasy windows and roadside kiosks. Whole cultures swallowed through the nose. She wandered, drinking in all she could varda, imprinting it on her memory. She hoped the children would remember this place; perhaps one would even return, someday. Cissie wouldn't mind if they liked boys. Honestly, she'd never quite savvied what all the fuss was about.

And herself? She was worried for the future, and no flies, but excited, nonetheless. She was a friend, and a mother, but aside from that she could troll anywhere and do anything. Maybe she could cut her hair and don overalls, working with her hands, feeling that satisfying ache at the end of each day.

It was her life, after all.

TIMELINE OF THE GAY REPUBLIC

1600s

"Parlyaree" develops as a slang among carnival performers. The slang is adapted by homosexual theatre actors, creating Early Polari. Polari becomes common in the "molly houses" (meeting places for homosexual men) of the early 1700s.

February 1726

Police raid Mother Clap's molly house in London. Though the raid is routine, the patrons fight back, marching through the streets in what is known as the "Molly Revolt." All participants are executed.

1800s

Secret clubs and societies of homosexuals are established in most major European and North American cities. Many are raided, often revealing participation by well-known personalities and political figures.

June 1888

Jane Addams, Oscar Wilde, and Karl Heinrich Ulrich co-publish *The Homosexual Haven*. The treatise calls for a homosexual homeland and is derided throughout the heterosexual press.

1914-1918

World War I changes the face of Europe, particularly Germany, which forms a federal democracy known as the Weimar Republic.

1918-1933

The Weimar Republic's lenient stance on homosexuality draws huge numbers of gay men and women to Berlin—

by the end of the Weimar era there are approximately one million gay residents (almost one quarter of the total population). Thousands of gay bars are opened. Magnus Hirschfeld establishes the Institute for Sexual Research, and in 1931 the first sex change surgery is performed.

23 March 1933
The German Reichstag passes the Enabling Act, allowing Adolf Hitler to rule by decree. With near-total control, the Nazis establish the Third Reich, headquartered in Berlin. The city sees mass demonstrations, which are subdued by force.

8 August 1933
Following Nazi attempts to shut down the popular gay Eldorado Night Club in Berlin's Schöneberg, an unidentified trans resident attacks an SA officer, sparking the Schöneberg Revolt. Thousands riot, first gathering at Nollendorfplatz and then destroying local Nazi party offices.

16 August 1933
The hundreds of thousands of residents marching through the streets are organised into brigades, beginning a campaign of guerrilla warfare against the Nazi administration. The Nazis are driven first from Schöneberg, and then Tiergarten.

28 February 1934
The Nazi government officially relocates to the Bavarian city of Munich. The gay brigades declare Berlin an independent city-state.

1934-1939
Berlin is the target of thousands of aerial and artillery bombardments by the Third Reich. The city remains

independent of Nazi control, though much of it is reduced to rubble.

1939-1947
World War II. With the Nazi forces focusing on their Western and Eastern fronts, Berlin remains depopulated and is largely ignored. On 5 November 1946 the city of London is devastated by a Nazi atomic bomb. The British government falls. The Allies—now consisting of just the United States and Soviet Union—liberate mainland Europe after a bloody and protracted campaign.

23 April 1947
Hitler commits suicide in his bombproof shelter in Munich. Two days later German forces surrender, ending the war in Europe. Germany is occupied by US and Soviet forces.

1 May 1948
The United Nations Plan for European Stability is implemented by the United States and the Soviet Union. The Plan dismantles the German state, dividing it into sixteen separate entities. Berlin is formally established as an independent city, and following an intense lobbying campaign, administrative duties are granted to the ruling gay brigades. The first homosexual refugees arrive.

7 August 1948
The city formally declares independence, officially establishing itself as the Gay Republic of Berlin. A federal constitution is drafted, with powers shared between the gay male Senate and the lesbian Assembly.

September 1948
Hundreds of thousands of Berliners are assigned categories, and the city is subdivided into seven districts. A council of architects and urban planners oversees plans

to create the world's first "vertical city," fit to house an unprecedented number of migrants. The project is known as the "Grand Say Oney."

17 October 1948
The first elections are held. Conservative parties are victorious: The Gay Patriotic League is the largest party in the Senate, while its sister party, The Demetan Union, dominates the Assembly. Trans groups are officially identified as subversive. Bisexuality is outlawed.

1949-1950
The categories into which residents are assigned become more stringent: a series of laws are passed by the Senate and the Assembly denoting exact criteria, information which is not released to the public. Those who fail to conform to a particular category join slums outside the central districts (later known as "Hetcarsey," "Gajo," and "Q").

12 December 1951
The Polari Grand Carsey is established to regulate Polari vocabulary and terminology.

November 1952
The first stage of construction for the seven central districts is completed. This three-dimensional network of transit lines, streets, and skyways is later identified as "hi-urban." Unofficial neighbourhoods rise alongside them, with construction firms taking advantage of the intense demand for housing.

1952-1953
Newspapers stir controversy over an alleged influx of migrants lying about their sexual orientation in order to gain citizenship, leading to a public outcry. Bisexual,

queer, and trans groups are accused of aiding in the "dilution" of the Gay Republic.

12 June 1953
The Migrant and Asylum Act is passed. Same-sex marriage becomes a requirement for full citizenship.

29 May 1954
The movie *Am I Not a Stranger?* is released. Starring Rock Hudson, it follows the story of a bigamous gangster who moves to the slum district of "Q" with both a husband and a wife.

28 June 1969
Bisexual groups undertake a series of protests in the "Q" district, which devolve into civil unrest (later known as the "Fencestander Riots"). Under pressure from left-leaning groups in both the Senate and Assembly, bisexuality is legalised exactly one month later, on 28 July 1969.

1981-1982
Berlin's Ministry of Health releases a report detailing an increase in rare cancers and infections in young gay men, particularly in the district of Twinkstadt. By the end of 1981, 500 people have died, rising to 18,000 by the end of 1982. The disease is first referred to as Disrupted Immune System Syndrome (DISS) by the Ministry of Health.

1983-1987
The death toll reaches the millions. Intense urban riots and political instability provoke a series of governmental collapses. Amid the confusion, NGOs and citizens' initiatives establish care centres, shelters, hospices, and support networks for the afflicted. This period becomes known as the "Great Embrace" ("Fantabulosa Aruma").

The situation stabilises by the summer of 1987.

5 February 1985
The Ministry of Culture releases its Media Production
Code (also known as the "Luvvie Code"), regulating
published and broadcast works in order to ensure they
"don't undermine gay or lesbian identity."

1987-1991
Having experienced severe unrest due to government
inaction in the face of the DISS crisis, many of the planet's
gay ghettos attempt to secede in order to join the
Gay Republic—a process known as the "Great Break"
("Fantabulosa Exita"). Many are successful, though some
only after protracted civil conflict. A few, such as Palm
Springs, California, later return to their former nation-
state.

1990s
Owing to poor housing conditions and a lack of political
representation, the outer districts of Q, Hetcarsey,
and Gajo see continual civil disorder. In response to
increasing threats from queer terrorist groups, the trans
neighbourhood of "Remould"—long thought to be the
epicentre of such movements—is surrounded by an eight-
kilometre-long wall.

GLOSSARY

From the Official Dictionary
of the Polari Grand Carsey

Content warning:

The vocabulary listed below is taken from the historical slang and may contain phrases which are offensive. Terms and definitions listed in italics have been invented for the purposes of this novel.

Numbers

Medza—1/2
Una; oney—one
Dooey—two
Tray—three
Quarter—four
Chinker—five
Say—six
Say oney; setter—seven
Say dooey; otter—eight
Say tray; nobber—nine
Daiture—ten
Long dedger; lepta—eleven
Kenza—twelve

Words and Phrases

AC/DC—a couple; bisexual
Acqua—water
Acting dickey—temporary work
Affair—relationship
Ajax—adjacent
Alamo—I'm attracted to you

Almond rocks—socks

Amore—love

And no flies—that's the truth

Andro dyke—lesbian who isn't masculine or feminine

Antique HP—old man

Arctophile—person friendly to bears

Aris—arse

Arthur—masturbate

Aruma—embrace (from Yiddish 'Arumnem')

Arva—have sex

Aspra—woman sex worker

Aspro—man sex worker

Aunt nell—listen

Aunt nells—ears

Aunt nelly flakes—earrings

Auntie—older gay man

B-flat omee—overweight man

Baby dyke—inexperienced lesbian

Back slums—dark room

Badge cove—pensioner

Bagaga—penis

Baloney—nonsense

Barbie—a scatter-brained drag queen

Barclays—to masturbate

Barkey—sailor

Barnet—hair; head

Barney—fight

Basket—man's crotch

Bat—dance; shoe; foot

Batter—sex work

Battery—attack

Battery carsey—knock on a door

Battyfang—attack; destroy

Beak—a judge

Beancove—young gay man

Bedroom—somewhere suitable for sex

Beef curtains—labia
Ben—good
Benar—better
Bencove—good friend
Betty Bracelets—police
Beverada—alcoholic drink
Bevvie—bar
Bevvy—to drink
Bevvy omee—drunkard
Bexleys—teeth
Beyonek—a shilling
Bibi—bisexual
Bijou—little
Billingsgate—swearing; woman
Billy doo—love letter
Bimbo—gullible person
Binco—kerosene flare
Bingey—penis
Bins—glasses (spectacles)
Bitaine—sex worker
Bitch—snarky gay man; complain
Bit of hard—male sex partner
Blag—hook up
Bloke—man
Blocked—to be high
Blow—oral sex on a man
BMQ—Black Market Queen (closeted)
Bod—male body
Bodega—grocery shop
Bolus—chemist
Bold—brazen
Bona—right; good
Bona nochy—good night
Bona vardering—good looking
Bonar for—excellent
Bonaroo—attracted to

Bones—partner

Booth—room

Bougereau—flamboyant

Box—buttocks

Boyno—hello

Brads—money

Brainless—good

Brandy—buttocks

Brandy latch—toilet

Bugle—nose

Bungery—pub

Bunny fuck—quick sex

Butch—masculine; lesbian

Buvare—a drink

Cabouche—car

Cackle—talk; tell

Cackling fart—egg

Camisa—shirt

Camp—effeminate

Capella—hat

Cant—talk

Caravansera—train station

Carnish—food

Carnish ken—restaurant

Caroon—crown (defunct currency)

Carsey—house; apartment; toilet; brothel

Carts—genitals

Catever—bad

Cats—trousers

Cavaliers and roundheads—circumcised and
    uncircumcised

Caxton—wig

Chant—sing

Charper—seek

Charpering carsey—police station; prison

Charpering omi—policeman

Charver—sex
Charvering donna—woman sex worker
Chaud—penis
Chavvie—child; son
Chemmie—shirt; blouse
Cherry—man's virginity
Chicken—hot young man
Church Times—a gay publication
Clean the cage out—oral sex on a woman
Clean the kitchen—rimming
Clear—100% gay/lesbian
Clevie—vagina
Climb the slanging tree—perform onstage
Clobber—clothing
Cod—wrong; bad
Coddy—bad; body
Cods—testicles
Cold calling—looking for company in a pub or bar
Colin—erection
Colosseum curtains—foreskin
Colour of his eyes—penis size
Commision—large shirt
Corybungus—buttocks
Cossy—clothes; costume
Cottage—public toilet
Cottaging—sex in public
Cove—friend
Crimper—hairdresser; barber
Crocus—doctor
Cruise—look for sex
Cull—testicle; idiot
Curtain—foreskin
Daffy—drunk on gin
Dally—kind; gentle
Dash—leave quickly
Deaner—shilling (defunct currency)

Dear—friendly but patronising term of affection
Deek—see
Delph—teeth
Dhobie—wash
Dickey—workplace
Diddle—gin
Diesel—masculine lesbian
(the) Dilly—Piccadilly Circus
Dilly boy—male sex worker
Dinarly—money
Dinari—money
Dinero—money
Dinge—Black
Dish—arse; attractive man
Dish the dirt—gossip
Dizzy—scatter-brained
Do a turn—have sex
Do the rights—get revenge
Doll house—drag club
Dolly—beautiful; lovely; intelligent and
    attractive youth
Dona—woman
Don't be strange—don't hold back
Doob—pill
Dorcas—someone who cares
Dosh—money
Dowry—much
Drag—clothes
Drag up—wear women's clothing
Drage—pull hard
Drear—dreary
Dress up—a bad drag queen
Drogle—dress
Dubes—pills
Duke—rich gay woman
Duchess—rich gay man

Ducky—darling
Dyke—lesbian
Ear fakes—earrings
Ecaf—face
Eke—face
Efink—knife
Eine—London
Emag—game
Ends—hair
Esong—nose
-ette—diminutive suffix
Fab—fabulous
Fabel—good
Fabulosa—fabulous
Facha—face
Factory equipped—biological male
Fake—do; make; erection; false
Fakement—thing; action
Fakements—jewellery; accessories
Fake riah—wig
Famble—hand; *feel; hold*
Famble cheat—ring
Fambles—gloves
Fang carsey—dental surgery
Fang faker—dentist
Fang crocus—dentist
Fangs—teeth
Fantabulosa—great; excellent
Far varda—distance; future
Farting crackers—trousers
Fashioned—fake
Fashioned riah—wig
Fatcha—face; apply makeup
Feele—girl; child
Feelia—girl
Feeliers—girls; children

Feely—young; child

Feely ome—young man

Fellier—girl; child

Ferricadooza—knock down

Filiome—underage youth

Filly—pretty

Fish—woman; feminine

Flagging—handkerchief code

Flange—vagina; walk

Flatties—audience of men; onlookers

Flies—lies

Flowery—accommodation

Flowery dell—prison cell

Fogle—handkerchief

Fogle hunter—pickpocket

Fogus—tobacco

Foofs—breasts

Fortuni—beautiful

Frock—dress

Fruit—gay man

Full eke—wearing makeup

Fungue—old man; beard

Funt—pound (currency)

Gaffer—entertainer

Gaffercarsey—cabaret; clubhouse; social centre

Gajo—outsider

Garter—edge; border

Gams—legs; oral sex

Gamming—performing oral sex

Gamp—umbrella

Gardy loo!—look out! (exclamation)

Gardening—sex in public

Gayle—South African gay language

Gelt—money

Gent—money

Gildy—fancy

Gillies—audience of women

Girl—term of address

Glamazon—drag queen

Gloria—God

Glossies—magazines

Goolie—Black person

Gollie ogle fakes—sunglasses

Grand—large; main; central

Grand Carsey—institute

Groin—ring

Groinage—jewellery

Grope—feel up; molest

Gutless—very good; very bad

Gylrig—attractive man; flirtation; sexy

Haldz—neck; throat (from Yiddish)

Hambag—money; gift

Hampsteads—teeth

Handbag—bag; money

Handle—name

Haponi—girl

Harris—arse

Harva—sex

Head—toilet

Hearing cheat—ear

Heartface—term of address

Herbals—herbal hormones

Hettie—straight man; *straight people in general*

High carsey—Skyscraper

Hilda handcuffs—police

Hobson—voice

Hoofer—dancer

Holy carsey—place of worship

Homies—men

Homie affair—husband

Homie ajax—neighbour

Homiepalonie—genderqueer/nonbinary

Hundred and seventy-fiver—homosexual

Husband—male lover

HP—gay man

Importuning—street hustling

In the life—homosexual

Invardible—invisible (from "varda")

Irish—wig

It—sex partner; penis (own)

Jarry—food; eat

Jarry the cartes—fellate

Jennifer Justice—police

Jew's eye—valuable item

Jim and Jack—back; buttocks

Jogger—sing; entertain; play

Joggering omi—street musician

Joobs—breasts; pectorals

Joshed up—dressed up

Journo—day

Kaffies—trousers

Kamp—Known As Male Prostitute

Ken—house

Kertever—bad

Kerterver cartzo—sexually transmitted infection

Khazi—toilet

Kosher homie—Jewish man

Lady—gay man

Lacoddy—body

Lag—prisoner; urinate

Lallie—leg

Lamor—kiss

Lappers—hands

Large—high quality

Lattie—house; apartment; room

Lattie on water—ship; boat

Lattie on wheels—car; taxi

Lau—put

Lav—word

Lavbats—poems (from "lav" and "bats")

Lell—take

Letch water—pre-cum

Litties—accommodation

Letty—bed; sleep

Libbage—bed; place to sleep

Lills—hands

Lilly Law—police

Ling grappling—sex

Lingo—foreign language

Lippy—foreign language

Lipstick—femme lesbian

Litter—spread; distribute

Lucoddy—body

Lullaby cheat—baby

Luppers—fingers

Lyles—legs

Madzer—halfpenny (defunct currency)

Madzer caroon—half a crown (defunct currency)

Mais oui—of course

Manjarie—food; eat

Manky—bad; tasteless

Manly—man

Manly Alice—masculine gay man

Maquiage—makeup

Maria—sperm

Martini—ring; hand

Marts—hands

Matlock mender—dentist

Matlocks—teeth

Mary-Ann—Catholic gay man

Maung—damage; destroy

Maunger—ugly

Mauve—possibly gay

Mazarine—mezzanine

Measures—money; wage; salary

Meat and two veg—penis and testicles

Meat rack—men's brothel/meat market

Medzer—half

Meese—ugly

Menge—dark; night

Mental—very good; very bad

Meshiginer—crazy

Meshiginer carsey—church

Metties—coins

Metzas—money

Mince—effeminate walk

Mincies—eyes

Minge—vagina

Minnie—gay man; walk

Mish—shirt

Moey—mouth

Mogue—mislead; lie

Molly—gay man

Mollying—sex

Montrel—watch; clock

Mother—me

Muck—makeup

Mudge—hat

Multy—many; much

Mungaree—food

Munja—food; eat

Mush—mouth

Nada—no; not; none; nothing

Naff—terrible; heterosexual

Namyarie—food; eat

Nanna—awful

Nanti—no; not; nothing; don't; beware

Nanti dinarly—poor

Nanti Polari—don't say anything

Nanti pots in the cupboard—no teeth

Nanti riah—bald
Nanti that—forget it
Nanti worster—no worse
Nantoise—no; nothing; never; inadequate
National handbag—government welfare
Nawks—bosom
Nell—hear; sound
Nellers—listeners
Nelly—effeminate gay man
Nellyarda—listen
Netters—news (from Spanish nyheter)
Nish—(variant of nix)
Nishta—(variant of nix)
Nix—no; none; don't; never; nothing
Nix mungarlee—no food
Nobba—person collecting for a street performer
Nochy—night
Nosh—fellatio
NTBH—Not To Be Had (unavailable; ugly)
Numba—number
Nuntee—no; none; don't; nothing
Ocals—eyes
Ogle—look; stare
Ogle fakes—glasses (spectacles)
Ogle filters—sunglasses
Ogle riahs—eyelashes
Ogle shades—sunglasses
Ogleliner—eyeliner
Ogles—eyes
Omi—man
Omi-palonie—gay man
Omni—heterosexual man
Onk—nose
On the team—homosexual
On your tod—on your own
Opals—eyes

Orbs—eyes
Orderly—leave; go
Orderly daughters—police
Outrageous—loud; camp
Oven—mouth
Oyster—mouth
Packet—man's crotch
Palare—speak
Palare pipe—telephone
Palaver—talk nonsense; argue; discuss
Palliass—buttocks; back (body)
Palonie—woman
Palonie omi—lesbian
Palonie affair—wife
Pannam—bread
Park—sit; put; give
Parker—pay; give
Parkering ninty—wages; salary
Parker the measures—pay money
Parlarly—speak Polari
Parlyaree—circus slang
Parnie—rain; tears; water
Pastry cutter—someone using teeth while performing
    fellatio
Pearls—teeth
Peroney—per; for each
Phantom—closeted gay man
Pig—elephant
Plate—food; feed; fellate
Plates—feet
Pogey—small; little; short
Polari—talk; speak; language
Polari lobes—ears
Polari pipe—telephone
Poll—wig
Ponce—pimp

Ponte—pound (currency)

Ponging—somersaulting

Poof—gay man

Pots—Teeth

Pumpmuscle—heart

Punk—young gay man; male virgin

Putting on the dish—putting on lube

Queen—gay man

Queeny—effeminate

Queen's dolly—woman friend of a gay man

Queer ken—prison

Queue—gay man

Quongs—testicles

Radfems—lesbian secret police

Randy comedown—horny

Rattling cove—taxi

Reef—feel; fondle; touch

Rent—male sex worker

Remould—sex change

Riha—hair

Riha zhoosher—hairdresser; barber

Rim—perform anilingus

Rogering cheat—penis

Rosie—rubbish bin

Rough—masculine man

Rough trade—thuggish sex partner

Royal—queenly

Rozzer—policeman

Salty—one penny

Savvy—know; understand

Scapali—escape

Scarper—run away; escape

Schinwhars—Chinese person

Schlumph—drink

Schmutter—clothes

Schonk—hit

Schooner—bottle
Schvartza—Black person
Scotch—deny; leg
Screaming—loud and effeminate
Screech—mouth; throat
Screeve—write; writing
Seafood—available gay sailor
Sea queen—gay sailor; man seeking sailors
Sedder—week (from Bosnian "sedmic"')
Sedon—nose
Send up—make fun of
Sharda—pity; shame
Sharpy—police
Sharping omi—policeman
Sharping palonie—policewoman
Sheesh—show off; fussy
Shietel—wig
Shush—steal
Shush bag—bag; handbag
Shyker—wig
Sister—close friend
Slang—perform on stage
Slanging tree—stage
Slap—makeup
Sling-backs—high heels
Smash—attractive man
Smellies—perfume
Smoke—city
So—homosexual ("Is he so?")
Soldi—money
Solicit—sex work while in drag
Sparkle—light
Stamper—shoe
Starter—lubricant
Steamer—client of a sex worker
Stiff—paper; forged document

Stimp covers—stockings

Stimps—legs

Stretcher case—exhausted; tired

Strides—trousers

Strill—musical instrument

Striller—piano key

Strillers—piano

Strillers omi—pianist

Strish—performance

Strollers—piano

Sweat chovey—gym

Sweet—good; right; exact

Sweet and dry—right and left

Swishing—camp

Tat—rubbish

TBH—To Be Had (sexually available)

Thews—arms; thighs

Three drags and a spit—cigarette

Tip—fellate

Tip the brandy—rim the anus

Tip the ivy—rim the anus

Tip the velvet—oral sex; rimming

Tittivate—make yourself pretty

Tober—road; circus

Tober omi—landlord

Tober showmen—street musicians

Todge omi-polanie—recipient of anal sex

Tod—alone

Toff omi—sugar daddy

Tootsie trade—two effeminate gay men having sex

Tosheroon—half a crown (defunct currency)

Town hall drapes—foreskin

Trade—sex partner; casual sex; sex worker

Traditional—concerning trade (see Trade)

Troll—walk; go; look for sex

Trollies—trousers

Trummus—buttocks

Trundling cheat—car

Turn my oyster up—make me smile

Tush—buttocks

Tusheroon—two shillings and sixpence (defunct
   currency)

Two and eight—to be in a state

Uppers and downers—drugs

Vacaya—loud noise; music player

Vaf—look (interjection)

Vaggerie—leave; go; travel

Vaggerie carser—travel agent

Valley drags—trousers

Varda—look; see

Vardavision—television

Vera—gin

Versatile—bisexual

Voche—voice; singer

Vogue—cigarette

Vogueress—female smoker

Vonka—nose

Wallop—dance

Wedding night—first night two men have sex

Willets—breasts

Winkle—small penis

Yews—eyes

Zelda—woman; witch

Zhoosh—clothes; arrange; *display*

Zhooshy—showy

Sources:

Alderman, Tim, "Gay History: How Bona to Vada Your
Eek! Polari – The Gay Lingo." https://timalderman.
com/2016/01/25/gay-history-how-bona-to-vada-your-eek-
polari-the-gay-lingo/

Baker, Paul, *Fantabulosa: A Dictionary of Polari and Gay Slang* (London: Continuum, 2002)

Denning, Chris, *The Polari Bible,* Chris Denning http://chris-d.net/polari/

Hajek, John, "Parlaree (aka Polari): Etymologies and Notes," *Spunti e Ricerche,* 6 (1990), 87-105

Richardson, Joseph Edward, Polari (Joseph Edward Richardson, 2014) [Mobile app, Version #3]

ACKNOWLEDGMENTS

Proud Pink Sky results from almost twenty years of involvement with LGBTQ+ communities: the "Lesbian, Gay, Bisexual Society" at my university, which I joined at eighteen; "Spectrum," the queer- and trans-friendly alternative we later founded; Queer Pagan Camp; the Radical Faeries; Queer Stories; and the many other groups, conferences, meets, and campaigns I've been a part of since. Meanwhile I debated my rights as a polyamorous person at University College London and was mocked in the tabloid press for daring to suggest that my family deserves the same rights as anybody else's. I've learned a lot about people and power relations over the past two decades in ways that have fundamentally shaped who I am—right up to my current point as a lipstick-wearing, beard-toting nonbinary giant some 198 cm tall. Both myself and this novel would not be possible without all of these experiences, the better and the worse.

I am ever grateful to Amble Press, the new imprint of Bywater Books, and to Michael Nava and Salem West for taking a chance on this story. Especially invaluable were Michael's insights and suggestions as my editor, immediately understanding the work and being intimately familiar with the social politics surrounding it. It means a great deal to me, and his numerous contributions to LGBTQ+ literature have benefited us all.

This novel's alternate history was sparked by my master's and doctoral research at Swansea University. My immense gratitude goes to my thesis supervisor, Prof. Caroline Franklin of the Literature Department—without her I would never have learned the discipline to become a novelist. Thanks also to my shadow supervisor, Doctor Dan Healey of the History Department, for his guidance on my research on the history of sexuality, and to GENCAS, the Centre for Research into Gender and Society.

I am thoroughly indebted to the artist Lindsey Marie Sheehan for her support with *Proud Pink Sky*, including the fabulous map of this alternate Berlin. I would also like to express my sincere thanks for the editing, proofreading, and insights for the many drafts and rewrites of this novel since its first inception in 2012: firstly to my wonderful partners Darren Cadwallader and Ismar Hačam, as well as Alex Goldberg, William Hillier, Peter Flynn, Claire Larkin, Doctor Olivia Plender, Doctor Mike Mantin, Doctor Paul Woodland, Vanessa Jupiter, Eleanor Tremeer, Sam a.k.a Morgan Wood, Thekla Altmann, Doctor Ritva Itkonen-Dolić, Mirza Dolić, Christoph Hartmann, Doctor Finn Ballard, and the Berlin Writing Group. I am also grateful to my parents, Ann Wrightham and Andrew Hemsley, for their support.

Finally, I would like to thank my late friend, the writer R.M. Vaughan (1965-2020). I miss our long walks, your observations on gay (and straight) culture, and the many hours we would spend sharing ideas. Sensitive queers have few role models, and I wish I'd told you that you were mine.

ABOUT THE AUTHOR

Redfern Jon Barrett is author of novels including *Proud Pink Sky*, a speculative story set in the world's first LGBTQ+ country (Bywater, 2023) and *The Giddy Death of the Gays & the Strange Demise of Straights* —which was a finalist for the Bisexual Book Awards and featured in *Paste Magazine's* "10 Audiobooks to Listen to During Pride Month (and Beyond)."

Redfern's essays and short stories have appeared in publications including *The Sun, Guernica, Strange Horizons, Passages North, PinkNews, Booth, FFO, ParSec, Orca,* and *Nature Futures.* Their writing has been shortlisted for Scotland's HISSAC prize, was a semifinalist for the Journal Non/Fiction Collection and Big Moose prizes, received an honourable mention for the Leapfrog Prize, and has exhibited at the National Museum of Denmark.

Born in Sheffield in 1984, Redfern grew up in market towns, seaside resorts, and postindustrial cities before moving to Wales and gaining a Ph.D. in Literature from Swansea University (Prifysgol Abertawe) in 2010. Redfern is nonbinary queer, and has campaigned for LGBTQ+ and polyamory rights since they were a teenager. They currently live in Berlin.

Amble Press, an imprint of Bywater Books, publishes fiction and narrative nonfiction by LGBTQ writers, with a primary, though not exclusive, focus on LGBTQ writers of color. For more information on our titles, authors, and mission, please visit our website.

www.amblepressbooks.com